SONG OF TIANANMEN SQUARE

This is David Rice's fifth book and second novel. A native of Northern Ireland, he has worked as a journalist on three continents. He has also been a Dominican friar. In the 1970s he was an editor and award-winning columnist in the United States, and returned to Ireland in 1980 to head the prestigious Rathmines School of Journalism. In 1989 he was invited to Beijing to train journalists on behalf of Xinhua, the Chinese government news agency, and to work as an editor with China Features. He was in Beijing during the massacre, and returned later to interview secretly 400 of the young people who had been involved at Tiananmen Square. His No. 1 best-selling *Shattered Vows* led to the acclaimed Channel 4 documentary, *Priests of Passion,* which he presented. He now lives in Co. Tipperary and teaches Writing Skills at the University of Limerick.

Also by David Rice

Shattered Vows: The Priests who Left
The Dragon's Brood: Conversations with Young Chinese
The Rathmines Stylebook: Guidelines for Writing
Blood Guilt (fiction)

A Brandon Original Paperback

First published in 1999 by
Brandon
an imprint of Mount Eagle Publications Ltd.,
Dingle, Co. Kerry, Ireland

Text © David Rice 1999

The author has asserted his moral rights.

ISBN 0 86322 251 X
(Original paperback)

This is a love story and a work of fiction. Although it is
based on very real and tragic events, the characters in the
book are fictional, and bear no relation to any living person.
Exceptions to this are the public figures associated with
Tianamnen Square: Li Peng, Deng Xiaoping, Wang Dan,
Chai Ling, Wuerkaixi, and Li Lu.

This book is published with the assistance of
the Arts Council/An Chomhairle Ealaíon, Ireland

Typesetting by Red Barn Publishing, Skeagh, Skibbereen
Cover design by the Public Communications Centre, Dublin
Printed by βetaprint, Dublin

Acknowledgements

Even though this is a work of fiction, I still must thank many people still in China, and a few who have got out, none of whom I can yet name: some ran considerable dangers to help me. I have my friends in Ireland to thank too, for so much help and encouragement: my brother Dermot; Catherine Thorne; my colleagues and my students at the Rathmines School of Journalism and at the University of Limerick; Lin Na (not her real name); Miriam O'Callaghan; Jeremy Addis and Jonathan Williams. Although I used thousands of pages of diaries and interview notes, I still must thank the authors of two wonderful books: Li Lu, whose *Moving the Mountain* put me right on so many things that happened, and Michael Fathers and Andrew Higgins *of The Independent* whose book, *Tiananmen: The Rape of Peking,* helped me get an accurate chronology of those terror-filled weeks. And Mervyn Cull, who helped me conceive this tale when we lived at the Friendship Hotel. And thanks too to the Macmillan Company for permission to use Chai Ling's speech to the hunger strikers.

For
Lin Na

PROLOGUE

I GAZED AFTER the boy as the truck carried him down the street. I gazed until I could no longer see his face. It was that face that had riveted my attention: never had I seen such an expression of horror and despair.

He stood in the back of a low-sided truck, a soldier on either side of him. A white placard hung from his neck, with large red Chinese characters on it. He wore a white shirt and blue jeans, and his hands were tied behind his back. He looked about eighteen.

The truck was one of a motorcade that passed slowly down that Beijing street one June afternoon in 1988. In my five months in the city I had never seen anything like it: first came several police cars with flashing blue lights; then a truck crammed with armed soldiers; then four trucks each with a handcuffed man standing between guards. More police cars and another truckload of soldiers finished off the procession, and the dee-dah sirens and the flashing lights faded slowly down past the Friendship Hotel towards Purple Bamboo Park.

Everyone in the cycle lane, including myself, had halted to watch the show pass by. I turned to a man beside me and mimed, 'What is it?' He grinned, and drew a forefinger smartly across his throat.

In the hotel dining room that evening, I asked old Norman Jenkyns, our resident Englishman and oldest inhabitant, what the cortège had been about.

Norman, as usual, had the answer. He had the answer to most things, and why wouldn't he, after nearly forty years in China? He had seen the parade from his hotel apartment which overlooked the street, and told our little dinner group exactly what it was all about.

'Tumbrels,' he pronounced, pausing to sip his beer. 'What y'saw were tumbrels, carrying the condemned precisely as in the French Revolution. Those men were on their way to their execution.'

'I wonder what they must have done,' I mused.

'It was quite clear what they had done,' announced Norman. 'The placards around their necks would have told you, young Paddy, if your Chinese lessons had done you any good. All four placards said the same thing – "The Criminal Illegal Drug-Smuggler" – and then the chappie's name.'

'I was not aware they actually kill you for drug-smuggling,' murmured old Madame Lukas, one of our dining companions. 'How do they do it?'

Norman was in his element. 'Those fellows were on their way to the Shang Yuan Gang execution ground. They'll be arriving about now. There'll be a couple of judges and public prosecutors waiting, and they'll ask each man if he has any last words, or messages for his relatives. There'll be a senior police officer with a red flag in his hand.

'"Kneel down!" they'll tell one of the fellows. He'll still

8

have the card around his neck when he kneels. There'll be a pause. Then the officer will lower the red flag – like this.' Norman snapped his soup spoon downward with a smart flick of the wrist.

'There'll be the crack of a pistol, fired right behind the fellow's neck, and the bullet will sever his spine at the base of the skull. It's almost surgical, y'know.

'The executioner's a policeman – they pick him for his nerves and his accuracy. He gets twenty *yuan* for each job. That'd be about three pounds in today's money, I daresay. Of course the dead man's family pays for it. Y'see, they get invoiced for the bullet.

'Then they move on to the next chap, and the procedure's the same. Except that he'll have wet his breeches by the time they get to him.'

Norman spooned the last of his French-onion soup. 'And don't think, young Paddy' – he glared at me – 'that you're safe just because you don't sniff any of that coke stuff. If indeed you don't. They'll shoot you for rape, too, remember. And if you manage to desist from raping, they can shoot you for any of thirty-seven other peccadilloes. Including, by the way, taking cultural relics out of China. So be careful what souvenirs you buy, Master Paddy, for the little lady back home. Or whomever it is y'keep back there in Dublin.

'Besides, it may not have been drugs at all with those chaps. The authorities might have framed them. They could be just political dissidents – but the authorities won't admit executing them for that. Thing is, we'll never know. No one ever knows here.'

Norman seemed to be the only one eating. He pushed aside his empty soup plate, mopped his lips, and drew towards him his pork and garlic sprouts. 'They'd be getting the chop right about now, I should imagine,' he said, inserting his chopsticks delicately into his dinner.

9

CHAPTER ONE

THEY BURIED MADGE Cranfield from the Friendship Hotel the day I arrived in Beijing. It was in early February of 1988.

'Precisely the same age as the century,' pronounced old Norman Jenkyns, presiding as usual at his table in Number Eight Dining Room of that vast compound miscalled a hotel.

'What did she die of?' I asked.

'She died of China,' Norman intoned. 'Most fatal disease of all. This wretched bloody country bewitches you, and y'simply can't leave. So y'stay – until y'die.'

'But she was eighty-eight when she died,' Sven Hansen ventured, pouring some more beer. 'Had to be a fairly benign disease.'

Norman glared at him. 'Y'want a monument to China? Look around you!' With a wave he indicated the vast dining hall. 'Look what China's done to this little lot. As you've heard me say, the Friendship Hotel contains four kinds of westerners – the fanatics, the failures, the chaps that are running away from something, and the chaps that have nothing to go home to. That's your kind, Hansen. You're fifty-five if you're a day, and your little wife is dying to see Norway. But what could you bring her home to? Who'd give you a job after writing lies on behalf of China for all these years?'

Sven looked sheepish and refilled his glass in spite of a nudge from his young Chinese wife. Norman's baleful eye turned on me. 'How about our new young Paddy here? Flotsam or jetsam, eh? Don't tell me – you're one of the running-away-from-something fellows. Betray the wife, eh? Or did she betray you? Cuckolded, eh?'

I could have strangled the old bugger. I felt the hotness hit my cheeks and I felt a momentary hatred for the grinning faces around the table – for beardedly handsome Sven Hansen, a good thirty-five years older than his pretty Chinese wife, who was now tugging at his sleeve under the table for him to come away; for Madame Lukas, that aged tarantula, Hungarian black eyes taking in everything in the whole dining room.

Mostly I hated that insolent old man, drawling his final vowels as if he had just come down from Cambridge, snapping his fingers now for the waiter as he must have snapped them for a steward on some slow boat to China more than forty years ago.

'A ship of fools,' he was intoning. 'This hotel is a ship of bloody fools, becalmed for ever in a sea of one billion Chinese peasants.' He turned to me. 'Do you know how many fools there are in this one ship, young Paddy? There are over three thousand fools, and all of them foreigners. Foreign experts, they call you. Hah! Called in to help the Chinese modernise. Hah! Offscourings, I would call you – scum of the earth. Heaven help the Chinese.'

'Hold it now,' Sven interrupted. 'You're one of us too.'

'I certainly am not,' Norman sniffed. 'I'm a Chinese citizen, and a long-standing member of the Communist Party. Here for more than forty years. I'm a part of China's history, I am. Dammit, Zhou Enlai knew me by my first name.'

It was then I remembered him. I had been too young to experience the furor when leading British Labour Party spokesman Norman Jenkyns had suddenly taken off for China, two years before the communist victory in 1949. But I had heard my parents reminiscing about it, and lately I had seen one of those Sunday supplements recalling 'Red Norman', and his departure for China, regarded at that time as tantamount to treason. A Cambridge contemporary of Anthony Blunt, as well as Burgess and Maclean, he was man hated and feared in those days, even long before he ever took off for China. Hated and feared for his merciless tongue in the House of Commons.

And now just a mean old man.

Still, I wondered, as I walked back to my hotel apartment, was Norman Jenkyns right about the *You Yi Binguan*? That's what they called the Friendship Hotel, or *You Yi*, for short. A ship of fools?

What an extraordinary place it was anyway – more like a vast university campus than a hotel, with its blossom-lined avenues, its 1950s-vintage Russian-built buildings, some of them eight storeys high, their solid shapes softened by Chinese roofs curving upwards at the extremities, reminiscent of ancient pavilions.

This was the Friendship Hotel, with its eight restaurants, its shops and stores, its tennis courts and swimming pool, its bars and pubs, its barber-shops and post office, its hotel blocks and apartment blocks, its armed guards at the entrance gates.

Within these walls the Chinese corralled their tame foreigners, those 'foreign experts' who sallied out daily to work
with local enterprises, or were introducing the Chinese to
computers, or were lecturing at Beida or Qinghua universities
or at dozens of other Beijing institutions, or were advising the
national television station, or were training the Xinhua news-
agency people in the idiotic ways of western journalism as I
had just come to do, or were sub-editing on *China Daily*, or
polishing the foreign-language news releases from Xinhua, as
Sven Hansen was doing.

From the time of Marco Polo, at least, the Chinese had
cannily corralled their foreign residents in one place. It was
partly to keep an eye on them, partly to keep them from mix-
ing too freely with the Chinese, and generally to keep them
under control by concentrating them in one spot.

But an extremely comfortable concentration camp was the
Friendship Hotel. On my arrival that afternoon I had been
installed in an apartment four floors up in Building Number
Four, with a double bedroom, a lounge as large as the one in
my Dublin semi, ample bathroom, balcony, colour television,
heaps of massive dark furniture and more wardrobes and
cupboards than I would ever fill.

I could have had an apartment with kitchen had I wanted
one, but those were mostly occupied by the married couples
with children. I was glad I had decided against the kitchen
when I saw the minuscule bill in the restaurant, where 'foreign experts' paid only half price.

The scent of blossoms was heavy in the air as I walked
back. I wasn't really mad at old Norman now – rather I felt
sad that the ferocious oratory that had been so feared in pre-
and post-war Britain had shrivelled to spite around a table in
a ship of fools.

Even my grief at all that had happened to me back in
Dublin was dulled in this warm, scented evening. I felt a

strange excitement, a sort of mellow near-pain that throbbed deep down in my gut (like the feeling I once had as a youngster when I realised a girl was actually going to give me my first experience of sex).

To be in China. And to be here now, when it was exploding with new ideas, opening up to the world, welcoming strangers, finally burying the grim legacy of 'The Ten Years', as they call the Cultural Revolution: that terrible time when the Chinese had shut out the world and had set about destroying everyone in authority, from government ministers down to the humblest teacher. All except Chairman Mao, who had egged them on to it.

All that was over now. This was the new China, vibrant and hopeful.

'Get yourself a bicycle, first thing,' Sven had said during dinner, and even Norman had agreed grumpily. Quickest way to get out among the people, they all said, and you can ride it to work. Sven told me he knew where you could get good bargains in second-hand bikes, just across the street from the hotel.

I'll get me a bike tomorrow, I told myself. And maybe I'll try learning Chinese too.

During those early spring weeks I wrote in my diary that I had found no better place to heal a grievous wound than the streets of Beijing.

These were just ordinary streets in an ordinary city. Well, an ordinary Chinese city, and therefore hardly ordinary by my standards, but a city experienced by me as profoundly peaceful: a place where I could come to heal my wound.

I am talking of an emotional wound, of a nightmare in which the solid ground on which you stand suddenly yawns into a chasm beneath your feet, and while you are clinging to its edge with only your nails, the person you care most about

strolls to the edge and smilingly draws a cavalry sabre across
your clutching fingers. And as your scream plunges with you
into the abyss, you know the nightmare is for real.

Maybe the abyss was not for real, but the betrayal was.
And the death that followed was real too. And as King Arthur
went to Avalon to heal him of his grievous wound, so came I
to Beijing.

I'm PJ O'Connor, by the way (PJ is short for Peter Joseph),
a sub-editor on Dublin daily papers for much of my thirty-
nine years. I had been supplementing my income with a couple of rather minor novels, and it had been a rather minor
supplement. And then one day my life fell apart.

Even eighteen months later, when I closed my eyes at night,
I could still see my wife's face. I could still hear the rumble of
the drawer when they pulled her out for me to identify. And
the clang when they rammed the drawer shut. I could still
smell the morgue odour, chlorine masking the formaldehyde
and dead flesh. And the faint Chanel perfume that lingered
after I had stooped over her face. It had always made me
think of Windowlene.

It had happened so suddenly. My dawning realisation of
betrayal, the screaming row, and Heather storming out to the
car to race across Kildare to her horseman lover.

Then the call from the Gardaí.

There wasn't a scratch on Heather's face. The steering
wheel had killed her instantly: it went into her heart.

In the year and a half that followed, I should have gone far
away, but I stayed and tried to cope, and finally lost my job.
So when I got offered this two-year contract to train young
journalists for Xinhua, the Chinese government news agency,
I thought it over carefully for one and a half seconds.

For me the Beijing bicycles were the most healing thing.
When I looked out of my high newsroom window at Xinhua,
I would discern a sort of leisurely lava flowing along each side

of the street, each molecule a man or woman perched on a bicycle.

The best moment of the day was when I would clatter down those five flights of stairs at 5 o'clock, identify my bicycle among the hundreds of identical black machines so like the solid old Raleighs of 1950s Dublin, and pedal gently out into the lava flow.

There's hardly a hill in all of Beijing, so cycling could be leisurely and pleasant. More than just pleasant, for the Chinese have the world's most beautiful women, and they were on bicycles everywhere around me.

At first I didn't look. I simply could not look at any woman. And the better looking a woman was, the more I wanted to turn away, with a sort of pain deep down in my gut. But in time Beijing began to work its magic. Maybe it was because its women are so different. They seemed almost like Dresden china figurines come to life, with their slenderness and their glinting blue-black hair and their tiny breasts and pale flawless complexions, and those almond eyes set in faces so strange and hauntingly lovely. They didn't seem quite real to me – just porcelain figures without any connection with love or betrayal or death.

So after a time I began to look at the women of Beijing. I even developed a routine. Cyclists really only see each other's rears, so the first thing I would perceive would be one of those neat rears, the tight denim pockets rocking gently with the pedalling. Or the occasional black miniskirt, tight as a drum. Or a summer dress flaring out like an orchid. But always the neat rear, and always the impossibly tiny waist.

I would adjust my pace to the vision ahead, and the joy was almost like the joy of gazing at spring's first crocus: so delicate, so exquisitely made, so incomparably lovely.

After a mile or so I would get curious about the face. Would it match the figure? My pedalling would speed up to match my heartbeat, and I would steal a glance as I passed. Rarely would the face disappoint, and mostly my heart would tighten at the almond loveliness of it. And I would look back for a full-faced vision.

The only thing is, I never got a smile. People didn't smile. Sometimes I might get a coquettish toss of the head, occasionally a glare of scorn, but nary a smile. However, I didn't try to talk in those days, if indeed anyone would have understood English. I needed to be alone. There was a kind of symmetry to it – I needed just to look, and those impassive faces exuded *noli me tangere*.

But even without the smiles, cycling through Beijing was healing for me. Still, healing is a slow process, and I had my bad times. There were times I had to tell myself to breathe, just to keep living. At nights I had a recurring nightmare where I was among Beijing's thousands of cyclists, and, when I turned around to look at them, they all had Heather's face.

CHAPTER TWO

WITHIN WEEKS I was well settled into the Friendship Hotel and learning what made for a smooth passage upon that ship of fools on its way to nowhere. Learning about Mayo, for instance. I had thought Mayo to be an Irish county or something you put on a deli sandwich, until I discovered it was the favourite utterance of those who ran the hotel. Actually it was *mei you*, but pronounced like the county, and it signified 'Don't have', 'Can't get', 'No way', with overtones of 'So-bugger-off-and-don't-be-annoying-me'.

For instance, cold milk was unheard of at breakfast. '*Mei you!*' the blue-jacketed *fu* would shrug when I requested it for my tea. (*Fu* was the short for *fu wu yuan*, the general term for the hotel folk who looked after us, including waiters, doormen and people who cleaned the rooms.)

'But if this is hot milk, it must have been cold once,' I tried to tell the girl, with Madame Lukas translating. I handed back the jug with its loathsome gobbets of skin. 'Simply don't heat the milk.'

'*Mei you!*'

However, at the end of breakfast she beamingly brought me another little jug, saying triumphantly, 'Cold!' Out plopped those gobbets of once-heated milk, now cooled by icebox.

I learned, too, how to double my income by a little deft and felonious exchanging. I was paid in FEC – Foreign Exchange Currency – a special hard currency for foreigners that could later be exchanged for dollars. If you could find an amiable money-changer on the black market, you could nearly double its value in regular Chinese currency (called *ren min bi*).

Our resident money-changer was Madame Lukas. One mooched unobtrusively along to her little apartment in Building Eight of the Friendship Hotel campus, and it was always a minor social occasion. The exchange was mostly transacted across Madame's bed, in which she would be sitting up with a glass of Talisker single malt beside her. The money came from a bag under the bed. A whiskey would then be proffered, accompanied by Madame Lukas' titillating gossip, which brought one accurately up to date on which hotel denizens were sleeping amorously with which. I called it the Gossip According to Lukas.

Madame was invariably and uncannily right. Sitting up in that bed with a black silk shawl around her scrawny shoulders, looking like a scaly old spider, she sensed the vibrations that came through threads that stretched far beyond the walls of the Friendship Hotel. Madame was our resident broker, exchanging money, gossip, contacts, influence, information, and God knows what else. If you wanted to learn Chinese, Madame found you a teacher. If your contract in China was ending, she knew which Beijing establishment wanted an English teacher or what government office needed a 'foreign expert'. And she knew where to get the required papers. And whom to bribe, and for how much.

Nothing was for nothing, and Madame Lukas knew how to ask for a return of favours previously granted. In fact the main commodity she brokered was that quintessentially Chinese thing known as *guanxi* (pronounced 'gwan-shee'). *Guanxi* is the Chinese equivalent of nudge-nudge-wink-wink, combined with who-you-know, but honed during four thousand years of feudalism and imperial rule.

In mastery of *guanxi*, however, the Chinese were only trotting after Madame Lukas. Fearsomely correct 'cadres' – Chinese officials, usually in Mao suits – came trotting in and out on visits to her, always just 'about to leave' when one came to change money; shifty-looking business types would drop in on visits from Hong Kong and whisk Madame off for a European meal at their lairs in the opulent Shangri La Hotel or the Great Wall Sheraton.

Lee was the shiftiest looking and most charming of all Madame's business acquaintances. A *hua qiao*, or 'overseas Chinese', of uncertain age like so many Chinese, Lee was something in that vast menagerie of import-export firms operating out of Hong Kong. He used to drop by the Friendship when he flew into Beijing a couple of times a month.

We wondered what was between Lee and Madame, because when Lee was visiting, Madame's door stayed shut and knocks went unanswered – unheard of at other times. However, details of any such relationship were not part of the gossip that Madame Lukas otherwise so copiously provided.

Lee could be amusing. Madame Lukas would sometimes bring him to our table for dinner, and he always had a couple of new jokes, sometimes about our Chinese masters. He could tell us what was really happening in China. That was a relief from the *China Daily* – the party line in English – and a welcome supplement to the BBC World Service and Voice of America, our only sources of real information.

None of us trusted Lee, of course, but we enjoyed him.

Even Norman enjoyed him, although heading to his room after dinner he might sometimes be heard to mutter, 'Goddam bloody spiv,' reverting to the argot of the postwar Britain he still related to.

I understood that Lee smuggled in banned books and videos from time to time, but I never knew if they were pornographic or politically unacceptable. Most were for an American professor over at nearby Beida (the popular name for the University of Beijing). Lee would sometimes leave a sealed packet of these books with Madame Lukas, who sent them across to Beida with my Chinese teacher, who lectured there.

My Chinese teacher? Ah, yes, I had one of those, but with precious little to show for it. Madame Lukas had found me Song Lan, Lan being her given name, which comes last with the Chinese. However, we mostly called her Song. It was arranged that she would come two evenings a week to my apartment to give me lessons.

Song Lan was about thirty-five, but looked twenty-one, as so many Chinese women do. She lectured in Chinese Language at Beida, and was trying to earn some money so she could study for a year or two abroad. With the regulation, but wretched, ten *yuan* per hour that I paid her (about £1.50), it was likely to be some time before she got there.

Song was a strict teacher. She dispensed with the Chinese written characters, which she said would be too hard for me at the start. Instead she wrote the phrases as pronounced, using the English alphabet according to the *pinyin* method. She gave me homework and checked every line.

Lessons began with an oral test on the previous lesson's material. When I disgraced myself, as was frequently the case, Song would gently give me the right answer, and that slender face would remain impassive. But if I performed exceptionally well, with those sing-song tones just right, I would be rewarded with an approving nod and a *'fei chang hao!'* – 'well done!' It worked: I found myself trying that little bit harder to earn another one of those nods.

I was grateful to Madame Lukas for finding me Song. It made learning Chinese a slightly less daunting experience, and I remember thinking that if I was going to give up one and a half hours, twice each week, to such an arduous task, I'd rather be doing it with someone like Song than with some fussy little man.

I had also been getting to know my trainees, and, although they were inclined to be in awe of the 'professor', they were gradually giving me insights into Chinese life. Kui'er and Ning were the two I liked best. Kui'er was twenty-four, with a wry humour and a puckish grin, always ready to take a rise out of me if I got pompous. I particularly appreciated the grin, because of its rarity among the Chinese.

Ning was twenty-three, fragile, bespectacled, and married with twin babies. It was she taught me what suffering could be like in China, and made me aware of a vein of cruelty that underlay the streets of Beijing with their placid cyclists. She was the most diligent of my trainees.

I would occasionally meet the tall, earnest young husband who cycled by to fetch her home. He had a tricycle with a chair at the back for Ning. I used to think there was something touchingly romantic about his pedalling away with Ning in the chair – a bit like the way we would carry a girl on the crossbar of a bike when we were young.

With only twelve trainees one noticed things, and for a few days I had been noticing dark marks under Ning's eyes. Maybe she had been weeping, I thought, or had had a sleepless night or two. Anyway it was none of my business, and it was probably some marital upset.

But one day there was Ning staring straight ahead, stock

still, with tears running down her cheeks. Her utterly blank face reminded me of that doll I once gave to my niece Lily, that wept tears when you squeezed it but never changed its expression. 'Tiny Tears' I think it was called. Ning's tears were not tiny and they cascaded on and on, from one class to another. The other students, even the women, seemed not to notice. Indeed they seemed to back away from Ning, except for Kui'er, who occasionally put a brief reassuring hand on hers.

I was supposed to stay out of my students' private lives, but after one entire day's weeping, as Ning was leaving I invited her into my office.

'I know it's none of my business,' I said, 'but I'm concerned for you. Is there anything I can do to help? Or would it help to talk about – whatever?'

Ning's dark eyes held mine for a long moment. Then she leaned over my desk, put her head in her arms and a terrible wail broke from her. The thin body shook convulsively. She grabbed her overcoat and pulled it over her head like a tent, and the overcoat shook as she sobbed inside it. Then she became eerily still beneath the coat.

Like many an Irishmen I'm a bit inhibited and not good at touching. Still, I did manage to pull my chair around beside her and put a hesitant hand on her shoulder.

Finally I got her to come out from under the coat – it was like trying to coax a little injured animal from its lair so you could bind up its wound. I poured her some tea from the urn, and waited.

Then she told me. Her fourteen-month-old twins were the problem. China only permits one child per family, and, since the twins were born, she and her husband had been under pressure to get rid of one of them. They had ignored the pressure and had been hoping the matter was forgotten.

Now her neighbourhood unit had sent a couple of nosey old women to tell her there was only going to be one place

24

in school, for one of the twins, only one medical card, one ration card for essentials like grain, oil and eggs. And only one *hu kou* – registration card. The other twin would be a non-person.

'Their birth was terrible, you know,' Ning said, starting to weep again. 'They had to cut me open. The twins didn't want to come out. They knew what was facing them, I think, and they didn't want to give themselves up.' She wept more.

Ning said they had told her and her husband to choose which twin to get rid of. I told Ning I couldn't believe this.

She stared at me and hissed: 'You don't live here. I do.'

'What will you do?' It was all I could think of saying.

'What can we do?' she wailed. 'We'll keep the boy, and send Hong down to the countryside, to her grandfather. She'll have no father, mother, brother. She'll grow up a peasant, with no education, with nothing. She'll be just dirt. Dirt.' The wails started again.

Ning glared at me. 'I want out of China! It never gets better. They keep promising, but it never gets better. We all just want out.'

It was one of the most shocking things I had heard in a long time. Had these authorities taken leave of humanity? And there was nothing I could do or say. I felt mute before this awesome cruelty.

'It's probably only a temporary measure, Ning,' I said finally. 'My guess is, Hong will only be away for a short while. You'll see.' I could hear my own inanity as I spoke.

She rounded on me. 'What do you know? What do you know about anything here? You live in that fancy hotel. You don't have rationing. And you can go home when you're tired of us. You don't know what it's like to live on eighty *yuan* a month. Ask anyone who's my age – they all want out. They won't tell you because you're a foreigner, but they all hate what's happening. They hate the corruption and all those cadres making themselves rich and driving through the streets in those Benzes with the dark windows. China's going to blow up soon. And I mean that. But it will be too late for my Hong!' She grabbed the coat and pulled it over her head again.

It was the most disturbing moment I had had since I came to China. If Ning was right, there was an underlying ferocity in life here that I had never before encountered. The next time I watched those couples strolling together in Tiananmen Square, I would wonder what they were really thinking. And what they were really suffering.

As I cycled home I was comparing myself with Ning, and my grief with hers. Cuckolded and widowed I might be, but I was going back to a comfortable hotel; I wasn't having children torn from me; I didn't have to live on eighty *yuan* a month – I was getting nearly 5,000, which was more than £800. And I could leave China when I got tired of it.

And I found myself thinking, too, how glad I was that that eleven hundred million population – the root cause of Ning's misery – was China's problem and not mine.

'But it *is* your problem!' Old Norman rounded on me, smiling his smug smile, when I uttered that same view over dinner that evening after telling the company about Ning and her twins. 'If y'think y'can walk away, think again, young man. That billion's not just China's problem: it's your little problem too!'

'So what has it to do with me?'

'O God or something, preserve me from these Christians,' intoned Norman, throwing his eyes to the heaven he didn't believe in. Then the eyes descended on me. 'Listen, young Paddy. If you weren't so busy saving your miserable Irish soul, y'might just perceive that China's a fifth of the human race. It's not China that's overpopulated – it's the globe. Your bleeding globe. What happens to China happens to you, and me. If y'd read John Donne instead of bloody Aquinas y'might have discovered that no man is an island. When that wretched woman packs her brat off to the back of beyond, she's doing it for you. And for me.'

'But what can I do about it?'

'Nothing,' he said sweetly. 'So don't even think about it. Just concentrate on saving that soul of yours. After all, as long as y'make it into heaven, China or anything else won't much matter in the long run, now will it? "Send not to know for whom the bell tolls," eh?'

Norman's ungracious words set me off that night on one of my periodic bouts of introspection. It angered me how his words could get to me. It was humiliating that his arrogant atheism could see the shortcomings of my half-understood Christianity, a Christianity I was being forced to explore more and more since Heather's death. It wasn't helping me much, but then all I had ever got was a legalistic set of do's and don'ts, nailed down by fear.

Those years in a Jesuit boarding school, did they teach me some sort of spiritual selfishness? To save your soul, that was all that life was about, and that was what they had hammered into us day after day after day. The alternative, hell for all eternity, made saving your own soul the only thing that really mattered in the long run.

So when you gave a cup of cold water to somebody thirsting, you were just adding an extra little bit of moisture to your own soul. Even when those China missionaries had gone off to save countless pagan souls, in the end was it all about collecting some sort of Green Shield stamps to be cashed in on the Last Day?

A cup of cold water here. Console a weeping mother of twins there. Thou shalt have thy reward. Every little good act gave an extra patina to one's own soul, to make the soul that little bit nicer on the Last Day. Like some prize dog being groomed for Crufts.

It all came down to oneself in the end. At least my kind of Christianity did, whatever the hell was wrong with it. Real Christianity had to be more than that.

What distressed me was that an old man, who believed in nothing himself, was finding flaws in beliefs I cherished – beliefs in which I was raised. And I didn't know enough about my own faith to refute him.

CHAPTER THREE

HALFWAY THROUGH MAY a fax came from my widowed elder brother Mick, who was news editor on the *Irish Independent*. His adopted daughter Lily was coming to study Chinese at Beijing University. She had wangled a fellowship from the Chinese government to study Mandarin, as the language is called. She was the first Irish student ever to have got such an award.

I knew that Lily had graduated from Trinity the previous autumn, but I thought she had read French and Russian. However, Mick's letter said she had been studying Chinese for some time at a night course in Trinity, and seemed to be brilliant at it.

My brother had taken Lily to Ireland as an infant, after his stint with Associated Press in Hong Kong. He had found her in some ghastly orphanage in South China and had got her across the border by copious bribing. Things were simpler in those days.

I remembered Lily well as a child and a teenager. I had always been intrigued by this otherwise typical, lively, attractive Dublin youngster – but with the almond eyes and the hauntingly lovely Chinese face. It had always seemed so strange to hear Lily's voice uttering Dublin English, from a mouth so surely shaped for the singing tones of Mandarin Chinese.

Now it seemed those lips would be framing the sounds they were made for.

Lily had been through a few things in the last few years. There had been something with drugs, nothing big, and she had got over it. She had been a teenage model for a while and could easily have made a career of modelling. However, Mick told me that in the last few years Lily had developed an obsession for China and had lived for the day she would get to Beijing.

Mick wanted to know, would I keep a mildly parental eye on her? Like, making sure it was hands-off where those billions of Chinese fellas were concerned? She was his only darling, and he dreamed of seeing her settled finally and happily in Ireland, presenting him with golden grandchildren. And make sure Lily didn't guzzle too much *Mao Tai* or whatever they call the stuff they drink in China. And were there drugs in China now? If so, keep them away from our Lily. Et cetera.

All in all a tall order. And God knows I had enough on my plate, like trying to cope with Ning's nervous breakdown. She had nosedived after they took away her child, and, of course, shrinks or counsellors were unheard of in Beijing. We all just had to try and help as best we could.

Still, Mick's request was understandable – the preoccupations of an adoring father on the other side of the world, and I didn't really mind taking Lily on. It was my first real chance to do something for Mick, who had done so much for me over the years. He had more or less brought me up after our parents died within a few years of each other and had been the caring elder brother ever since. It was he who paid for my boarding school, and who later got me into journalism, putting me through Rathmines and getting me my first job at the *Evening Press*. And he was the only one I could turn to after what happened in my marriage.

Poor old Mick had been a single parent twice, first raising me and then having to cope with Lily after his wife Kate died. Lily had been a dazzlingly attractive child. She had been fond of me, and I had always had an affection for her, especially as I had no kids of my own. As Lily grew towards womanhood she had grown extraordinarily beautiful, and her voice had grown husky and gravelly. But her beauty had made her proud. In the last few years Lily had discovered she had a sharp tongue and seemed intrigued with the power it gave her. People hesitated to take her on, and she became more and more accustomed to getting her own way. I had become slightly in awe of her. I didn't doubt Mick was too.

Anyhow I faxed Mick that I'd be delighted to be mildly parental, but mild would be the operative word. Lily was a stunning girl, and I wasn't going to be her chaperone. As regards *Mao Tai*, the Chinese were a lot more sober than we were. In fact, they were the world's most sober people. Besides, beer was the students' gargle. And, as regards drugs, if Lily had managed to put them behind her in Dublin, she'd have no trouble here. Come to think of it, warn Lily not to bring anything like that with her, as I hear they take a very dim view indeed of drug smugglers.

By the time Lily arrived in the middle of June, I had discovered an eminently satisfactory way to weasel out of my commitment to supervise her. My teacher Song Lan would do it for me. She actually volunteered to help Lily find her feet. It made sense: Song lectured at Beida and shared a tiny room

31

there with two colleagues. Lily was coming to Beida, so would be in a dormitory on the same campus. So Song would keep an eye on Lily, and it would be a chance for Song to practise her English. With that in mind, I invited Song to come with me to the airport to let the two young women meet and to see how they got on.

Lily looked stunning. She was in the full bloom of her 21 years. She wore the regulation Trinity fatigues – Levis and leather Docs – but she had topped them off with a beige Calvin Klein shirt with more buttons open than strictly necessary. She had tiny pearl ear rings. Men were looking at her and I noticed how Lily held their gaze. This one had style and all the self-assurance of Ireland's younger generation.

I felt some misgivings as I became aware of the heap of suitcases she had on the pushcart. Chinese face or not, was this exotic creature going to fit into no-nonsense Beijing?

As I introduced Song to Lily I noticed both were about the same height. Not quite the same build, however: there was a spareness about Song's frame that suggested some past period of want, whereas Lily exuded robustness. Years of Irish meat and potatoes there, I thought.

I also became aware, for the first time, of how simply, even severely dressed Song was. She wore black pants of some very thin cottony material, a simple white shirt with short sleeves, and small black, low-heeled shoes. Yet Song was far from dowdy. That shirt was flawless and spotlessly clean, and the pants were slender and creased like razors. Clothes hung well on Song. Both these young women had a natural elegance, but had it been a contest, Song might have won by a nose.

I had been hoping the two would get on, and it seemed I need not have worried. By the time the taxi had covered the 20 miles of tree-lined avenue to Beijing, the two in the back were chatting away in Chinese, Lily of course doing most of the talking. Chinese has to be sung to be understood, as different tones have different meanings, and I was fascinated at how the tones sounded in Lily's gravelly voice. By contrast Song's voice was the ringing of a glass bell.

As we drove along, I found myself thinking how those two Chinese women stood for quite different worlds, even in their body language. I had noticed at the airport that where Lily's catwalk strut exuded assertion, if not aggression, Song's movements were as controlled as if she were walking a convent cloister. It was the faces, however, that had said more than anything. Smiles and laughter chased across Lily's magnificent face like breezes across a meadow, followed by a frown or a flash of scorn as she told me of her father's old-fashioned ways that had been getting on her nerves. Song listened and spoke gently, her face showing almost no expression, except perhaps attention to Lily's words. And Song's minor-key beauty seemed to come not so much from splendid facial features like Lily's, but from a sense that behind that impassive visage lurked warmth, maybe even flame. Lily's face could dazzle; Song's might intrigue if you let it.

A couple of days later, when Lily and Song came over to the Friendship for dinner, Lily was indistinguishable from any young Beijing cyclist. Her dark pants and white blouse had obviously been got in Beijing. And Song was wearing a pale blue sweatshirt emblazoned with *Trinity College*. The blue gave an agreeable translucence to her skin.

That's how it continued. I was able to sit back and let the two women get on with it. I was glad to see Lily making a real friend, in spite of the fourteen years between them. Indeed Song's relative maturity might enable her to give some guidance to Lily. And for me it was a relief to see that Lily was keeping her cutting tongue in its sheath.

Not indeed that I noticed much about Song in those days, beyond the fact that she was a great help with Lily, and a damn good Chinese teacher to boot (whatever boot is).

There were those around, nevertheless, who were beginning to hint that I was indeed noticing Song, if one were to believe the Gossip According to Lukas and the sniggers around the Friendship Hotel. It took quite a while before it dawned on me what they were hinting at.

The first hint came from Lee. I was emerging from Madame Lukas' flat with a packet of books to pass on to Song, when I met Lee coming up the stairs. We stopped and chatted a moment, and I asked when he was heading back to Hong Kong. He said tomorrow. Then Lee asked how Song was doing, and I said fine.

'You got yourself a sweetie there!' Lee said, with a smirk. I said yes, surely, and thought to myself, not for the first time, that Lee was an odd sort of fish.

A couple of days later Sven got up at the end of dinner and headed off with his young Chinese wife. She had been tugging at him as usual under the table not to pour himself another glass of beer, and for once had prevailed.

When they were out of earshot, Madame Lukas murmured, 'Of course you know who he's bedding now?' She hitched her black silk shawl around her shoulders and waited.

'You mean he's finished with that Hun woman?' Norman asked. 'The big Bruennehilde one? Can't say I blame him.' He snorted. 'Those Hun squaws were always too hefty by far for me.'

'It's Xia Ruimin, now. The little one from Shanghai.'

'Then Dr Hansen had better watch himself,' Norman said. 'The Chinese don't take kindly to anyone playing around with their women. It can be declared illegal, and y'can go to jail or to slave camp for it. And the Chinese like it even less when for-eign devils are at it.'

I became aware they were watching me. Not directly, of course. I found myself recalling that phrase, 'with hooded eyes'. Melodramatic, no doubt, but it described what they seemed to be doing. My cheeks hotted up and I felt myself getting angry, but I said nothing. I just poured some beer and let the conversation resume.

However, walking with me back to Building Four, Norman came back to the point with his irritating directness. 'Are y'poking that teacher of yours?' he asked.

I stopped and faced him. 'Norman, I certainly am not, uh, "poking" her, as you so delicately put it. I'm not doing anything to her. In fact there's – she's – she's just my teacher. Besides, it's none of your goddam business!'

'Just so long as y'remember what I said,' the old bugger replied imperturbably. 'The Chinese are very jealous of their women. God knows why – there's plenty to go around. And besides, the women are as prudish as an Irish Catholic, so it's jolly hard work, and hardly worth the risk.'

Norman put a match to his pipe and turned to walk on. I walked with him and bade him a curt goodnight at the lift. It was dawning on me that the whole miserable dining room was sniggering behind my back, just as they were sniggering at Sven.

Now I don't know whether the Gossip According to Lukas put the idea into my head, or whether it was already in my head and the others sensed it before I did. Whichever, I found myself noticing Song.

I think it began one late afternoon, when I was gazing out of my window awaiting her arrival for my lesson. Then I saw her, some distance away, moving down the pathway towards the building. Sometimes when you look down towards someone from a height, you see them differently. For some reason Yeats' words came to me: "I saw a young girl, and she had the walk of a queen."

Her gait did seem regal. She wore a long black skirt that swirled about her ankles. In her right hand she swung the light canvas bag that held her books. The dark hair to her shoulders gleamed almost like metal in the evening sun and, as I watched, the left hand came up in a graceful arc to push the hair back. I realised then I had often subconsciously noted and admired this little gesture, so peculiarly hers. And I realised for the first time that she was left-handed, a *citóg*.

Even with the ankle-length skirt, it was clear from her stride that she had the long legs of the northern Chinese. I remembered Hansen's remark that some of these girls seemed to have legs all the way to the navel. She moved out of view, and as I waited for the crash of the lift doors down the corridor that would announce her arrival, I found I was aware of my heartbeat.

Now, that I had not allowed for. Song was just my teacher, and a friend of my niece, which is how I wanted it to stay, but it wasn't easy during that lesson. I noticed her voice again, and it really was like a glass bell, especially when she was uttering Chinese words. I could have listened to that voice all night. I noticed too that her eyes weren't slanted at all, but the shape of almonds. However, the impassive face helped me keep my perspective.

And yet every movement, every arcing of the hand to toss back the hair, spoke of some repressed spontaneity. I wondered once more did a smile lurk somewhere back of those lips, or a sparkle hide within those dark eyes?

'Where's the Trinity sweatshirt?' I asked her, on the spur of the moment.

'Too bright,' she said. 'Can't wear things like that. People would notice.'

'So what if they do?'

Song looked at me and sighed. 'Here in China,' she said, 'if a tree grows taller than the rest, it's chopped down. If a nail sticks up, it gets hammered back.'

From that day on I found myself looking forward to Song's Chinese lessons in a way I had not before. There was one day we were sitting together for the lesson, and Song Lan had a light summer dress on, in some sober colour as always. Beige, I think. At one point I just looked down and noticed her bare knee. I remember thinking, foolishly, it's just like an Irish knee. What else should it be like? But somehow or other that knee made me aware that this was just another human being beside me. Not Chinese, just human. The knee was slender, but somehow solid looking. Well, I could hardly expect to see through it. I suppose what I am trying to say is, I wanted to put my hand on that knee.

But I didn't. Because this was a teacher-student relationship? Because I was Irish and hung up? Because she was a Chinese and somehow out of bounds? Because of her Chinese Cold Face? Or because I just didn't want to start anything after all I'd been through? I don't know. I do know I kept my hands to myself. But I thought about that knee when I was going to sleep that night.

Then came Chen.

One day Song arrived over to the Friendship in the company of a handsome Chinese giant, about thirty years old. He stood six five, and Song told me he had been a basketball player for the PLA (the Chinese military) before he came to Beida. He was now doing a PhD in English Literature.

Lily came with the pair of them, and as we stood at the foreign experts' bar with a crowd from the hotel, the gravelly voice exuded high humour. No sign of the sharp tongue I dreaded. Indeed I was the one inclined to be sharp. I was in one of those black moods that occasionally come down on me, and there seemed nothing I could do about it. It must have been unpleasant for the others. I could hardly smile, and when I did, it emerged as a sort of grimace. I tried terribly hard to be nice to this Chen fellow, but that didn't come off well.

I simply didn't like him. While respectful and polite, he was extremely self-assured, and what irritated me was that he had plenty to be assured about. His English was flawless; he could discuss Yeats and Synge with me, and even knew a lot about Joyce (whom I regarded as my personal property, at least among the cultural gorillas of the Friendship Hotel). Chen had the temerity to finish the last sentence of *Finnegans Wake* when I started quoting it, bringing it full circle right back to the first sentence of the book.

Now I don't especially like folks who can finish my Joyce for me. Especially when they're Chinese and oughtn't to know Joyce at all. Still less do I like it when they're six foot five and towering over me while doing the quoting.

I liked Chen even less when he started giving off about the Chinese government and the party. I felt he should not have been running them down to a foreigner, and I wished he would keep China's dirty linen to himself.

'Look,' I said, 'no other country in history has ever managed to do what your government has done – to feed one billion people. And to clothe them, and give them all a roof over their heads. India hasn't succeeded: thousands die on the streets in Calcutta. People live in cardboard boxes in Brazil, and more children die there every year than five hydrogen bombs would kill. Your government has eliminated all of that, and you should give them credit.'

Chen talked as if I were a child, or so I felt. 'But it is time to move beyond that, Mr O'Connor,' he said. 'So, we are no longer hungry and no longer cold in winter. Well and good. But our government and party is riddled with corruption. It is time for democracy: from now on the people must decide. Not the party and not a few people in some politburo.'

'And would you like to explain to me, since you seem to know it all, how one billion people are going to decide anything?' I asked. 'When eighty per cent are goddam peasants, and seventy per cent can't bloody well read or write? Do you have even the beginnings of a notion of what democracy is really about? None of you have a fucking clue!' Now that I had beer in I was getting aggressive as well as morose.

Song had never seen me like this. I knew she was watching me, but I would not catch her eye. Finally she came over to me. 'Are you all right, PJ?' she asked gently.

'I'm *fine*, thank you. I'm just discussing democracy with your democratic friend here. I do hope that's all right with you?'

'Well, I need to talk to you now,' she said with surprising firmness. 'Please come with me.'

I let myself be led outside, where we both blinked in the evening sunlight.

'Why are you unfriendly to Chen?' Song asked. The face was impassive.

'That's nonsense!' I blustered. 'I'm perfectly friendly to him. I told you, we were just discussing democracy.'

'No. You are not friendly. And it will upset Lily very much if she notices. She wanted so much for you to like him.'

'Lily? But I thought – uh – I didn't know –'

'He's Lily's new boyfriend. Could you not see that? She brought him here today to meet you. That's why we came.'

'Well, uh, I didn't know that. Nobody told me he was, uh, anybody's boyfriend. How was I expected to know?'

'You didn't give anyone a chance to tell you,' Song said quietly. 'Why don't we go back in, and you can try to be nice to him this time? For Lily's sake, yes?'

We went back in, and to tell the truth I still didn't like Chen, but I was nice to him for Lily's sake. However, I was delighted to see his face glowing bright red from the beer. It's something that happens to some Chinese men, to their embarrassment, because they lack a certain enzyme that breaks down alcohol. Now that would cramp Chen's style and help him lose a little face. It meant he couldn't hold his liquor. It meant he wasn't so goddam marvellous.

It was after this I realised that the gossips were right, but only to a point. I did like Song, and while I found her strangely attractive in spite of her inscrutable face – or perhaps because of it – there was no way I was going to get involved, emotionally or sexually, or any other way. No way was I going to leap from an Irish frying pan into a Chinese fire. Song was a good teacher and interesting to be with, but that was all. And would be all.

CHAPTER FOUR

THAT EARLY AUTUMN in Beijing was an idyllic time. July and August, however, were far from idyllic. That was the period between my two courses when I went to Hong Kong to earn a few dollars, sub-editing for the *South China Morning Post*. The subbing was all right, but I hated every minute of Hong Kong. The damp heat was stifling. The harsh Cantonese language grated on my ears. The people seemed only about half the size of the tall northern folk, and their frenzied lifestyle contrasted harshly with Beijing's more tranquil ways.

It was like living in an anthill. Everything seemed to be a lunatic chase after money, and the honking taxis and the blaring fast-food joints, and the skyscrapers towering over everything, and the mountains closing off every side gave me a fearsome sense of claustrophobia.

My mind kept coming back to Song and her beautiful face. And that almost feline body. Like a cheetah. Chinese women had that catlike quality – even Lily had it. But if Song was a cheetah, Lily was a Siberian tiger that could gut you with a swipe of its paw. Tiger Lily.

And I wondered over and over again what lay behind Song's strange, cold face. Song's hint about hammering back the nail was a clue, and I started reading all I could about China. With little else to do in my spare time, I was reading a lot.

My reading helped me realise that Song was far from unique with her cold face. It was a syndrome that came from thousands of years of feudalism. The Song and Ming dynasties had enforced utter conformism under pain of ferocious penalties. During the Qin Dynasty, which had unified China, historical and philosphical books were burnt, and intellectuals were buried alive lest they might encourage independent thought. In the end no one dared utter an original thought, betray an unacceptable emotion, or show any originality or achievement. Inscrutability became the only escape, and the cold face evolved as protective colouring.

Communism gratefully built on that feudal control, adding its own brand of terror to enforce it. Add to that the awfulness of the so-called 'Cultural Revolution', only a few years back, when a mad communal frenzy led friends to betray friends, wives to sell out their husbands, children to turn in their parents, so that trust simply died.

And if that were not enough, even today you have to live among one billion people, where you can never be alone except when you sleep, where it's dangerous if people get to know you well, where mystery is your only safeguard, where 'your best friend is the one who betrays you'.

'We have to be like those Muslim women with masks over their faces,' a woman had once told me.

I think I was beginning to understand about Song. But would it be worth the effort to lift the mask? Would there be anything behind it after four thousand years, or would it be empty like that death mask of Tutankhamen? Could anything be left beneath the coldness?

But instinct told me that human nature endures, can never be destroyed. And I remembered my sense of some kind of fire behind Song's strange, cold face.

I longed to get back. It became an obsession. I longed to be cycling Beijing's Chang'an Boulevard with Song beside me – if she would ever consent to cycle out with me. I dreamed of strolling with her in the vast space of Tiananmen Square. It seemed to me that you could have plonked the whole of hateful Hong Kong into Tiananmen Square and there'd still have been room for us to stroll there. I just longed for Song Lan.

And not having her, I began to brood about Heather. During the months in Beijing I had gradually come to terms with her betrayal of me, and her death. But the memory was not gone, only lurking. In that Turkish bath of a Hong Kong summer it came back with a vengeance, and I brooded endlessly over whether I was to blame for what had happened.

I had loved Heather so much: I had loved her wheat-coloured hair and her long legs, and I had come to accept her devil-may-care assumption of the down-at-heel gentry that everything exists for their use and benefit. Even people. Even me. It seemed to me I had given Heather everything and given in on everything.

It shouldn't have been a shock. The whole of County Kildare knew about my wife and her Austrian horseman long before I did; at least Heather's horsey crowd knew. It was just denial on my part. It was like having one of those Lippizaner stallions in our living room, and myself stepping gingerly around it as if it wasn't there.

I'd have had to be blind not to notice there was something between Heather and Johann, but I didn't know for sure they were lovers. Or maybe I didn't want to know. And then

finally (to put myself out of my misery, I suppose), I had
used the oldest trick in the journalist's book – pretending to
knowledge I did not have. I said to Heather, one night over
supper, 'How long have you two been lovers?'

Her eyes widened, and she said, 'Since I started running the
stables for him. Six years.'

I actually felt dizzy. I thought I might keel over.

'How did you find out?' Heather asked.

'You told me.'

'When did I tell you?'

'Just now.'

That's when the screeching began. It's strange – she was the
one that was screaming and furious. Whereas I was just
numb, so great was the shock. And that's when she told me I
didn't know the first thing about even beginning to learn
about love. It was the last thing she flung at me before she left
in a fury to go to her lover. Ten minutes later her car ran into
that striped wall by the canal bridge at Hazelhatch.

Maybe Heather had been right in what she said. In that
steam-bath that was Hong Kong, I brooded again over it.
Maybe I didn't know how to love. Was loving a woman just
another version of my Jesuit-induced notion of loving God?

Loving God had been a sort of grooming of the soul,
checking with the handbook to see if the grooming was being
done correctly. Was my loving of Heather the same, checking
in some imaginary handbook to see if I was doing it right?
Flowers for her birthday; being especially understanding once
a month; not letting the sun go down upon our anger. Like
some perfectionist lecher checking in some ceiling mirror on
the aesthetics of his copulative writhings?

So that in the end was I grooming myself as the ideal lover,
just as I had groomed my soul for the Great Doggie Show in
the Sky on the Last Day? Was it all about Me the Lover,
rather than about Heather the Loved One?

Maybe if I had flung rule-book and mirror out of the window, and screeched and roared some uncouth real love, maybe if I had sulked or raved or smashed crockery or even Heather's ribs, she might have felt at least I was real, at least that I cared about her and not just about me.

But even these very thoughts were about me, not her. Was there any way for a Me like Me to flee my Me? No more than I could flee the hell of Hong Kong.

However, after I did finally escape Hong Kong for the cooler spaces of Beijing, that last half of September became an idyll.

In the north-west of Beijing there lies a park full of strange stone ruins. It is called Yuan Ming Yuan. The ruins are from an imperial palace that was destroyed by French and British troops at the end of the second Opium War in 1860 – when those countries incredibly went to war to force drugs on the Chinese and create nine million addicts. And then make a fortune selling them opium.

Today the ruins lurk like dinosaurs among the rustling trees.

On a Saturday of that September, Song Lan walked with me there. It was the first time we had ever walked together. I was just back from Hong Kong, and after my Chinese lesson I simply asked her to come. And she came.

The trees around the ruins were turned to autumn red, and each leaf glowed as the sunlight came through it.

'In China we call those trees *huang lu* – yellow beeches,' Song said. 'They're supposed to be yellow in autumn, but they're always red, like this. Still, I think I prefer them red.'

The park is so vast that the Beijing skyline is not visible, and we had the sense of walking in a remote and beautiful part of the countryside. Rowing boats followed the canals that meander Venice-like throughout the park, connecting shimmering lakes and pagoda-crowned islands. Hundreds of willow trees line the edges of the lakes, their fronds dipping towards the water. Here and there a slender, curved bridge spans a waterway or reaches across to an island topped with a circular pavilion.

As I stood with Song on one of the bridges, suddenly I realised why I had this sense of *déjà vu*. 'When we were children,' I told her, 'we had dinner plates with a scene like this. Lots of people had them. People called them Willow Pattern plates. They had a picture of a pavilion and a little bridge and a willow tree. I loved to finish my food and look at the picture. I wished I could get right into that picture – to be with those little people crossing the bridge to the pavilion. Now I have stepped into that magic picture and you are one of the people on the bridge.

'We kids used to recite a poem about the Willow Pattern plates:

> Two pigeons flying high,
> Chinese vessel sailing by.
> Weeping willow hanging o'er,
> Bridge with three men
> If not four.'

'You say "weeping willow"?' Song asked. 'We also think they are sad – because they mean farewell to us. See how those willow branches droop down and move in the breeze? For us they are lovers waving farewell with their long imperial sleeves.'

Some days could never have been planned, and this was one of them. And some days could never be forgotten, and I knew as we walked along that this too was one of them. This was another Song. The face was still impassive, but I sensed a germ of joy somewhere behind those gentle features.

Music came softly from speakers hidden in the trees, and

we would stop to listen. I would look at those strange eyes now closed as Song listened.

The left hand came up to push the hair back. 'I know that song,' she said. 'It's a Red Guard song I used to sing. The words are silly, but I love the music.' She started singing along with the music, and I could understand then how that song had once set uniformed youngsters stepping out on their marches.

Song recited a poem as we walked along. The meaning was inaccessible to me, but I did not mind, for the sound was as of a dove cooing among the trees.

Towards late afternoon we found ourselves sitting beneath the willows at the edge of a lake, gazing out across the water to where the distant outline of the Fragrant Hills filled the horizon. The hills were eggshell blue. The water was smooth, save for a ring where a fish had jumped. A line of slow sparkles led across the water to the sun. I leaned back for a moment and looked up to where a mare's tail of cloud was moving slowly past the willow over our heads.

Song's hands were in her lap. I reached across and took one. It was dry, and the palm was not as soft as I had expected. Almost rough. Then I felt her nails and ran my thumb over the cuticles. I lifted the hand then to study it, palm downwards, and I thought this is the first oriental hand I have ever really looked at. The fingers were slender, with the faintest golden sheen to the skin, which made my own hands seem strangely pink. I turned her hand over and noticed how the palms were the colour of my own.

'You have circular whorls in your fingerprints,' I said. 'You must be special.'

'You know what we say in China?' Song murmured back. 'One circle means you will marry a poor man. Two means a rich man. Three means you'll end up selling bean curd and never marry at all.'

There was a pause. 'I have three,' Song said.

I turned to look at her. There was a single tear half way down one cheek.

'Three's OK,' I whispered.

'But it's true,' Song said. 'I am too old to marry now. No Chinese man would have me. I am 35.' She lowered her head in shame.

'That's still young, Song,' I said gently. 'But what happened? Why did you never marry? You must know you are beautiful.'

'The Cultural Revolution,' she said. 'It destroyed me, and millions of women like me. It destroyed our lives. And our parents' lives too.'

She turned to look at me. 'When I was fifteen years old, they broke up my home and took me away from my parents. They sent me down to the countryside, to work with the peasants. I slept in a mud hut, and there was ice on the inside of the walls at night. When I came back from the fields at night and pulled off my work gloves, the skin would come away from my hands.'

I found I was pressing one of those hands tightly between my own. Now I knew why the palms were rough.

'My parents were sent to the countryside too, because my father was a professor of English. That made him a class enemy – "the stinking ninth category". That's what they called intellectuals. They burned my father's whole library of English books – the ones he taught me to read as a child. They forced him to watch. Then they beat him so badly he's paralysed down one side and still blind in one eye. My mother died of pneumonia down in the countryside. I never saw her again, and I didn't see my father for more than ten years. And after years in the fields they made me work in a factory. It was only after that I got back to school again, just when the schools had reopened. And I was lucky – most of my generation never got an education, because the schools had all closed. Most of them never recovered. They call them the Lost Generation.'

'But did no one ever ask you to marry?'

'Oh yes. And it was the worst thing that happened to me. The headman of the village, the party leader, wanted to marry me. But I refused him.'

'But you would have married a powerful man. He could have done so much for you.'

'I could never have married him,' she said fiercely. 'Can you imagine how crude these peasants are? You have no idea. And if I had married, I would have been left in the countryside for the rest of my life.' She sighed. 'But you are right: he was powerful. So powerful he put me in the local jail until I gave in. First he tried to bribe me. Then threats. Then the jail. That's how powerful he was.'

'But you never gave in?'

'*Never.*'

'So what happened?'

'I was in the jail seven months. Then I refused to eat. I almost died, so he had to let me out. The party forced him. That's when he had me sent away to work in a factory. I was an embarrassment to him before the whole village.'

'But you must have got other offers to marry.'

'Yes. But I didn't want to marry a worker any more than a peasant. It would have finished my chances of ever getting back to school. So I held out and said no every time. I was determined that some day I would finish my schooling. And I did.' She sighed. 'But by then it was too late for me to marry. Girls here don't marry after twenty-four. Nobody would have them.'

The sun had moved, and the sparkle was now a golden pathway across the water to the Fragrant Hills, lately turned to mauve. I reached across and put my arm around the slender shoulders. They started to quiver, and I realised she was sobbing.

So Song could weep. I wondered if some day I might see her smile. A fish plopped in the water, and the rings widened silently.

At some point shortly afterwards we started to hold hands. At first it was as strange for me as it was for her – Heather had never been one for touching.

And then for the rest of that September, Song and I wandered hand in hand. Dear God, how wonderful it was just to hold hands with someone. Hand in hand we strolled past Zhongnanhai, down past Tiananmen Square to drink tea at some cheap little place in an alley beyond the Beijing Hotel. Holding hands we puttered across the blue lake of Bei Hai in a puttery electric boat. It was only later I realised that Chinese women do not lightly hold hands in public, and what a compliment Song had paid me.

As we wandered the streets we watched the old men strolling with their pet birds, swinging them in their cages as they walked and hanging the cages from the trees in the little street-corner parks where they met their cronies for cards or *mahjongg*. The parks sounded like forests filled with birdsong.

And we listened to that other bird sound, the strange whistling that comes from flocks of doves wheeling overhead. Each dove is fitted with a tiny bamboo whistle, so that when they all fly together, they give off this ethereal sound.

Song gazed up at the doves, listening. 'That's what we all long to be like,' she said, 'but instead we're like these.' She pointed to the birds in the cages.

We meandered through Purple Bamboo Park one Sunday morning, looking for English Corner, where all Beijing's English-language enthusiasts congregate to practise their English.

A girl of perhaps eighteen dropped into step with us. 'Good morning, Sir,' she said. 'Let us speak English together.'

I was slightly taken aback, but I said OK.

'Very well. We start now. How old are you?'

'Ulp. I'm thirty-nine, if you really want to know.'

'Oh, that's very old. How many children you have?'

'None that I know of.'

'Oh, that's terrible. Is this your wife?'

'Well, no. Look, young lady, that's enough of the questions. How about showing us a shortcut to English Corner?'

'Sure, I take you.'

That near-child was gentle, shy, yet with a quality that could give lessons to any western assertiveness-training course. Those questions, of course, would be quite normal among the Chinese. This was the newly assured generation that was growing up in China – a generation Song had missed by a good fifteen years.

English Corner turned out to be a misnomer. It's not a corner at all, but a clearing in the trees, and there were hundreds of mostly young people chattering away together in English. Or in the nearest they could manage to English.

As soon as the foreign devil was spotted they gathered around, until we found ourselves surrounded by a crowd pressing in from all sides. The youngsters vied with each other to ask me questions: how old was I and how much did I earn, and did I know how equal pay for everyone (the 'iron rice-bowl') was destroying initiative and making everybody lazy? And did I think that China had corruption in high places and not enough democracy in low places, and did I know how many 'Benz' cars the leaders had here in Beijing? Far too many, everyone seemed to agree.

Little Miss Assertion seemed to have got lost or trampled under all the 'Benzes' and the longings for democracy, for we didn't see her again. But I did see Kui'er, and he gave me a cheery greeting.

It was when someone said, 'You must be making love to lots of women because you're starting to go bald,' that I blushed and Kui'er grinned. The trouble really began when someone started asking if western penises were really bigger than Chinese ones. I tried to brush it off by saying that the only way to find out would be to compare.

Then that monkey Kui'er, with a grin on his face, said, 'OK, let's compare!' And he stepped forward, unzipped and pulled out his willy. Two other young fellows immediately stepped forward and did the same. I was flabbergasted. Their willies curved down like small pink caterpillars and looked servicable enough to me. The crowd, men and women, waited attentively.

'You must!' hissed Song in my ear.

I had no option. I unzipped and pulled it out. There was a sort of gasp from the crowd, and then they began to applaud. I pushed it back in. Mercifully it hadn't stood up.

I said we really gotta be going now, and pushed my way through inner and outer and outermost rings, tugging Song the while, until we breathed again. Jesus, I wanted to kill that grinning little creep Kui'er. Just wait till class tomorrow. And in fact nothing had been proved, because I had known from schooldays that I was more than usually endowed in that quarter, even by western standards.

And then I saw something I never thought to see. Song was grinning. Grinning from ear to ear. And it transformed her. Grinning at me, who had just made an almighty exhibition of myself. Well, if it took that to crack the cold face, so be it. I grabbed her and I hugged her. And she hugged me. We hugged until it almost hurt.

The next day Kui'er didn't bat an eyelid. And nobody else was grinning, so I knew he hadn't squealed. So I said nothing either. Indeed I felt I could at least trust him, little devil though he was.

The Summer Palace became our favourite haunt. It is not so

much a palace as a domain. Coming up to October 1, the National Day that commemorates the coming to power of the communists, the whole vast terrain becomes a red forest of flags. On one pleasantly warm day we found ourselves pushing through the crowds in the narrow alleyways between the pavilions.

What an experience suddenly to emerge on to Kunming Lake, choppy like a sea, with a cool breeze coming off the top of the waves, then to be strolling along what seemed miles of brilliantly decorated open corridor with the lake on our left, and to see those gentle impassive faces, and people standing their little ones against some pillar to take a snapshot and to realise that no one is begging, no one is trying to sell anything, no one is bothering us at all.

And to be hand in hand with someone like Song – this was summer in any month, and we were in a palace.

As we walked she told me about her grandmother. 'Grandma's feet were only the size of my finger, about three inches long, and her toes were twisted back in under her soles. Like this' – Song made a fist. 'She could only hobble. When she'd wash her feet I'd try to see them, but she'd get mad. And the smell was awful.

'Her mother bound them when she was a tiny girl, to stop them growing and force them to be crooked. It was done to all the women: no one would marry them if they hadn't tiny feet. The men told them it was a mark of beauty, but it was only to keep them from leaving the house.'

She told me how the Cinderella story had come from China and was about those same small feet. That the glass slipper had been a mistranslation by the Frenchman who collected the story. 'It wasn't *glass* – it was *tiny*.'

She told me too how every man had had to wear a pigtail, which must never be cut, as a symbol of his submission to the emperor.

53

And she told of all the wonderful things China had invented when the world was young – like gunpowder, the compass, and printing and paper. 'We wasted every one of them,' she said. 'Like the compass. The foreign devils stole it and used it to guide their ships. And they built great navies and discovered the world. Do you know what we used the compass for? For aligning tombs in the right direction. And for finding buried treasure.

'And gunpower. The foreigners stole that too, and conquered the world. We used it for fire-crackers, for the emperor's ceremonies. You know we've never had a Nobel prizewinner yet? Out of a thousand million people?'

I let her talk on. I felt her anger, but it seemed that if she was starting to name these things, to utter them, to express her anger, it could only be good.

That day we wandered the length and breadth of that vast area they call the Summer Palace, past the crazy but lovely Marble Boat, great hull carved in stone, beached from the day of its creation, its impossible marble paddle-wheels frozen for ever in the shallows.

'A symbol of China,' Song said. 'Never moves.'

We climbed the hill to the Pavilion of Buddha Fragrance that crowns the top, wandered up and down steps and over bridges, and gazed out over the lake where dragon-headed barges floated, one containing a full orchestra, from which drifted the music of Händel.

At one spot along the shore is a life-sized bronze statue of a reclining ox, and just beyond it a gracefully curved seventeen-arch bridge leading to an island. We were just passing when I noticed Lily and her boyfriend standing on the bridge, about ten yards away. They did not see us, and I was about to go up to them, when Song pulled me sharply away.

I stopped for a moment to look. Chen was holding Lily against the parapet. Her head was back and her eyes were closed. They were doing just about everything short of making love, right there on the bridge.

As we walked on, I sensed that Song was disturbed.

'They shouldn't do that,' she hissed. I was noticing that Song hissed when she was upset. It was about the only sign she gave. 'Did you see how people were looking at them? People do not do that here, and they are being insensitive. Chen should know better.'

She stopped and turned to me. 'PJ, I do not want you to be upset, but Lily is trouble. She is not good for Chen. And she is trouble among the students.'

I felt a lurch of guilt, realising I had hardly thought of Lily since I came back from Hong Kong, except to ask Song if she had seen her. Song had indeed seen her, but had said little about it. Now it seemed I was to hear more.

'She has been taking Chen to sleep with her at night,' Song said.

Well, Lily, you little minx, I thought. You didn't waste much time, did you? You gave your dad a few grey hairs back in Dublin, and now you're going to give me some.

'But surely Chen's big enough to look after himself?' I said to Song.

'Of course he is. But Lily keeps leading him on, and it's becoming the talk of the campus. It's not like in the West. People just don't do it like that here. And the thing is, we need Chen very much – he is one of the best student leaders we have, and if we are ever to make changes here on campus, or in China itself, we need leaders like him. Now he's losing respect.'

She paused and gazed out over the lake. 'But that's not all. Do you know that Lily goes to all the political meetings among the students? She goes with Chen. She's very active and tells them they have to learn to organise and go on strike, just like Irish students. And to have no respect for their teachers. And they listen to her, especially because she's a *hua qiao*.'

'A what?'

'An overseas Chinese. Not a foreign devil like you! It's
what they call Chinese who live abroad. In a way she's still
one of us, but she's bringing these ideas we're not used to.
And our students are very naive – they think that if students
can change things in the West by marching and demonstrat-
ing, as Lily says they do, that it will work here too.'

'Well, why shouldn't it?'

'Perhaps it can, but I doubt it. Our government's not like
the West. Here change doesn't come from below. But, on the
other hand, our leaders have grown more open in the last ten
years, so maybe they will listen to us when we tell them about
all the bad things in China.'

'Have they really grown that open?'

'Well at least they're better than during the Cultural
Revolution. People say the older leaders have grown benign.
Like that stone lion outside Zhongnanhai – he seems fierce
until you take a good look at him, and then you see his face
is kindly. I think some of these old men – not all of them, of
course – want democracy as much as we do. Maybe some of
them even want us to push for it. They need our help.'

'So what's the trouble with Lily?'

'The trouble is she is a foreigner in the eyes of the government. She is not the only one: there are westerners teaching
and studying here that are telling the same things to the students. There's a Norwegian man from your Friendship Hotel,
called Hansen, who is saying all the things like Lily, and even
saying the students should use violence. He goes to all the
meetings. That makes the government think, it's only the foreigners stirring up trouble.

'If there's to be change, it has to come from the Chinese
people only, and the foreigners should keep out of it. They are
not helping us at all. Instead they are just making clear water
muddy. And Lily's one of the worst.'

I resolved I would endeavour to fulfil my long-neglected *in-loco-parentis* duties towards Lily, and I looked forward to it with little relish. In fact I dreaded an encounter with her tongue. So far she had not used it on me, and I would have preferred such a situation to continue.

But what happened in the next few days quite put Lily out of my mind.

CHAPTER FIVE

I T WAS ON October 1, 1949, that Mao Zedong had stood on the balcony of Tiananmen – the Gate of Heavenly Peace – and proclaimed the People's Republic of China. Each year since, that date has been a time of celebration.

It has also been a traditional time for China to say thank you to her friends, in particular the 'foreign experts'.

No one knows better than the Chinese how to say thank you with generosity. Thus it was that on October 1, 1988, I found myself invited, with fifteen hundred foreign experts and their friends, to a banquet in the Great Hall of the People that forms one side of Tiananmen Square. 'No bringing of bags,' the invitation had stipulated.

Through Norman I had managed to weasel a second invitation for Song. We felt awed as we walked past the hard-faced sentries at the north entrance of the Great Hall, that enormous shrine to the people of China, across the hushed red carpet and up the magnificent ceremonial staircase.

It is a remarkable experience to sit down to a meal with 1,500 people. We were in a vast upstairs hall, with windows looking towards the Gate of Heavenly Peace. The hall was crammed with circular tables, ten people to a table. Banks of built-in floodlights and spots ran the length of the east and west walls, just below the ceiling, and those lights were coming on and off in clusters to meet the need of the television people who moved among the tables with shoulder-held mini-cameras.

On the south wall of the banquet room was the circular red and gold seal of China – five stars above a bas-relief of Tiananmen Gate. The seal was surrounded by furled red flags, like rays from the rising sun. I was thinking it must be the devil of a job to get the dust out of those flags.

Inevitably I found myself stuck at the same table as the old Friendship gang. Norman was holding court, just as if it were the hotel, and Hansen was already at the beer, his wife vainly signalling him to go easy on it. There were the usual hangers on and a couple of strangers. Only Madame Lukas was missing, and the one empty place at our table had her name on the card.

All the lights came on at once, and there was a burst of applause as a line of dignitaries filed in and took their places at a raised long table only yards from us. I recognised the horn-rims and owlish face of Premier Li Peng and the cheerful countenance of Party Secretary Zhao Ziyang. Li was in a formal Mao suit, while Zhao wore a light grey western suit and tie. It was a curious sensation to be sitting close to people whose faces were familiar from television. They looked ordinary. At the VIP table a silver-haired man in olive uniform was bowing in our direction, and I realised Norman was bowing back.

'So you really do have friends in high places?' I whispered to Norman.

'How many times have I told you that?' he growled.
'Trouble with you sods, y'don't appreciate your elders and
betters.'

'How do you know him?'

'Used to be my jailer in the Cultural Revolution,' Norman
said. 'Now pipe down and sing up!'

Everyone was standing for the 'Internationale', to the
accompaniment of loudspeaker music. Zhao Ziyang then
went to the rostrum below the flags and talked interminably
from a sheaf of notes.

Finally we got to eat. The meal was a medley of quite deli-
cious morsels like spiced beef and crispy duck, alternating
with loathsome frogs legs and jellied horrors like slugs and
sea-cucumbers that sent shivers down my spine. One simply
spun the movable centre of the table until the preferred good-
ies came one's way, and left the horrors to Norman who
benignly wolfed his way through them, sliding slugs down his
gullet with panache.

We each had a large glass for beer which was continually
replenished, and a tiny stemmed glass for Great Wall wine, to
be used for the various toasts towards the end of the meal.
Norman explained that they used to serve that ferocious spir-
it called *Mao Tai*, 'but so many of you damn foreign experts
disgraced yourselves that the Chinese daren't serve it to you
any more.'

A glance at Sven, already catatonic from mere beer, left me
in no doubt of the truth of this.

The toasts seemed as interminable as Zhao's speech had
been, and then a ferociously hot damp towel was placed in
front of me. 'What's this for?' I asked.

'A subtle hint,' Norman said, 'that the party's nearly over.
No more food coming your way, young Paddy. Just eat what's
on the table. And remember, if y'can, that a gentleman in
China leaves something on the plate.'

61

People were starting to visit each other's tables, and I saw the silver-haired police officer coming our way. He greeted Norman warmly, sat briefly beside him in Madame Lukas's empty chair and chatted in Chinese. Norman introduced us with a wave of his hand as 'our foreign devils from the Friendship Hotel'. He added, 'This is Colonel Wu.'

Wu rose slightly, smiled and bowed to each of us. His eyebrows rose slightly when he saw Song, but he bowed especially graciously to her.

The two men resumed talking, and Norman's face suddenly grew grave. I recognised the words *You Yi Binguan* (Friendship Hotel) several times. After a couple of minutes the colonel left, with another bow and a smile to our table. But Norman wasn't smiling.

'What was that about?' I asked.

'Later,' Norman said.

'So what was it?' I asked again in the taxi on the way home – which Song and I shared with Norman.

'Wu told me Lee was arrested last week. Said it would probably hit *China Daily* in the next few days, so he didn't mind telling me. They know he always stayed at the Friendship and probably had friends there. I had the feeling he wanted me to warn those friends, though I am not quite sure why.'

Norman turned around to us as the Nissan purred past Muxidi.

'It seems,' he resumed, 'Lee was picked up at Beijing airport, coming in from Hong Kong. He was carrying half a million dollars worth of heroin. Oh, and Wu also said he had been distributing heroin through Beijing University. He had some messengers, apparently, who smuggled packets of heroin in there for him.'

We were still in the car when the implication of Norman's

words hit me. I felt dizzy, and wanted to vomit at the same time. I reached for Song's hand, and it was damp and trembling. I put my arms around her shoulders, and she clung tightly to me, and she was shaking.

In the front seat Norman was busy with his own thoughts. When we got to the Friendship, Norman stopped the taxi at the second roundabout, near Building Eight, paid the man and, without speaking, walked quickly off towards entrance Number Twelve. We followed him in silence, and again I wanted to vomit and I could feel Song's hand trembling. Norman was climbing the concrete staircase to the second, third, then fourth floor, until we were outside Madame Lukas' door.

He knocked, but there was no answer. He hammered loudly, about five times. Then he just stood back and nodded to me. I kicked the door in. I went in first, Norman behind me. I don't remember if Song stayed on the landing. The place smelled of stale cabbage.

There was no one in the little lounge. I pushed in the bedroom door: the bed was unmade, and there were piles of clothes on it. The horrid black silk shawl lay on top.

The kitchen was empty and dreadfully untidy. That left only the bathroom. The door was slightly ajar, so I pushed it in. Madame Lukas lay, naked as the day she was born, floating in a full bathtub. She looked like a wizened Ophelia, her hair swirling about her head like grey water weeds.

I was reaching over to her when Norman grabbed my arm. Silently he pointed to the electric flex that snaked over the side of the bath, near Madame's feet. We followed the flex back through the door to the wall socket just outside and unplugged it. Then Norman went to the bath, reached into the water and lifted out Madame Lukas' electric cooking ring.

He went to the lounge and lifted the telephone. Song and I followed him.

'Can y'remember Security's number?' Norman asked me.

I put a finger on the telephone cradle. 'Before we do that, Norman,' I said, 'there's something you should know.'

He stared at me.

'Song has been delivering packets for Madame Lukas,' I said. 'To some American up at the university. Packets that Lee brought in from Hong Kong. Sealed packets. Song thought they were banned books. I thought so too.'

Norman looked at us, from one to the other, like a bleary old lion. 'You blithering idiots,' he finally said, and it was almost a whisper. 'O dear God in heaven. You pathetic, miserable, blithering idiots. O dear God in heaven.'

Somehow, Norman invoking God put the frighteners on me more than anything else. He looked at Song, standing there, head down, hands clasped in front of her. Then he turned to me.

He stood up. 'Get out of here. Get her away from here. I'll deal with this mess. Take her to your apartment and stay there until I get back to you in the morning. Just GO!'

There are a few times in life when one is numbed. I remember being so at ten when my mother died. I felt that way again the day I identified Heather's body. But this was the first time I had felt numb for a living being right there beside me.

Song and I sat side by side on the edge of my bed, upright and staring forward, like those two statues at Abu Simel. I just kept squeezing Song's hand in mine, and I could feel the spasms of shuddering that ran across her frail body, like aftershocks of an earthquake.

Helplessness combined with horror. One moment I would think, I must get her out: there has to be a way – where there's a will there's a way – maybe through Hong Kong, or some kind of forged passport at the airport: there has to be a way.

And then my heart would lurch and I would realise there was no way. No way at all. I would have visions of Song kneeling on the ground, arms twisted back into the jet-plane position, and someone putting a pistol to the nape of her neck (that slender nape I would glimpse when the breeze lifted her hair), and the officer lowering his red flag. And another spasm of trembling would signal that Song was envisioning all that too.

Then I would lurch towards hope. Maybe they don't execute women. I remembered reading how they sometimes give suspended death sentences. Or maybe they'll never connect Song with anything. Or she could say she really thought it was books. Which is true anyway. Perhaps the American she delivered them to would speak up for her. Or is he an American? Jesus, I don't even know who he is.

Then a lurch back to horror. What if a knock came on the door right now? Those cold faces under olive peaked caps taking Song away. Christ, maybe taking me away too. Now stop that: she's the one needs help. But I'm scared too. Ah. Feeling sorry for yourself too? Never change, you creep. Me, me, me, my, my, my . . .

Suddenly Song was sobbing as if her soul was coming up, and I was holding her and her head was on my breast, and then we fell back on the bed, and she sobbed and shook and rocked herself and clung to me, and her tears tasted salty.

We lay entwined for hours. Maybe we slept a little: I am not sure. Maybe we felt cold, and awakened. I just remember that suddenly I was gazing into those dark eyes that gazed unblinkingly back at me. The faintest tang of perspiration touched my nostrils. My heart was drumming like horses' hooves, and then I realised hers was too, because I could feel it, and then my mouth was upon hers and we were devouring each other like starving people. I felt the thin cotton of her blouse and was tugging at the buttons and she was helping me, and then helping me with my own buttons and zip, and then we were clinging together, raw and desperate and terribly vulnerable. She pushed me back a little to look at me, and her body seemed lightly brushed in gold dust, and I marvelled at how perfect her small breasts were.

'Help me,' she whispered. 'It's the first time I ever – I've never —'

I held her tight. 'It's a first for me too,' I whispered. 'First time with someone who's never —'

We were wakened the next morning by a key rasping in the door and the door banging open. We both sat bolt upright, pulling around us the bedclothes under which we had later crept for warmth. I don't think either of us knew for a moment where we were, although the sun was blazing through the thin curtains.

Standing in the bedroom doorway, staring in, was the tall, unfriendly *fu wu yuan* that looked after our floor. In one hand he held a bathroom mop and in the other a thermos of hot water. His glasses glinted.

We stared at each other for what seemed an age, and no one said anything. The *fu* gave a slight bow: '*Dui bu qi*,' he said, and went back out, closing the door gently behind him.

We looked at each other and burst out laughing. It was the first time Song had ever laughed. Then her hand went to her mouth and the horror came back, and both our laughters died like quenched fire. The fear was pain now – a cancerous thing that throbbed deep down in the belly, no matter how you twisted or turned or tried to force yourself to think of tolerable things.

We were strangely shy of one another. Song wrapped the bedspread around her and took her clothes to the bathroom with her. I telephoned the journalism school and cancelled my training session. I said I was unwell. God knows I was. When Song had showered, I took a shower too.

Norman rang the bell just as I was combing my hair. It was the first time he had ever been to my apartment, and the old curmudgeon looked almost benign in the unfamiliar surroundings.

'Go back to Beida,' he said to Song. 'Go on with your life as if nothing has happened. Give your classes; tutor your students. And don't go looking for that American: he won't come looking for you, I assure you. Indeed he could be arrested by now.'

He sat down on the bed. 'Oh, and come down here as usual to give young Paddy his lesson. In other words, don't make any change in your routine. Even if you're involved with any of this student-movement stuff, stay involved. No obvious change. Is that clear?'

He was surprisingly gentle with Song. 'Now be off, young lady. I need to talk to Paddy, here.'

When Song was gone, Norman turned to me. 'It could be very bad. The amount these people know, that they never even use, is incredible. And Wu hinted at something rather alarming. He said there might be other dimensions to the affair – far beyond drugs. Political dissidents. Or espionage. It could even be tied up with the power struggle going on right now. Zhao versus Li Peng.'

He sat down and fumbled for his pipe. 'Or it could be there were never any drugs involved – they could be using drug charges as a cover to get at the dissidents. That's the problem with China: nothing is ever what it seems. And you never know how much the authorities really know. Or whether they are just waiting. That oriental patience is a very real commodity – don't you ever underestimate it.'

He struck a match and pulled on the pipe. 'On the other hand, perhaps they really do know very little. Wu told me he understood it was only a spot check at the airport. But how much does he know? Wu's under pressure too at the moment.'

'What would happen if – if it did get bad?' I asked.

'Then I'd tell Wu what I know. That the wretched woman thought it was books. I'd ask him to pass it on to the right quarters, and then start hoping. And y'could start some of that praying – you're supposed to be one of those bloody Christians, aren't you? But I'm not sure I'd bother Wu unless they actually came for Song. I'm going to do some thinking about this.'

As he left, he turned at the door: 'And will you for God's sake grow up fast, young Paddy. And learn to take care of your women!'

I did try hard to take care of my one woman in the weeks that followed. They were weeks of great beauty, with the trees around the Friendship turning yellow and red, and warm November days like summer in Ireland. But fear was a tiger curled inside our bellies that would suddenly sink its claws into our gut, and we would shriek silently with the agony of it.

Two policemen walking towards us in the hotel grounds were enough to make us dizzy. A knock on my door when Song was giving me a Chinese lesson left us so disturbed that we could not finish the lesson.

And that was when we were together. I will never know how much that woman suffered when alone. I can only guess what it must have been like in that tiny Beida dormitory room with colleagues she dared not confide in, or when she was called in for an unscheduled meeting with her work-unit director. I do know that for a while it seemed as if her tiger was gnawing her insides clean away.

It was worst the day we learned of Lee's execution. Just a white poster on a wall near the campus – a list of names in Chinese characters, and a red slash-mark opposite each name. Song told me one of the names was Lee's.

But if Song grew frailer, the bonds between us grew stronger. I had never heard of fear as a nourishment for love, but maybe fear shared could create bonds that nothing else might ever have done. We were glad and grateful for that first night together. I remember Song once saying, 'We've planted a tiny acorn. Now we must water it and watch it grow, and the water we use is kindness.'

There wasn't all that much sex at first. I would have liked lots. In spite of my Catholic upbringing my natural drive was to make love at every opportunity, even if I got twinges of conscience afterwards, as I occasionally did when the black moods came. But Song didn't always encourage lovemaking. She said that when you're getting to know someone, sex could be a distraction. It's just so all-absorbing that you hardly get time or energy to notice anything else about the person, she said. Well, maybe. I'd have taken my chances.

Yet perhaps she had a point. Even in the midst of terrible fear, there were so many tiny facets of Song's personality which I might hardly have encountered had I been constantly mesmerised by that incomparable body. And I might not have encountered the quirks and flaws of her character either, and I needed to know those too.

Still, as I say, I'd have taken my chances on it. And I rejoiced at those times I did plunge deep into Song's golden body. Like the day we went to the Fragrant Hills.

We almost forgot the fear that morning. As our bus from Beijing approached the Fragrant Hills, the forested foothills lay layered in ever fainter shades of blue, one behind the other, like a Chinese silk painting. It was a warm late-November day and the slopes with their Buddhist temples were swarming with people picnicking under the trees. We passed through the crowds and found a forest track leading upwards.

We just kept on going for several hours until finally there were no more people. It was an easy climb, and birds were singing and the forest murmured all around us and the light filtered through the red and yellow leaves that still remained on the branches over our heads. Each leaf lit up and glowed like a tiny church window. There was the fragrance of warm earth about us, and the leaves under our feet crunched and crackled as though they were Chinese crackers.

Song stretched up to a branch to pluck a red maple leaf. There was an unconscious grace in the way she reached up with her left hand, her head back with the hair cascading down, one foot off the ground behind her, white shirt dappled by the leaf-filtered sunlight. I can see her stretching still.

And I can still see the wonder in her face as she sat there on the carpeted track, holding the leaf against the light so that it glowed and its skeletal tracery showed like a crimson x-ray.

She looked at me and uttered in English the words of the old Tang Dynasty poem:

> Deeper yet deeper into the mountains go;
> Drain every beauty there of hill and dale.

I was sitting close to her when she said this, gazing at her face. And I noticed things I had never quite grasped before – that oriental eyes do not sit at the back of hollows as ours do, but lie almost flat on the surface of the face; that the whole face, even with its nose, is strangely flat, and that the head, from cheekbone to cheekbone, is wider than ours, but shorter from forehead to the back of the head, like the statues of the Buddha I had seen. And then something seemed to go 'click' inside my mind, and I suddenly saw how incomparably beautiful such proportions are. I needed to weep.

I moved closer to that splendid face until it filled my vision and the almond eyes were gazing into mine. Song's scent touched my nostrils – the fragrance of warm clean flesh. Lips touched and opened, and the taste was like that fragrance.

My heart was thudding as we spread our clothes on the crackling carpet of leaves. I put my arm around her and gently laid her down. It seemed as if her splendid body had been lightly brushed with gold dust.

She was lovely beyond all utterance.

Song seemed different from that day on. The change was infinitesimally slow, and subtle at first, as though the lips that I had parted that day were getting the courage to part in a smile. I had only ever seen her smile once, at my ridiculous exhibitionism in Purple Bamboo Park. And she had only laughed once, for a tiny instant before terror quenched it. Now I would occasionally catch her in a smile. And how it transformed her face.

Her innate humour began to show. It was kindly, and frequently at my expense. She would sometimes pronounce my name as 'Pee-Joe' instead of 'Pee-Jay', which created hilarity among our friends. Even Norman snorted into his glass when he heard it. Finally it was he told me she was actually calling me *pijiu*, which was the Chinese word for beer. I didn't much mind, and it delighted the Chinese.

She could imitate my walk, which I had never thought in any way peculiar, but it made our friends chuckle. She would sometimes tease me about my nose – our prominent western noses being objects of fascination and indeed hilarity to the Chinese. They perceive them as something akin to axe-heads projecting from the face. '*Da Bizi*' (Big Nose), she would chuckle, and pull her own neat nose outwards and upwards, as though that made the slightest difference.

Yes, she could chuckle, and the first time I heard it it sounded to me like the ice of the cold face breaking up. And from that she progressed to occasional giggles – and eventually to joyful laughter. How I remember that first peal of laughter that was without terror: to me it was the peal of a bell announcing good tidings.

None of it happened overnight, of course. The changes came almost imperceptibly, over a long time, with an occasional sudden increment like that first laughter.

I think I was changing too, but I didn't know it then.

They were good times, all in all, even if the fear never left us. Surprisingly, during that time I found myself growing to like old Norman. Not that he had changed in the least: he remained the same mean-mouthed old curmudgeon who bullied everyone by the fear his tongue inspired and snapped at any hand that dared to proffer even a hint of friendship.

Yet I was beginning to realise we were all his friends, even if the old man chewed us up and spat us out and dominated us and bullied us. Norman had a bad dose of British stiff upper lip (or, as I called it, stiff upper buttock) and had never learnt to show feelings. He hid them all in a snarl or a growl or in that biting humour.

But the façade had slipped ever so slightly, that night of death, and I had had a glimpse of the caring man who had left the England he loved, to give his life to helping an infant dragon break out of its eggshell. And who had stayed with that growing dragon even after it had mauled him badly during the Cultural Revolution.

CHAPTER SIX

I WISH I could say there came a day when the fear was gone, but that never happened. And I wish I could even say that it just 'faded into the light of common day', as the poet said. But that did not happen either. The fear simply lurked. Waiting.

Time passed, and they still didn't come for Song, but we never knew if or when they would. The Chinese being a people of infinite patience, they were well capable of waiting months or years before they struck.

So we simply got on with our lives and doing just that gave to those lives a semblance of normality. And it also gave us the opportunity to learn more and more about each other.

There was one thing I gradually learned about Song, which I didn't particularly appreciate: that there was a part of her life where she did not want me to intrude. Her life on Beida campus was, for all practical purposes, out of bounds to me.

Finally, after a lot of badgering from me, she invited me one Saturday evening to her living quarters so she could cook *jaozi* for me – a sort of ravioli. I don't know how much of her salary the food cost her, but I know her salary was a minuscule eighty *yuan* a month (about £13 sterling).

To get to Song's room I climbed cluttered concrete stairs with wooden crates on the landings and picked my way along unglazed corridors around tea chests, cardboard boxes tied with rope, bicycles, pots and pans, barrels of paraffin, gas cylinders, all stacked as neatly as space allowed. Song told me these were the tenants' possessions: there was nowhere else to store them. People were cooking at little paraffin stoves on tables in the open corridors, through which a cold wind moaned.

Song's room in that Beida dormitory was the size of my hotel bathroom, into which three bunks were crammed, one double-deck and the other single. Her roommates, two other women lecturers, had discreetly buggered off to give her some space.

Song did the cooking outside in the freezing corridor on a tiny pot-sized paraffin stove, like the Primus stove I remembered from childhood. My initial feeling in Song's room was one of claustrophobia. And then it struck me that this would be Song's lot for the rest of her natural life. No western jail would warehouse its prisoners so tightly, and Song had a life-sentence. I grieved for her.

But that gave way to profound admiration at how Chinese people cope with well-nigh impossible conditions. The room had the tight tidiness of a submarine's sleeping quarters. Nothing out of place: every cubic centimetre of space was used, were it under the bed, on shelves above the bed, on the back of the door, or in a net hanging from the ceiling. Books had their place; clothes were tightly folded as in the military. The room smelled clean and fresh and feminine.

I realised once more that simply coping with one thousand million fellow citizens was the primary and overwhelming task that every Chinese person faced in life, and, cold face or not, I was humbled in amazement and admiration at how well they did it.

Song's friends dropped by soon after we finished eating. Some of them carried jam-jars full of jasmine tea, from which they proceeded to sip, topping up with hot water from Song's giant thermos flask. This was their equivalent of an Irish pub: there was no money to go out and drink beer. Nobody even seemed even to think of alcohol. Yet the *craic* seemed as good as in a pub back home, though different in form and content.

More people came until the tiny room was crowded. They sat on the floor, on the top bunk with their feet dangling, on the bottom bunk with backs bent to fit. Some came and went; some came and stayed. Some were Song's students – earnest lanky young men, who clearly never had to shave; and those agonizingly lovely young women. Others were Song's colleagues: an efficient, professional-looking woman in her 40s; an elderly professor with a long wisp of beard, whom everybody treated with respect.

Smiles were few, but there was a friendliness here that perhaps only exists behind closed doors in China. Maybe here is when the masks come off, I thought.

This was another facet of Song that was new to me. Although she said little, it was evident that she was both respected and popular. At first I had rather conceitedly thought these folks had come to meet me – until I realised that this was a regular Saturday evening. A Chinese combination of intellectual salon and Thank-God-it's-Saturday, and it seemed Song was a natural hostess.

Lily came (Christ, I had nearly forgotten about her), and she had that bloody Chen in tow. I sensed that all was not well between Lily and Song, and that Song did not really want her there. But our Lily has nothing if not a thick skin. And Chen was on the top of his earnest, bespectacled form, regaling me as usual on what he considered wrong with China.

'Did you ever try to get on a bus at rush hour?' he asked me.

'Practically every day.' Which wasn't quite true, for I loved my bike too much to spend much time on buses.

'Then you know how people rush and fight and scramble and use their elbows, and how the old women are nearly trampled?'

Yes, I knew, and it was one of the most frightening things about commuting in Beijing. It frightened me every time I got into one of those loose ruckuses, and I had indeed heard children screaming with fright.

'That's what's wrong with China,' Chen said decisively. 'We don't pull together. We don't care about each other any more. Not since the Cultural Revolution. It's everyone for themselves.' Chen was fast reaching the soapbox stage. 'But why are we like that? Do you know what happens when you put too many rats in a cage? They fight.'

So that was the other side of China, I thought. The other side of the neat dormitories and the carefully folded clothes. The shadow side. People were rats in a crowded cage. I sometimes felt it myself. I had even seen Song use her elbows with gusto in a bus-queue ruckus.

'But people don't seem angry or upset,' I said. 'Maybe they don't smile, but they seem to cope.' I was trying to get back my cherished early vision of placid Beijing streets, which I hoped was at least partly true.

'Be sure they're angry. Do not doubt it. Everyone is angry. But they have to hide it. That's why they show the cold face.'

'So what are they angry at?'

'They are angry at those who control our lives and should be helping us. And who instead are helping themselves.'

I could sense the depth of his bitterness.

'One of your Europeans said it years ago – Max Weber, I think – that people in power end up serving themselves instead of serving the people they were put in power to serve.'

'That's not only China,' I said reasonably. 'European officials are just as bad. We even have TV comedies about it. All over the world people in power look after themselves. Power corrupts.'

'But in Europe you don't depend on such people. You can pass them by and work hard to make a success. But here in China hard work gets you nowhere. Talent gets you nowhere. *Guanxi*'s all that matters – connections to powerful leaders. Most people don't have those connections, so they're angry. What *guanxi* really means is that your abilities don't count. Which means you don't matter as an individual.

'That's why nobody works hard. There's no point. Know what they say? *Yi bei cha; yi zhang bao* – a cuppa tea and the newspaper. That's what we do all day at work. But look at the overseas Chinese, in Singapore or Malaysia: they're the hardest-working people in Asia. And the richest: they call them the Jews of Asia. Yet here nobody works. It's useless, and that's why we're angry. Look around you: everyone in this room is angry.'

Song said something in Chinese in a tone that clearly conveyed, 'That'll do, Chen. Put a sock in it!'

Later that night, when everyone had gone home, I strolled with Song around the campus lake. I said I had been astonished at the anger among the students. Did ordinary people feel the same way?

'Even more angry, but they cannot express it as students can. They haven't the words or the education. And they are still afraid, even though the very bad times are gone. The students are starting to express their anger for them.'

'I'd like to see a lot more of your friends, if I may.'

'You cannot,' Song said bluntly.

'What?'

'I do not want you to see my friends.'

'But that's ridiculous. Why not?' I was hurt.

'Listen.' Song stopped and turned to me, as she did when she wanted to make a point. The hand brushed back the hair. 'The students are angry. They're looking for ways to protest and to get our government to move against all this corruption. But if foreigners get involved with our students, the government will just say it is all foreign agitation. Already there are far too many foreigners coming to our meetings. I don't want you to be one of them.'

It was a bit of a slap in the face to be told that in all the exciting things that were simmering on Beijing's many campuses, I was not just useless, but a nuisance. But, as Norman was always saying, getting to know China is like learning to ride a bicycle. When you think you can ride, you fall off your bicycle.

'And, PJ,' Song was saying, 'will you try and talk to Lily? Ask her to back off and leave us alone. Please.'

I got nowhere with Lily. I took her to lunch at the Friendship, which I didn't particularly want to do, as Lily's figure and voice could arouse a sexual twinge or two in me, which isn't really that comfortable when it's someone who's practically a relative. That day she was in tight, black, glove-leather jeans, and that didn't help. So maybe I was a bit uptight around her. Anyhow we had rather a row, in which I came second.

'I'm twenty-two years old, PJ,' the gravelly voice reminded me. 'And I'd like you to bloody-well remember that. I'm not the little girl that used to sit on your knee. And I'm not the teenager you used to talk down to a few years back. Remember that too.'

'But your father —'

'And that's another thing. I'm well aware Daddy asked you to keep your eye on me. And it's just as well you haven't bothered much. Just keep it that way. Daddy had no right to ask you, and I don't want you fucking around in my life.'

It had long been a mystery to me how Dublin girls of good class all seemed to swear like troopers. Lily was no different. For some reason the gravelly voice made me think of digestive biscuits. At least it took my mind off sex.

'Just let's be friends, OK?' Lily's suggestion was enforced by a peck on the cheek, delivered with that charm she could switch on when she chose. Nevertheless I persisted.

'But you've got so involved with the students, Lily. It's not good for an outsider to —'

'Song's been on to you, hasn't she? There, I knew it. Get this into your fuckin' thick head, PJ – I'm *not* an outsider. I'm Chinese, like everybody else. It's a personal accident I was brought up in Dublin. Maybe an advantage, 'cause at least I've learnt about organising and agitating, and they need that here.'

The tone changed, and Lily became persuasive again. 'They're so *passive* here, PJ. So fatalistic. They want change, but they don't think it can happen. And they don't seem to realise it's they themselves can make things happen. That's what I'm trying to get across. Now I've got to run; I've a class at 1.30. Bye!'

Another peck on the cheek and Lily was gone. Well, it was a relief that she hadn't been too nasty. Tongue had stayed more or less sheathed, and instead Lily had used the technique she had long practised on her poor father. Namely, after she won an argument she would abscond before you could muster your second thoughts.

As usual, Lily left my mind in a whirl. What if she was right? Maybe students here were indeed too passive. And their teachers, too. Was Song passive? She cared deeply about her students – that I knew – but did she have any concept of being able to change things? I remembered once trying to explain to her how I had been trained to make decisions with the head, trained to list the pros and cons, and how I had always made wrong decisions.

'There are two ways to decide anything,' I had told Song. 'With the head or with the heart. I know now I'm a heart man.'

'Here in China there's a third way,' Song had replied. 'What the Party tells you to do. And that's the only way that counts.'

Those words had brought home to me the fatalism that is China. And it was not simply forty years of Communist Party rule, but four thousand years of imperial rule, plus a century of European exploitation, that had embedded deep down in Song and her compatriots that pervasive sense of hopelessness.

I felt so sad one day when Song and I stopped off for a coffee at the Great Wall Sheraton, that monstrosity of chrome and glass in North Beijing. We locked our bicycles in the parking lot and walked towards the great mirroring glass doors where a flunkey in resplendent uniform was on duty. I could see our reflection in the doors as we approached, and I noticed how Song bowed her head and looked at the ground as we passed the doorman.

'Why didn't you look at him?' I asked her when we got in.

'I always look away. They've stopped me so many times before, even when I came to give someone a Chinese lesson. You see, ordinary Chinese aren't allowed in these western hotels.'

'But goddammit, woman, it's your country. China belongs to you now. That's what the Revolution was about.'

Without saying anything, Song slowly turned full circle in the foyer, and I let my eyes follow hers. A crowd of loud westerners, the men in cowboy hats, the women bulging out of their polyester suits, were clustered around the hotel desk. A group of elegant European businessmen were talking over beers at a bar table. Westerners were whooping it up at every table in the sunken foyer.

The only Chinese were the bar hostesses in their *cipao*s – those graceful, long split skirts – and the quintet playing Mozart, which could hardly be heard over the guffaws and loud western voices.

I felt a sudden loathing for those chrome pillars that rose up out of that foyer like metallic redwoods, for the gurgling indoor fountains and the carpets like wheatfields and the acres of polished marble – for all this obscene opulence that not even emperors had enjoyed and that few westerners ever had inside their own homes. I felt choked by such a loathsome level of luxury, but, more than anything, I felt ashamed.

For there were still two worlds in China, and I belonged to the privileged one. And Song and most other Chinese belonged to a second world where people lived three to a tiny room and got paid a monthly salary that wouldn't buy an *hors-d'oeuvre* in a hotel like this.

'*Hua ren yu gou bu zhun ru nei*,' Song whispered.

'What?'

'"No dogs or Chinese allowed here." Used to be written outside the Europeans' park in Shanghai, before the Revolution. It's still true.'

'Let's go,' I said, and we went back through those glass doors, both of us looking the doorman right in the eye. We ended up eating marvellous noodles for two *yuan* at a wooden table in a pokey, smoky little eating house run by a minority-race family who looked like European gypsies.

I had got a whiff of China's fatalism that day. Maybe not fatalism, but a subtle sense that I was not always master of my fate.

There was the sense of being watched. When I was out with Song, I certainly was watched, and people left us in no doubt about it. Seeing a Chinese girl walking with a foreign devil, men would turn to stare, and the stares did not seem friendly. I asked Song about this.

'They say to each other,' she said, 'there's a Chinese girl trying to marry a foreigner, so as to get out of the country. Or that she wants to have a good time at the big hotels. But I don't let it worry me.'

I developed a custom of saying a cheery *ni hao* (hello) to any man who turned to stare. It was always a man, who would usually nod curtly and bugger off about his business.

On the rare occasions that I went into the Beida campus with Song, she would not let me cycle beside her. I had to go in front, or well to the rear.

'I have to live here,' Song explained, 'and people here gossip. Or someone will get jealous and give me a bad time. I could even get called in by my work unit and be asked to explain who you are and what I am doing with you.'

Song would only come to the Friendship on the two evenings a week when she gave me classes. I tried bringing her to eat in the dining room on those days, so as to get a bit more nourishment into her slender frame. She finally agreed to come, but reluctantly, as she was terrified the Friendship staff might report her for being seen too often with this particular foreign devil.

Our sense of being watched was not helped when we heard what happened with Sven Hansen. One night he had been out dancing until midnight with his Shanghai girlfriend (leaving the wife at home in bed), and the taxi was stopped by a couple of policemen. They questioned the girl about what she was doing with a foreigner and reported her to her work unit (she was a nurse in a Beijing hospital). The work unit called the girl in and fired her.

Finally the feeling of being watched got right into my bones, along with the fear that had never really left us since Madame Lukas' death. I found myself being careful what I said to Song on the telephone; stopping short of the Beida gate whenever I saw her home; no longer holding hands with her when we walked through Purple Bamboo Park. I even found myself convinced there were microphones in the ceiling of my apartment. All of which cramped our style considerably.

Nevertheless Song and I tried to be happy, the way the Chinese try to be happy in spite of everything. And we tried hard to keep a sense of hope alive inside ourselves. Indeed all around us there seemed to be some strange hope developing, especially on campus, a hope that paradoxically seemed to flourish side by side with the fatalism, taking its nourishment from the same soil.

There was a feeling in the air that somehow the government authorities might have grown more tolerant – no, less powerful, perhaps, and therefore less dangerous. And people felt that perhaps some government members genuinely wanted to see an end to corruption, but dared not say so. And, perhaps, were looking to the young people to speak out. There was a sense that Someday Soon Something Must Happen. Nobody seemed to have any notion what that Something might be.

It recalled for me the words of St Paul: 'All creation groans as if in travail, waiting for birth.'

CHAPTER SEVEN

OUTSIDE MY FRIENDSHIP Hotel window was a tree, the branches of which reached right to my fourth-floor balcony. Birds chirped among its leaves, and I watched those leaves grow yellower and lovelier as that unusually late autumn drew towards its close. Then one day there came a wicked wind from Mongolia that took all those leaves away.

It was a harsh enough winter, even if it was brief, yet it must have nurtured joy in me, for, by the time the first spring buds appeared on that tree by my window, I knew I loved Song more than I had ever loved any human being.

If any one word conjured up Song for me, the word was 'tenderness'. It took a considerable amount of time before I encountered this tenderness, as if it were a sub-cutaneous layer below the cold face. But after I broke through that hard outer shell, what awaited me was warm, yielding, enwrapping, cherishing and loving quite beyond measure. I had not known that love of such intensity could exist. I had never met it in marriage. For the first time in my life I was aware that someone truly cherished me, was thinking of me night and day; that my well-being was paramount to that person; that such cherishing was expressed in ways that were gentle and tender and imaginative.

I had feared tenderness. I had been brought up to see softness as somehow unmanly, but now Song was showing me its place in a man's life.

One day I told her how my wife had died. 'But I must try and be strong,' I said, 'if I'm to survive the anguish.'

'Don't try to be strong. Strong, hard things break; soft things do not break.' She took my hard old hands in hers. 'You must be yielding, because softness is only the other side of strength.'

Song explained to me that wonderful Chinese concept of Yin and Yang, in which things are not opposed to each other, need not clash and destroy each other, as they do in the West. 'Things are not opposite,' she said, 'but one thing curves into the other, as a man curves into a woman. And what you call opposites really need each other. Highness needs lowness; light needs darkness. Hardness needs softness. Male needs female. And in each there is the seed of the opposite.

'Look. If it's midnight – the darkest hour – already light is beginning. If you say you are happiest, already sadness is beginning. So we say, never be too happy; never be too sad. And PJ, you must never be too strong, because I don't want to see you break.'

One Sunday I had to make an emergency visit to a dentist and Song came with me to the dental hospital near the Friendship Hotel. Of course it was closed, and I was turning away in cowardly relief when Song led me to the porter's gatehouse, and to my horror I was taken into a tiny emergency room, complete with dentist's chair and a dauntingly young dentist.

I wanted to come back another time, any other time, but I also wanted to preserve my machismo in front of Song and this young dentist. So I stayed. I lay back in that dentist's chair and thought of the Empire. Or of Mother Ireland. Whatever. Sweat came out on my forehead when the young man said he would drain the abscess – without anaesthetic, unless it started to hurt badly.

All of a sudden I felt my right hand gripped and held by Song's two hands. She was beside me, and every time I felt the drill come near a nerve, her hand squeezed tighter on mine. I don't know how she knew when it hurt, but the pressure of her hands ebbed and flowed with the pain.

Then I remembered Song's words – 'You must not be strong' – and I just let myself go, let myself be afraid. Suddenly I was completely relaxed, and there was hardly any pain, and I almost wanted it to go on and on, just to have the pressure of those hands go on and on.

It was incidents like that which gave the wheel of our love another small turn, so that the bands that were starting to fasten us would tighten imperceptibly. Our love came in increments.

But life with Song was by no means all softness. One day at the Fragrant Hills I wanted to buy a few of those plastic cards with a red autumn leaf sealed inside. Song was like a fishwife. She would bargain with the stall owner, throw the cards contemptuously down on the stall and march off to another stall. There would be more words with that stall owner and a flash of scorn from the magnificent eyes, and off we'd go to another stall, or back to a previous one. I traipsed meekly along behind.

'It's because of you,' Song said. 'They see the foreign devil, and they say, hah, here comes money. Do you know how much they're trying to ask?'

Lord knows it wasn't more than a couple of pence they were asking, but Song would have none of it. And we ended getting far better quality leaf cards, for about a quarter the asking price. Song told me we finally paid what the locals would pay.

I too got a dose of the flashing eyes. Once we had decided to visit Beijing's 360-degree cinema, where the screen is all around the viewer. I had forgotten my foreign expert's 'white card', which allowed me to pay less than a tourist, so the woman at the box office demanded seven *yuan* instead of four.

'We will not,' Song said. 'We come next week, when you have your card.'

'But I don't mind, Song. Let's do it.'

'We will not. We come back, maybe tomorrow. Seven *yuan* is too much.'

I was about to become a spoilt small boy stamping my foot and whimpering that I wanna go today when I realised I was about to make an idiot of myself. But it was my money and I did want to go in, and to tell the truth, I didn't like being bossed. I half realised it was our first clash of wills: not that I felt any need to win such a clash, but I felt it was only fair I should be let spend my own money.

I put my hands on both her shoulders and said, as earnestly as I could, 'Song, it's my fault, I know, forgetting that card. So I suffer, OK? And it's only three *yuan* more. It's worth it to me. OK?'

'That's because you're rich,' she sniffed. The left hand pushed the hair back.

'I'm not rich, and you know it. I just want to do this very much. And I'm too tired to cycle anywhere else. Come on, Song: say yes!'

'Hinh!' she said, with the tiny contemptuous snort which showed that she was particularly unimpressed with something I had said or done.

Anyhow I went ahead and bought the tickets. As we

walked in she said, 'You're a rich man. Spend your money as you want.'

'Now you're angry with me.'

'I'm not angry. But you are rich'.

Inside, waiting for the performance to start, I whispered, 'Look, it's only three *yuan* more.'

'Only? Only rich men say "only".' I could feel her scorn.

The strange thing was, even that little incident seemed to bring us closer. I think maybe we had glimpsed each other's shadow side and found it not too awful.

Later that afternoon we wandered into the Temple of the Great Bell, and Song was singing as we walked through the courtyard among the hundreds of bells. Her voice could have been one of the bells.

'I always feel happy when I'm with you,' she said suddenly. She turned to me and put her closed fists together, with the knuckles hitting off one another. 'With many people I feel like this.' Then she slightly shifted her fists, so the knuckles of one fitted into the hollows between the knuckles of the other. 'But with you it's like this!'

We wandered among the bells until we came to the Pavilion of the Great Bell, that twenty-foot monster of which the clangour can be heard thirty miles away. There is a six-inch hole in the top of the bell, into which people toss coins for luck. We climbed the steps to the top of the bell, with coins clutched in our fists. I threw one and it went straight into the hole. Song clapped with delight. Then she threw a coin, left-handed as always, and it went in too. This time several onlookers applauded. An old woman called out something, and I asked Song what she had said.

'She says it almost never happens like this. She says we are surely going to be very lucky.'

Try as we would, we could get no more coins to go into that hole in the bell.

Beijing can be gloomy when it's cloudy, but some of the emotional clouds during that short winter, I am ashamed to say, were supplied by me. An unhappy consequence of being betrayed is that one stops trusting people, even those who deserve one's trust. And no one deserved mine more than Song.

The doubt began with that mother of twins and trouble, Ning. Ning began to cheat in her student work, and to cheat in a quite original way. She would first pop the articles she wrote for me into one of the dozens of sub-editors' trays at Xinhua, the government news agency where our training also took place. A sub would then edit and polish the article as part of the day's work, and Ning would quietly pick it up at the other end of the conveyor belt. She would then retype it and pass it up to me as her own work. Of course she was starting to get higher marks, and I was considering recommending her for further study abroad. It worked like a dream until a sub-editor caught her at it.

When I tackled Ning about it she burst into tears and began screeching that all she wanted was to get the hell out of China, just as everyone else wanted to get out of China. And they were all cheating in one way or another, she said. She was just doing it her way; others were chasing Westerners and pretending to love them, and wasn't that cheating too?

I should have fired Ning from the course, but I just chewed her up and gave her a warning. What else could I do? They had taken the poor creature's child from her and she had not been the same since. She had been a promising journalist, and I kept hoping the training course would somehow give her something to cling on to, something to work towards. But what could substitute for a child? So I simply tried to be as understanding as I could.

Instead I took it out on Song. When a man has been cuckolded, he loses trust in himself: he begins to wonder if anyone could love him. And so suspicion grew, as love had, from the

90

tiniest of seeds and started choking that flower that was to have been watered with kindness.

I was wondering if maybe, just maybe, Song wanted out of China too. Sure she might love me, but how could she herself be sure of her own motives?

I am deeply ashamed now that I could have doubted for an instant a love so intense and tender and giving. I was behaving like an ill-treated mongrel snapping at the hand that caresses it.

In my professional life as a journalist I had long learnt to doubt and question. But I shouldn't have done it with Song. That was my private life.

I must have grown perceptibly less open, ever so slightly remote. Song noticed, of course. She tried to get through to me once about what was wrong, and it just sent me into one of those black moods in which I could hardly say anything. If Song had simply shrugged and walked away, I could not have blamed her. I could see the harm I was doing to our relationship, but felt powerless to do anything about it.

Christmas is meaningless to the Chinese, and for western-ers there would be few depressingly Teutonic gatherings around Christmas trees in German or American households at the Friendship, only relieved by a hectic party or two at the Irish Embassy. I made Song's first-ever Christmas even bleak-er by casting this shadow over it.

During the January break (which coincides with the Chinese New Year), Song took off for Heilongjiang Province, a thousand miles north, to visit her elderly father, who, she told me, lived in a room shared with two others. I met Song at the station when she got back, and she could not stop talk-ing about the old man. I had not realised she loved him so deeply. 'That's one reason I could never leave China for good,' she said. 'I could never leave my father alone and helpless when he gets really old.'

Inside my perverse heart relief mingled with dismay: dismay at the thought that I might have to choose life in China if I chose life with Song; relief at the thought that Song had no hidden agenda. And mingled with both was a deep shame.

But the clouds lifted, and, even though that winter grew more cruel, there was no longer winter in our hearts.

When the weather grew really harsh, out came the fur coat, Song's most treasured possession. I'm not exactly sure what it was made of: it seemed a tired-looking bit of rabbit skin, but Song told me she looked forward to every winter just to be able to wear the fur coat.

Song had been saving earnestly for ten years, in the faint hope of being able to get a year or two's study abroad. In those ten years she had amassed the princely sum of one thousand *yuan* – about £166 at that time. Then inflation struck and there was a bout of panic-buying. Song had held fast, and found her one thousand *yuan* was now worth only about seven hundred and fifty. After another panic, in which she again stood fast, her nest-egg was now worth half.

'Well, when the third panic came,' she told me, 'I just ran and took out all my money and spent it on this fur coat! Don't you think it's a nice coat?'

I folded her, coat and all, in my arms and hugged her, and felt a lump in my throat. I told her I liked the coat more than any coat in the world.

We cycled all that winter, even if sometimes we felt our ears would fall off with the cold. But as the streets warmed up with the approach of spring, cycling became for me more of a joy than ever.

As we rode the streets of Beijing I began to realise what cycling skills the Chinese had developed. I marvelled how a young woman could balance so gracefully side-saddle on the carrier of a bicycle, leaning back without support, feet held high to balance as her man pedalled along at high speed.

I carried one such welcome burden for a few days while Song's bike was in for repairs. I realised the skill involved the first time I halted my bicycle for her to climb on.

'Don't stop,' she said. 'That's not how to do it. Start cycling without me.'

'But how –?'

'Just start pedalling. I show you.'

I started off at a reasonable pace, and I could hear Song trotting behind me. There was an almost imperceptible wobble and I realised Song was now perched on my carrier. I hardly felt the difference.

I heard many tales about the things Beijing folk manage to carry on their bicycles. The only thing I never saw was a piano being carried, although I had heard of such a feat.

Perhaps the piano went by three-wheeler. As well as bicycles, Beijing was thronged with tricycles: highly functional machines with a small goods platform at the back. The amount of freight the Chinese could get on to those platforms boggles the mind. I used to meet one young woman every morning tricycling with five kids to school, and all of them squatting behind her on the platform. I suppose some were neighbours' kids. On rainy mornings the little ones, in their bright plastic capes and hoods, were like a flower garden on the back of her trike.

Some of the platforms had a tiny wooden hut built on top, and if one looked carefully one could see a child peeping out, protected from the elements. Other platforms supported a chair – sometimes rudimentary, sometimes a sumptuous armchair. The locals joked that it was the ambition of every Chinese to sit in such a chair and have someone else do the puffing and pedalling.

Whenever rain came, and it could come suddenly in spring or autumn, the whole street would be transformed within a minute into a garden of brightly coloured capes, each like a giant fuchsia, pixie-hooded at the top and flaring to cover both bicycle and rider. Under the gloomy sky the street would look festive with its procession of reds and yellows and greens and pinks.

I still gazed in wonder at the splendid women that thronged the streets. However, since I had one of the loveliest riding beside me I no longer raced ahead to peep at someone's face. Song didn't seem to mind: 'It's OK to read the menu!' she would say with a smile, a quip she had picked up from me. Nowadays she could even smile in the street.

One day that spring Song arrived down to the Friendship wearing her first-ever pair of blue jeans, Levi 501s, in dark indigo with white stitching. She just looked stunning. I guessed the jeans had come out of Lily's mountain of suitcases, because there was no way Song could have afforded Levis. The jeans must have been skin tight on Lily, because they fitted Song like a glove. I couldn't believe how they changed her appearance; the severity had simply dropped away and she looked refreshingly casual and relaxed.

In fact she was far from relaxed, as she told me later. She had been in an agony of shyness and self-consciousness. 'I felt nearly naked when I put them on first,' she told me. 'I pulled them on twice, and took them off again, before I got the courage.'

'But why feel that way?'

'Older people here think only bad girls wear jeans. Look –' She pirouetted, running her hands down over her lovely haunches. 'They show everything. They show the shape you are.'

'Aren't they supposed to?'

'But here a girl has to hide the shape of her body. Until lately, anyway. Especially if she's slim, because she'd be thought too weak for work and a man wouldn't marry her. It's changing, of course. But even now jeans are seen as dangerous. They could make you feel independent, like those cowboys in America – make you feel a real individual. And around here that's not allowed.'

Maybe Song was right, but she stuck with her blue jeans.

Soon she was wearing that bright blue Trinity sweatshirt again, the one Lily had swapped with her that so became her skin colour. And then one day she arrived with her ears pierced, wearing miniature pearl ear rings, and it was astonishing how such tiny things could so set off that lovely face.

As Song grew more colourful she continued to grow less solemn, her innate humour bubbling up to the surface more and more. It was great to hear her infectious giggle. It was as if a girlishness was coming out in her – maybe from the girlhood she had never had. Probably a lot rubbed off from Lily, because, in spite of occasional coolnesses brought about by Lily's political involvements, that friendship had seemed to endure. I hoped it would, for Lily seemed to be good for Song, even if she wasn't good for me.

I felt enwrapped by Song's love, but it didn't overwhelm or suffocate; it was like being bathed in light. And I do believe I was at least beginning to learn how to return such love. Hindsight tells me it was around then that I threw out the invisible rule book. Now I simply loved. I no longer checked to see if I was getting it right. I no longer observed myself performing my caring functions. I just let go and loved this splendid creature with all my heart and soul. I lived to be for her, and I lived to be with her. That was all.

I realise now I had never actually encountered love until then. I had not witnessed my parents' love: my father was gone before I reached awareness, and my mother died when I was ten. Perhaps I got a bit of my Ma's love when she wasn't drinking, but it didn't leave much of a mark. Of course my brother Mick showed love when he saw to my education, but that's different. I hadn't seen *Love* – that awesome thing that sears and burns and welds two human souls. And not having seen it, how could I recognise it or ever have it myself? So with Heather I had to guess what love must be like, and all I came up with was a set of rules I invented for myself. Rules that didn't work.

But when this woman of China loved me, I simply loved her right back.

As I cycled the streets of Beijing with Song, I often found myself humming that line from *South Pacific* – 'Once you have found her, never let her go.' It was Song I didn't want to let go, of course, but I think I began to be in love with China itself as well. How can you be in love with one billion people? I don't know, but I think I was. I certainly was in love with the streets of Beijing. I felt a warmth towards those quiet people for ever cycling the streets of their city. A man in love thinks he loves everyone.

I did my share of hating too, as I cycled those streets. I hated the big, bullying buses, hinged in the middle, that writhed through the streets like Chinese dragons, with their loudspeakers yelling for me to get out of the way. I hated the cars, especially the taxis that hurtled through eleven million cyclists as if they did not exist, and treated pedestrian crossings with disdain. I hated how they honked through crowded alleys with the arrogance of an imperial mandarin in his sedan chair, yet infinitely more menacing.

Most of all I hated those long, official limousines with the invisible eyes peering out from behind dark windows. I hated them because, for both Song and me, they brought back the fear.

But the limousines would hiss away and the fear would recede, so that, all in all, that winter and spring was a happy time in both our lives.

Then one day in April I came down from the hotel dining-room and saw a notice on the bulletin board. There was a lot of black around it and a man's picture at the top. I guessed it was an obituary, and that the man had been important. Norman came by and I asked him what it was about.

'Hu Yaobang is dead,' he said.

'Who's he?'

'He's nobody now,' Norman sniffed. 'He's dead. Dead people don't exist – haven't y'heard? But he used to be Communist Party Secretary, until they sacked him two years ago for being soft on student protest. I knew him in the old days.'

Norman peered at the notice. 'Damn Chinese characters. Let me see – yes, says he died early this afternoon.' He turned to me. 'This means trouble – you mark my words. Trouble.'

CHAPTER EIGHT

NORMAN WAS RIGHT as usual. I sensed it the very next day when I went to the Beida campus to pick up Song. It was a Sunday, and we were going to spend the day in the Fragrant Hills. As I came in through the university's south gate, strings of white flowers, seemingly made from tissue paper, were blossoming on every tree and fluttering from every window and balcony.

It looked cheerfully festive, but Song told me it meant mourning.

We met Lily coming out of the foreign-student dormitory, and together we walked to the nearby *San Jiao Di*, the triangular college yard where Song said the wall-posters always went up at times like this.

There was an unusual hush in the air, not of foreboding, but almost of sadness. But there was an expectant edge to the sadness. It reminded me eerily of those annual retreats we used to have in my Jesuit boarding school, where everyone walked head down in silence, praying or meditating maybe, but knowing that after three days we would erupt into noise and activity.

At the wall people were three deep in places, poring over the posters, some copying them into notebooks. We had to elbow our way in. The posters were hand done in large black or red Chinese characters. Lily spotted Chen pasting up a poster and tapped him on the shoulder. He smiled when he saw us and read the poster for my benefit: 'A true man has died, who should not have died. While false men live, who should have died.'

I heard Song's breath hissing inward. 'He should not have written that,' she whispered to me. 'It's too dangerous.'

'Why is it dangerous?' I was whispering too.

'He means Deng – Deng Xiaoping. Our top leader.' Her breath hissed again. 'It's dangerous.'

'But I thought Li Peng was premier,' I said.

'Deng's the power behind them all. He doesn't need a title: he just tells them what to do.'

'I thought you once told me the leaders were growing benign?'

'Deng's not benign. And neither is Li Peng. Maybe Zhao Ziyang – really we don't know any more.'

'Well, Chen hasn't signed the poster, has he?' I said comfortingly. I had my own comforting thought of Chen being lugged off to some slave camp in Xinjiang where I'd never have to suffer him again, but kept the thought prudently to myself.

We moved off, leaving Chen and Lily to their poster, and elbowed our way along the wall. Song murmured translations of some of the other offerings. It seemed Chen was far from alone in his sentiments:

'Deng Xiaoping enjoys health at eighty-four,' said one of the posters. 'Hu Yaobang has died at seventy-three. The wrong man is gone!'

Another: 'If Li Peng can be Premier, who can't be?'

Another: 'Beloved Hu Yaobang, China was in your heart. And that is why you died of heart attack, knowing how sick our China is.'

Song's hissing grew almost shrill as she read the one about the bottle: 'Will someone please smash the Little Bottle?' That, Song hissed, was like insulting the emperor.

But how? I wanted to know.

'Deng Xiaoping's nickname is "Little Bottle",' she hissed. 'That's what his name sounds like.'

As if in answer we heard the sound of breaking glass, and a student was hoisted up to place a smashed *pijiu* bottle on top of the wall. There was a brief cheer, then the eerie silence fell again.

The next day we adjourned classes early. My trainees were restless and wanted to go to Tiananmen Square to see the mourning wreaths for Hu Yaobang. Ning and Kui'er took me along with them. They were still the two trainees I felt closest to. Kui'er I enjoyed for his grin and his humour. I had forgiven him the thing with the willies. And he was really great with poor Ning; he could josh her into some semblance of cheefulness as no one else could.

We left our bicycles at work and walked the couple of blocks to the square. Ning had picked up her remaining twin from the creche and had him in a sling on her back.

I could never see Tiananmen Square without marvelling at its bleak immensity. It is a concrete prairie of 110 acres, the size of several Trafalgar Squares, dotted with clusters of tiny human figures that seem to fade into the haze. I found myself thinking that it's designed to make humans look, and feel, minute, like ants in an anthill.

Across the top end of the square – its north side – runs Chang'an Boulevard, the city's east-west artery. Beyond that, closing off the square, is the red bulk of the Gate of Heavenly Peace (Tiananmen), not so much a gate as a balconied edifice with upward-curling Chinese roofs and perforated by five tunnel-like archways leading to the Forbidden City. From above the largest archway a portrait of Mao stares across the boulevard and down into Tiananmen Square.

For the moment Mao wasn't doing all the staring. A ten-foot-high portrait of the deceased Hu Yaobang stared back at him from the Monument to the People's Heroes. Whoever had erected Hu's picture – and it certainly wasn't the author-ities – had a nice sense of symbolism and was up to no good. The monument stood a quarter way into the square, a two-hundred-foot stone obelisk atop its plinth and surrounding steps, to commemorate the Communist Revolution. It was bedecked in those white paper flowers.

I stood beside Hu and stared back at Mao myself, trying as always to orientate myself in this vast space. On my left the Great Hall of the People bordered the west side of the square. I recalled our banquet beyond those pillared porticoes a few short months before, the night I had first learnt the fear China can engender. I felt a twinge of it now, unsure why. On my right, the History Museum closed off the square to the east. And far behind me, at the bottom end of the square, would be the pillared tomb of Mao. I turned to look for it, but it was no more than a rectangular silhouette in the smog.

Tinny music sounded somewhere. A straggling bunch of young people was making its way into the square from Chang'an Boulevard. They carried white banners. It surprised me to see policemen stopping the traffic to let the marchers enter the square.

They were quite far away in that concrete vastness, but I guessed there were several hundred marchers, and they moved slowly down the west side of the square past the Great Hall, in the direction of Mao's tomb. A girl in white shirt and black pants swung one of those ghetto-blasters, presumably the source of the tinny music. People seemed to be carrying lots of white wreaths. Those in the front row held square white cloths in front of them, each with a single black character on it: among the leaders I could make out the tall figure of Chen. At least he's not just talk, I thought. I'd have preferred to think of him as full of hot air.

'Yaobang lives for ever,' said Ning.

'Huh?'

'That's what those characters mean – the ones they're carrying in front.'

'Oh.'

I was only half listening. I was looking at the girl with the ghetto-blaster. Godammit, it couldn't be. Lily, you bloody little hellion. Christ, I'll have your hide. Would you ever cop yourself on.

I was going to go after Lily, then realised I could hardly create a scene in the middle of Tiananmen Square. And a scene there surely would be, if Lily could help it. The marchers receded into the haze at the southern end of the square, and the tinny music faded.

I was so agitated I could hardly attend to what Ning and Kui'er were saying. I think they were telling me what had been on the various banners. Then we could hear the music again – it was the 'Internationale' – and the marchers were coming up along the other side of the square. People began to sing along with the music, including Ning and Kui'er. The singing was hesitant at first, then picked up. I didn't know the words, either in Chinese or English, but I was too upset to sing anyway.

The marchers turned across towards the Monument to the People's Heroes, passing close to us. Except for Lily, they had a slightly mousy look about them, as though astonished at their own daring. Lily saw me, treated me to a large wink and

swung the ghetto-blaster. I didn't doubt it was the one I had
bought for her second-last birthday.

The marchers clustered on the steps of the monument, and
people gathered around. A young man scaled the obelisk like
a cat and hung a white banner from the pediment's top ledge,
right below the picture of Hu.

Chen's voice sounded shrilly across the square, without
benefit of loudhailer. I needed an oration by Chen like a hole
in the head. Time to go home, PJ. Ning's husband arrived to
collect her and the twin, so I said goodbye to them all and
headed off to Xinhua to get my bicycle.

'"The new-born calf doesn't fear the tiger" – old Chinese saying,' pronounced Norman. 'Those young idiots had better
learn to fear, or they'll be taught how, in no uncertain terms.
You mark my words.'

We were at dinner that evening at the hotel, and Norman
was holding court to the usual bunch, including Sven and his
wife, the regular hangers-on, and Song (who was still coming
to dinner the evenings of my Chinese lessons). We had been
telling the old fellow about the events at Tiananmen Square.

'Of course these bloody Chinese never learn,' Norman
went on. 'Using mourning as a mask for protest. They tried it
when Zhou Enlai died. Y'd think they'd remember what happened then. And time and again. Can't they remember this is
a dictatorship – a Communist dictatorship, certainly, but still
a dictatorship. And y'don't take on dictators.' He forked
some noodles. 'Or y'can take them on,' he muttered with full
mouth, 'and wonder why you're all over the place in small
pieces.'

'There's another march tomorrow,' Sven ventured.

'How do y'know?' Norman's muzzle came around like an
ancient pointer.

'I'm helping organise it.'

'You're – WHAT?'

'I'm – I'm involved up there. Up at Beida.'

'And just how, pray, are you involved?' I was beginning to feel scared for Sven. His wife had her head down, gazing at the table.

'They seem to appreciate my western know-how. I'm organising loudhailers, parade marshals, armbands. I may be Norwegian, but you forget I went to Kent State years ago . . .' Sven's voice dwindled.

The table was silent. Norman was staring at Sven. 'Y'do remember what happened there, don't you? How many died – four, wasn't it? In a place that at least claimed democracy.' A bony finger pointed. 'They make no such claim here. Here you may multiply your Kent figure, not by ten, *not even by a hundred*. Doctor Hansen, do you understand what I am telling you?'

In the silence that followed, Song's hand felt for mine. But Norman wasn't finished.

'I have always thought you stupid, Hansen, but I never thought to plumb such depths of stupidity as I do now. It has not even crossed your mind that your involvement with those young Chinese is the one thing guaranteed to destroy whatever it is they are attempting. You – you personally – are their kiss of death. China's leaders need only point to foreign agents, particularly westerners, fomenting trouble among their students, and the students' case is finished.'

Norman leaned back in his chair and pushed his plate away. 'I happen to know they are already pointing,' he said quietly. 'I just didn't know it was at you.'

'Listen —' Sven started to say something, but the wife, near to tears, had got up and was pulling him away. Norman dismissed him with a wave of his left hand.

No one was eating. Song was gently squeezing my hand beneath the table. Norman snapped his fingers at one of the *fu*s, who hurried over with the dessert menu. Norman reached for Sven's unfinished litre of beer and poured himself a glass.

'Lily's involved too. She's actually been marching,' I said to Norman.

'Then get her out.'

'She won't heed me. She never does. Norman, you've no idea how headstrong she is.'

'Then you're going to have to tell her father what's going on. Perhaps indeed it's time he came to see for himself.' He turned and looked at Song and his voice became gentler. 'I seem to recall you're a friend of the young lady. Could you not – persuade her?'

Song turned to me, eyes wide. 'I didn't know she was marching, until right now.'

'I only found out today. I'm damned upset, believe me. I just didn't see you to tell you before dinner.'

'My dear young lady,' Norman said, 'I meant what I said to that utterly foolish fellow. Every single word of it. Foreign involvement is truly the kiss of death for those young people. Even if your friend looks Chinese, it will not be enough. They know where she comes from.

'You'll find, however, that she will not be touched. Nor will that idiot Hansen. For the moment, that is. Why? Because the authorities need foreigners to point to.'

'He's right,' Song said to me. 'And they'll point to us teachers if we get involved too. They'll say we're egging on the students. But there's no way I can talk to Lily either. She listens to nobody, not even Chen. It's the other way round – Chen listens to her.'

'So where does that leave me, then?' I asked. 'It was my trainees took me to the square today. Just to watch, of course. Are you saying, Norman, I should stay away from now on?'

'Observe, by all means. You're a journalist, aren't you? The point is, not to get involved.'

CHAPTER NINE

BEIJING BREATHES RUMOUR the way its people breathe smog. It's all there is to breathe. *Xiaodao xiaoxi* they call it – 'alley news'. There is no other kind: anything official is propaganda, which nobody has believed for decades. So during this time of 'turmoil' – as the authorities were starting to call it – there was simply no information available locally. Nothing. Except the rumours.

The only way we could know what was happening a few blocks away was via London – courtesy of the BBC World Service. Indeed, as the weeks went by, the boom of Big Ben and the station's jaunty 'Lilliburlero' signature tune heralded our only tidings of reality, except for Voice of America, which performed a similar service.

But during that first week of protests, either the stations were still getting their act together in Beijing or we hadn't started listening systematically. Besides which, the stations could only give the broad picture: alley news provided the detail. The problem was knowing which detail was for real. During the rest of that week Beijing's rumour pumps had us so smothered that, by the time Hu's funeral came around, we had little notion of what was really happening.

Some rumours claimed the leaders has grown benign. Hadn't the police just stood by during Tuesday's march and even halted the traffic so the marchers could get to Tiananmen Square? They would have had their orders from above. So what then were these stories about police using their belts on students outside the gates of Zhongnanhai where the government leaders lived? And that was just up the street from the square. Or even using electric cattle-prods to force students into buses and then carting them off? And where to? Had anyone come back? Or had they ever gone? No one seemed to know.

And had students outside Zhongnanhai really yelled for Li Peng to come out and face them? 'Come out! Come out!' they were supposed to have yelled through the great red-lacquered gates. So rumour had it.

But no rumour ever said he came out.

And then Song came down from Beida to announce she had actually met someone who had actually met someone who had been beaten bloody by police outside Zhongnanhai. 'The Martyrs', people were calling the students who got beaten. So Song said.

The fact that I worked within China's state news agency (albeit as an instructor) gave me no informational edge whatsoever. Xinhua had little concern with mere student defiance of the government – it was far more concerned with reporting important matters like increased production of sorghum, sugar, soap and soya bean. Rumour seeped through the agency corridors just as anywhere else, until finally I found my news-agency colleagues turning to me for information.

I was the only one who had any, and I got it by sending out

my trainees. By halfway through the week a few of the good ones like Kui'er and Ning were nosing out real stories from Tiananmen Square and the college campuses. By Wednesday they reported 30,000 students at the square, and could report that Qinghua University, Beijing Normal College, and even the Communist Party's own university, Renda, had all joined the marches, along with scores of other Beijing colleges and institutions, and that the numbers of protesters were growing exponentially in spite of the torrential rain. They confirmed that police had indeed used belts and clubs outside Zhongnanhai, and that western journalists had been frog-marched away by police.

Not that Xinhua officially gave a damn, but since Wednesday I had been filing copy for Associated Press. As soon as I grasped that something unusual was unfolding in Beijing, I had contacted AP's London office. Their Asian desk had jumped at my offer to file copy. I got it out through the Friendship's fax desk, as I could hardly dare use Xinhua's own fax machines. How long the hotel would permit this I did not know.

However, my easy source of stories dried up all too soon when my superior at Xinhua called me on the carpet and warned me about my use of the trainees. 'You are putting their careers in jeopardy for your own selfish gain,' Mr Xiao told me bluntly.

'But this *is* their career,' I said. 'They'll never get better practice than right now!'

'Besides,' Mr Xiao went on, as though he hadn't heard me, 'you are leaving them open to arrest by the security police. Yes, I can see you did not know that. Now listen: I care too much about these young people to let that happen. I should wish you also to care about them, at least as much as you care about Associated Press. You will cease to encourage them in this way again, please.'

I was astonished that Xiao already knew about my AP contacts: it seemed Xinhua could gather news when it chose to. Presumably I was watched and reported on at the Friendship Hotel. The fear was back. Now I was afraid not only for Song and myself, but for my trainees, who were far from happy when I called them off.

Meanwhile, back at the Friendship, Norman continued his growling dinner-table commentary on the information Song and I brought him. His cup was full when Wednesday's *Renmin Ribao* newspaper declared that 'a small number of people with ulterior motives, including foreign nationals, have taken advantage of the mourning activities'.

Norman looked around balefully for Sven Hansen, presumably to slap the paper down in front of him with a growled 'I-told-you-so'. But I knew that Sven and his wife now waited each evening until Norman had finished dinner and gone before they had their own dinner.

Norman guessed, however, and by Friday night, standing beside me on a street corner outside the hotel, he delivered himself of the observation: 'Can y'believe it, Paddy? I do declare, I believe that Norwegian chap is sulking.'

It was the eve of the funeral, and Norman was on the footpath with Song and myself watching the students file through the darkened streets on their ten-mile route to Tiananmen Square.

What we now saw was light years from the stragglers of the previous Monday. These came in their disciplined thousands out of the darkness of every street: quiet, purposeful columns from Beida and Renda and all the other campuses, merging right in front of where we stood. In their soft sneakers the feet made no din. The chants were rhythmic and hypnotic. Marshals carried electric loudhailers, or linked hands in protective cordons around each group of marchers. In the light of lanterns the faces beneath the headbands had the sternness of gothic saints. It was eerie, but extraordinarily beautiful. These young people clearly needed help from no one.

There was no sign of Lily or Chen, but we had missed the start of the march and they might already have passed. That Lily would be marching I did not doubt. Song had in fact tried to talk her out of it, telling her how worried I was. She mightn't have bothered. Lily had simply told Song to tell me to take a running jump at myself, only she had expressed it in the somewhat more robust language of the streets of Dublin.

'Will the God protect them now, PJ?' Song asked with a wry smile.

'He might even protect you, you little heathen,' I replied.

We gently joked, but the fear was in us both. It was 7.40am and we were waiting in Tiananmen Square as the minutes ticked slowly towards the 8am deadline when the authorities were to clear the square. The tension among the thousands of youngsters around us was palpable, and growing with every moment.

We estimated from the crowd in the square that more than 100,000 had marched through that long night, for the sole purpose of gatecrashing Hu's funeral (later reports said it was 150,000). Now they were all around us, between the Heroes' Monument and the Great Hall of the People, in ordered ranks, grouped according to college, sitting lotus-position on the pavement behind their campus banners or squatting in that inimitable way that comes so naturally to the Chinese. Like Muslims facing Mecca, all faced the Great Hall of the People, within which Hu lay awaiting his obsequies.

We had not been able to resist coming to the square. After the parade had passed and Norman had bade us a gruff good-night, we had scurried for our bikes and set off. I was in need of stories to file, and Song wanted to watch. She especially wanted to see how her Beida students were faring.

'We'll not get involved, of course,' Song said.

'Absolutely not. We'll be there to observe.'

During the ten-mile ride through the night we had seen hundreds of young people hurrying in the wake of the marchers, on bikes, trikes and on foot. We had also observed olive-drab columns of police heading in the same direction. Lights were on in many of the high-rise apartments, and people leaned out to watch and often to wave. Around Muxidi, where many of the high officials live, most of the lights seemed to be on and there were clusters of people at the windows.

When we reached the square the students were already drawn up in serried ranks in the lamplight, while hundreds of police waited in the side streets. We had sat on the pavement and waited for the night to pass.

Sometime after 5, as the sky grew pale, three figures could be seen moving up the steps to the Great Hall, and everyone fell silent. The figures looked tiny as they passed beneath the columns. One of them was a slightly built young woman. It clearly wasn't Lily, for which I thanked heaven.

'That's Chai Ling,' Song whispered. 'One of the student leaders. The two men are Wang Dan and Wuerkaixi.'

Everyone waited quietly. Minutes later the three figures emerged, came down the steps, and we could see them heading towards the Beida campus banner.

Chen's voice came harshly over a loudhailer. Song interpreted for me.

' . . .Have refused us permission to honour Hu . . . Our three demands refused . . . Ordered to leave . . . Police to clear square by 8 o'clock.'

Something like a moan went up from the crowd, and Song's breath hissed.

Chen's voice again, vibrating with emotion: '*Zan men zou ma?* – Do we leave?'

112

'*BU ZOU!*' roared the crowd.

'Do we stay?'

'*LIU XIA LAI!*' roared the crowd.

Everyone spontaneously broke into the opening words of the 'Internationale', which even I understood: 'Rise up, you who refuse to be slaves.' And all of a sudden all had risen to their feet, and Song was singing as if her lungs would burst.

From that point on, time seemed to crawl towards the 8am deadline. The crowd continued with slogans shouted in unison – *Down with Corruption! – Long Live Democracy! – Sell the Benz limousines!* As Song translated each one for me, I thought *Long live Hu Yaobang* a bit much, given we were attempting to attend the poor fellow's funeral.

The shouts grew sporadic towards the deadline. People began to sit again. Finally silence fell. There is no clock in Tiananmen Square.

All of a sudden hordes of olive-green soldiers were swarming down the steps of the Great Hall. I glanced to the right and saw more soldiers racing through Tiananmen Gate. They were coming from behind us as well, across the square from the History Museum. They were running and within a minute a three-deep cordon had surrounded the still-sitting mass of students, who seemed in shock.

Shouts went up, then a cheer.

'What is it?' I asked Song.

'*Mei you qiang!* They've no guns! NO GUNS! They're UNARMED!' She did a little dance of joy. There was relief on many faces.

Abruptly the soldiers sat down, lotus position, three rows deep, facing the crowd. And there they stayed. The soldiers' faces were devoid of expression.

Shortly before 10am an olive-green ambulance backed in at the front of the Great Hall, in the space between the soldiers and the steps. Surely they weren't going cart poor Hu away in an ambulance, I thought.

'It's a sign they're coming,' Song whispered. 'They always have an ambulance ready when the very oldest leaders come out.'

She was right, for a few minutes later black-windowed Mercedes stretch limousines started arriving, one immediately after the other, backing in along the bottom of the steps in several rows. Soldiers were opening all the doors simultaneously, and dark-clad figures moved up the steps. They all wore those old-fashioned Mao suits. At the top some of them stopped and turned to stare down at the hushed crowd, which stared intently back.

The figures on the steps turned away and passed beneath the columns. Doors moved in the shadowed portico. The crowd erupted, and I could hear shouts of 'Li Peng!'

'They're saying Li Peng's not there,' Song said. 'And neither is Deng or Zhao.'

'But they'd have to come,' I said. 'It's a state funeral.'

'They're already inside – I'm sure of it. They'd have come through the underground tunnels. They wouldn't be able to face our insults.'

It was only then I realised the enormity of the affront the students were offering Deng Xiaoping and his minions. *Lèse majésté* was the only expression that might encompass it. That the emperor with his mandarins had to scurry like moles beneath the ground, away from the light of day, for fear of humiliation at the hands of what they saw as hooligans, and that thousands of such hooligans had gatecrashed the most solemn of imperial rites, had to be a loss of face more monstrous than they had ever endured.

Once again the fear sprang in my gut. Song, who could now read me like one of those big-character posters, looked at me. 'They will not forgive,' she said.

I had no idea what kind of service was taking place inside, except that it was hardly likely to be Solemn Requiem Mass. Outside in the square Chai Ling and Wang Dan took turns in leading us through our own ritual, which appeared to be the Chinese equivalent of 'Whaddawe want? Democracy! When do we want it? Now!' I knew it was Wang Dan only because Song recognised the voice over the loudhailer. These chants alternated with the singing of the 'Internationale', followed by that wonderfully proud song, 'Children of the Dragon', about how the people of China had been spawned by some great, invincible, primaeval dragon, from which came their greatness. Then came the Chinese national anthem, and even some of the communist songs from the Revolution.

The whole thing must have lasted a couple of hours, then suddenly there were the Mao-suited figures scuttling through the portico and down the steps. One after the other the black limos slid away. It happened so quickly the crowds hardly had time to react. They were left staring at an empty portico.

A howl went up from thousands of throats. 'Li Peng!' they howled over and over. Then the rhythm changed, and it was '*Li Peng, chu lai!* Li Peng, come out! Li Peng, come out!' For some reason the focus was moving to the premier and away from his emperor and master, Deng.

Now anger had entered in, waves of anger chasing across the crowd the way wind chases across a hayfield so you can see its passing. The cold face had slipped, and students around me were banging fists on the pavement in frustration, shaking fists into the air. 'We'll leave our blood here on the square,' I heard one of them say.

This was escalation. It was the first time I had seen the protesters truly furious. On previous occasions it had been more a ritualistic utterance of grievances, but this was fury. I sensed a turning point: I think it was the moment I realised that whatever was happening in Beijing was not going to fade away.

Song beside me was hissing like a little serpent. She seemed to hiss under various emotions, but I had never seen her as angry as she was now. 'The fuckers!' she hissed. 'The big fuckers!' I guessed she had picked that one up from Lily. I resolved that at an opportune moment I would counsel Song on utterances appropriate to a lady.

A hush fell, and Chai Ling was moving up the steps again with her two companions. At the top step they fell to their knees and raised their hands above their heads. In Chai Ling's hand was a white paper.

'A petition,' Song whispered. 'Like they used to make to the emperor.'

The three remained a long time kneeling before that empty portico, but no one came out from the Great Hall of the People. Finally, after perhaps an hour, the tall figure of Chen was seen moving up the steps towards the kneeling figures. He bent down to speak to them. The three stood up and came down the steps with him.

CHAPTER TEN

THREE DAYS LATER, on Tuesday morning, I was facing my class of trainees at Xinhua. They all wore the cold face. There was some embarrassed coughing, and Kui'er stood up. He had a slip of paper in his hand.

'The class deeply regrets to have to inform you,' Kui'er read, 'that as and from now, they are striking.' A cough. 'The class wishes to assure you that this striking state is not intended for you to lose your face, but that we are part of a universal striking throughout every college and learning institute within Beijing. It responds to the refusing of the leadership to meet us, and will continue until they do meet us and take our conditions.'

What a lousy training job I must be doing, was my first thought. Was this their best attempt at writing English? Where did they get this ridiculous 'as and from', which had always annoyed me when it crossed my desk back home? I consoled myself that Kui'er, while an effective news gatherer, was hardly my most gifted writer of English.

My second reaction was of relief. I would be free to roam Beijing and gather my stories on the extraordinary events unfolding. Unless, of course, Xinhua packed me off home. Or stopped paying me. Or kept me inside to write its twaddle about increased production of night soil.

I need not have worried, as Mr Xiao simply said he would let me know when the strike was over. Which would be in a couple of days, he said. I had my doubts about that. The youngsters at Tiananmen Square seemed in for the long haul, and China's leaders would surely manage to infuriate them further.

They did so before the day was over. I had just got back to my hotel room after dinner when the phone rang. Norman was on the line. 'Drop over to me, would you?' he said.

He was watching China TV's *News in English* when I got there and motioned me into an armchair. It took me some time to grasp what the newscasters were on about. It seemed an editorial was to appear in tomorrow's *People's Daily* which was far from reassuring. They were reading an extract which called the student protest 'a planned conspiracy and turmoil', which would have to be withstood and destroyed, because this deliberate turmoil had the express aim of 'destroying the leadership of the Communist Party of China and the whole socialist system'.

'In other words, treason,' Norman said. He switched off the sound and turned to me. 'Y'understand what's happening?'

'Can't say I do,' I said.

'The gauntlet is down. It's a declaration of war on the students.'

'So what happens now?' I asked.

'I've no idea.' Norman looked tired. 'But it's a fight to the death.'

'Can you be sure? After all —'

'Listen to me, Paddy. I happen to be aware of a secret speech Deng gave yesterday. He said they must do their best to avoid bloodshed, *but it might not be possible to avoid it.* Those were his words. He also said they had millions of soldiers, so what were they afraid of? Those were his words, too.'

'What do I do, Norman?'

He gave me the bleary look. 'Well, you've two women to look after, don't you? That's your first job.'

'Song's OK. She's mad as hell, but she won't get involved. In fact she's trying to persuade her students to stay out of it. They're only kids.'

I suddenly remembered I had made no effort to persuade my own trainees to stay out of things. I had been so delighted with my new-found freedom that I had thought of little else. Well, they were an older bunch, and would do their own thing anyway.

'What about your niece?' Norman asked.

'That loose cannon? Lily heeds nobody. I can get nowhere with her.'

'Did y'contact her father?'

'I sent him a fax last night. Asked him to come out here right away.'

The phone rang. Norman lifted it, listened and handed it to me with an expressionless face. It was Lily. They all knew where to find me if I wasn't at home.

'I'm up at Beida,' she said. 'Could you come up here right away?'

The Beida campus was now red instead of white. Gone were the white flowers of mourning, and scarlet banners hung vertically from windows and were strung from tree to tree across the avenues.

The atmosphere had changed too. There was a buzz about the place which differed from the melancholy of the days

119

before the funeral. Students talked animatedly at every corner and buzzed like bees around the posters. An air almost of euphoria belied the metallic menace of the loudspeakers, which were broadcasting over and over what I guessed must be the key phrases of the editorial.

A note on Lily's door directed me to Chen's dormitory. The light was fading as I crossed the campus to where he lived and clambered over the usual detritus on the stairs to get to the third floor. The crowd in the corridor clustered around a door from which yellow light came out. I pushed my way through and stood blinking in the light of the room.

It was packed with young people. They were sitting squeezed together on the top bunks with their legs swinging; they were sitting hunched on the bottom bunks; they were squatting on every square foot of the cement floor. Chen and Lily were standing by the open window, papers in hand, and several others stood with them. One was Song, with her impassive face back in place. She gave me a nod. A respectful space had been left around the group, which had evidently been arguing.

The raised voices had paused as I picked my way across the floor. Chen's legs-apart posture reminded me of a military commander in his tent before the battle. The arrogance in the stance was already starting to irritate me, but when he grasped my hand in both of his, I felt the man's power.

He introduced me to the others in the group. They included the three who had knelt on the steps of the Great Hall. Chai Ling was petite and somewhat unkempt, in beige chinos and wrinkled white blouse. She looked too harassed to have had time to comb her hair. But she could smile and a warmth came from her, and, for one so petite, a kind of natural authority. Wang Dan wore glasses with light-coloured frames. Wuerkaixi was taller and had curly hair, unusual among Chinese.

Beside Song a heavily built young man called Ujun had the look of someone losing an argument. Song had that look too.

'PJ,' Chen addressed me, 'we asked Lily to invite you because we need your help. I know it is an error to have a *yang guizi* – a foreign devil – here among us at such a time, but you are a journalist. We want to ask if you will tell the world what we are saying and thinking.'

I nodded in a non-committal way. Chen continued: 'The day after tomorrow, Thursday, all the city's students will answer this editorial by marching to Tiananmen —'

The argument exploded again, and I was ignored as angry voices rose. Finally Ujun, impassive face slipping badly, banged his clipboard on the windowsill and stormed out of the room, clambering over the squatting bodies as he went. Several students got up to follow him.

Chen turned to me with a shrug: 'He tried to cancel the demonstration without asking any of us, because he's head of the union. Well, *was* – he's just resigned.'

'I still believe he was right,' Song murmured. She turned to me: 'You know the leaders have banned demonstrations, public gatherings, speeches, all we have been doing. It will become very dangerous. I can't encourage my students to take such risks.'

'It's democracy now, Song Lan.' Chen was gentle after the raised voices. He spoke English, presumably for my benefit. 'Our vote here says we march, even if the Qinghua leaders have backed down. And the students know the risks. Some of them are already writing their wills.'

Song said nothing, and the face remained expressionless. Chen turned to me and became businesslike: 'We won't keep you long, PJ. Very briefly – you are already reporting on the demonstrations for the foreign press?'

'Well, AP is taking my stories, yes. So they would be appearing around the world, I presume.'

121

'Couldn't be better. And you report on what you see in the streets?'

'What I see, yes.'

'But not on what the students think?'

'I would, if they'd tell me.'

'That is exactly what we are offering you.' Chen sounded like a salesman. 'Listen. We are offering you regular briefings on what we're thinking, our demands from the leadership, our replies to their lies, and what we plan next. We need someone we can trust, who will not distort what we say.'

I nodded. I might not like this overbearing fellow, but I was flattered.

'We might not always be able to meet,' Chen went on. 'When we cannot, Song will deliver to you a written bulletin. Or Lily will.'

It struck me Lily hadn't said a word the whole time. She was nodding now, in silent agreement with Chen. By God, maybe Chen might be the one to tame that shrew.

But what would her father say when he came?

CHAPTER ELEVEN

THURSDAY, APRIL, 27 was the day the miracle began. It was as if grace had dropped down upon the young people of Beijing. And not just upon the young.

It was the day the cold face melted.

The first inkling came about 10am outside the back gates of Beida. Song and I were among the waiting street crowd, watching with apprehension the massed ranks of police blocking the campus gates. The growing sounds of the 'Internationale', from inside the walls, told us the march was advancing towards the exit.

All at once the police lines parted like the Red Sea, and there were the marchers coming through. Rhythmically they swung left and down the street towards us. The leaders were about nine abreast, among them Chen, Chai Ling, Wang Dan and Wuerkaixi. They carried at waist level a scarlet banner that stretched the full width of the march. Their arms were linked together and they moved at a measured pace to the beat of the music. The faces, although singing, were stern and impassive.

Spontaneously the street crowd broke into applause, then began cheering and cheering. People were holding up two fingers in the V-for-victory sign.

As we watched, the cold faces of the marchers simply melted. First they went wide-eyed with astonishment at the cheering reception in the street, then they burst into smiles, then there was laughter, and youngsters began hugging each other as they marched along. Some were wiping away tears, and others were weeping unashamedly.

I looked back and some of the police were smiling and some were holding up their fingers in the V-sign.

The crowd was moving with the march, and, as we trotted alongside, I sensed that the rhythm of the marchers had changed subtly. There was a flourish to it. The step was lighter, the pace a little faster, shoulders were back and chests were out and heads were high. And all along the way the crowd caught the smiles and tears and laughter, and smiled and wept and cheered as if the cold face had never been.

At the junction with Fucheng Lu a shout arose: approaching down the street was another column of students behind a flaring red banner.

'The Qinghua students,' Song shouted. 'They've defied their leaders.'

Among shouts of 'Qinghua! Qinghua!' part of the Beida column halted to let the newcomers move in and take their place. Down the other street came a column headed by a Renda University banner. At another intersection a column joined in from Beijing Normal College, as well as a column from the Foreign Language Institute. It seemed groups were waiting at every intersection, behind banners of medical schools, schools of aeronautics, nursing, teacher-training, indeed of most of those myriad institutes that are the pride of Beijing.

The windows along the route were full of cheering, smiling people. Hard-hatted workers clustered on scaffolding and cheered and waved two fingers in the V-sign. As we passed the stalls of street vendors, they came running across with ice-cream cones, bottles of cola, and dumplings in paper bags as gifts for the marchers. I recalled the vendors' reputation as the most tight-fisted of all Beijing citizens – and the dourest. They were smiling today as they parted with their wares.

Just beyond Muxidi a three-deep police line was drawn across Chang'an Boulevard. Shouts went up: 'The people love the people's police. The police love the people.' At first the police looked impassive, then bewildered, then melted into smiles, and the sea of olive green became one more Red Sea that parted gracefully. I saw a police hat being tossed around like a Frisbee.

The same happened all along Chang'an Boulevard, at Fuchengmen, Xidan, and Liubukou. When we reached the red gates of Zhongnanhai, where China's geriatric leaders dwell like the gods in Valhalla, the marchers were singing to the tune of the French ditty, *'Frère Jacques'*. It was only later I learned the meaning from Song, which was approximately

'All our leaders, all our leaders,
Telling lies, telling lies!
Lying to the people, lying to the people,
Very strange, very strange!'

The final line of police defence, where the avenue entered Tiananmen Square, was hardly likely to behave like one more Red Sea. It was a sea of open military trucks, each one crammed with soldiers.

The march faltered for a moment. Song grabbed my hand. Then the marchers surged ahead, and the trucks were engulfed in a sea of youngsters, all chanting, over and over, 'The people love the People's Army. The People's Army loves the people.' As hundreds of hands reached up to touch the soldiers, Mao's portrait gazed down upon this unaccustomed spectacle.

The trucks started moving, one behind the other, infinitely slowly and gingerly through the swaying, chanting crowd. A few soldiers gave furtive V-signs. Once free of the crowd, the trucks accelerated and roared off down East Chang'an Boulevard.

The top of the square became a mass of cheering, hugging, weeping, smiling, conquering youngsters. There wasn't a cold face in sight. And Song was hugging me.

Euphoria by definition is a temporary phenomenon. That is why that Beijing spring was a kind of miracle. Not so much that the euphoria stayed, but that it transmuted itself into something richer and more enduring.

In the weeks that followed it was as if the shattering of the cold face had released an outpouring of generosity and mutual caring, even of love, that had been pent up at least since the Cultural Revolution. It showed not only in the youthful protesters, but as time went on, it was manifest in people of every age.

The paradox is that communism had always aimed at such solidarity and care for the common good, but had produced instead generations of head-down individuals resolutely minding their own business and tending their own little patches. So when China's youngest were seen putting their lives on the line for the common good, perhaps it triggered in all of us insights into our own selfishness. I say 'all of us' advisedly, because the Beijing spring touched us foreigners too.

I particularly recall those two weeks before the state visit of Soviet President Gorbachev as a period of hopes raised and dashed again – the size of the various marches always reflecting the current level of hope or anger.

It was encouraging however that maturer faces were appearing in the marches: construction workers in hard hats, doctors and nurses in white coats and some of the students' own teachers. This was the people, not just students any more.

When the journalists came out it was seen as the biggest break of all. At the May 4 demo there they were in their hundreds, behind a yellow banner proclaiming, 'Our mouths cannot utter what we think. Our pens cannot write what we know to be true.' I was delighted to see Xinhua colleagues among them.

After that the newspapers began reporting the demonstrations and outlining student demands. The reporting was hesitant at first, but gradually grew in confidence. State television followed.

Norman of course pronounced it a temporary phenomenon. 'Don't you believe it, Paddy,' he told me. 'Don't imagine Li Peng is giving them a longer leash. He's just too busy for the moment, slugging it out with Zhao. And they're both feeding stuff to the papers to get them on their side.'

That was the night I got another insight into the cold face phenomenon. I had brought a bottle of Canadian Club along to Norman's lair, and Norman was expounding on the cold face. 'It's not gone for good, y'know. Has to come back eventually. Chinese need their masks.'

'But why can't they stay more open, now that they've learnt to trust each other?'

'Because, old chap, it's a matter of population. Had there never been a Cultural Revolution, there'd be the cold face. Simple maths: d'y'realise the population of Ireland is born in China every four months? A thousand million people cannot have privacy, so they must create their own private walls. Up at that university where you hang out, you're aware there are four people to every nine-square-yard room. And they're the teachers – the ones with privileges. No matter how much of this warmth and caring y'go on about, they daren't leave themselves too open.'

He took a slug of his rye whiskey. 'The Chinese have a saying, "You've got to be like a well-cooked duck – warm and soft inside, but with a hard beak."'

I was on my third whiskey – a potion I'm not much used to – and I got a fit of giggles. 'That's you,' I said. 'A perfect description. Norman is a well-cooked duck!'

'What the dickens do you mean?'

'I never thought of it till now, but you've got the cold face too, just like the Chinese. Only your lot call it the Stiff Upper Lip!'

'Stuff and nonsense, Paddy.'

The liquor was making me combative. 'Do you deny you're soft inside? That you need friends? That you feel lonely for England sometimes? There's a daughter back there somewhere, isn't there? Ever long to see her?'

Norman was that stone lion outside Zhongnanhai. 'Listen to me, PJ. I live here gratis, yes. Guest of the nation, and all that. But my pension's Chinese. That is to say, minuscule. I could hardly visit Tienjin if I wanted, never mind England.'

We were silent for some time, while my big mouth hung open. When eventually I got it closed, I said, 'But you still need friends.'

He gave me the bleary look. 'Friends leave, PJ,' he said quietly. 'They go back to bloody Ireland – places like that. Haven't you noticed?'

What I had noticed was that he had called me PJ. Come to think of it, he never called me Paddy again.

CHAPTER TWELVE

THE BEIJING SPRING was in essence a flowering of courage. Hindsight convinces me of that. The splendid things that happened in those few weeks could be reduced to a facing up to fear by the Chinese people.

The casting off of the cold face was itself an act of courage. It took courage to show joy or sorrow in a society where gladness could arouse envy, and grief could signal vulnerability; where any kind of enthusiasm provoked suspicion.

The upsurge in caring took immense courage for people who had learnt from infancy that the only loyalty was to family, and that to save someone's life was to be responsible for that life for ever.

It took courage, too, to trust, so few short years after that frenzy of spying and mutual betrayal that Mao had engineered, and which he had the effrontery to call a Cultural Revolution. It took courage to face one's shortcomings, especially to put aside mutual jealousy and envy, so as to grow and work together, as many protesters did. Above all, it took courage to put one's life on the line.

It was the facing one's shortcomings that is one of my most vivid memories, but in my own case it was hardly a matter of courage. It was thrust upon me. And, as might be expected, the thruster was Lily.

All hell broke out when I told Lily I had invited her father to Beijing. I had at last managed to get up the courage to invite Lily for a drink in my rooms for the purpose of breaking this news.

'What the hell have you got against Chen, anyway?' she demanded.

'Christ, Lily, it's nothing to do with Chen. But your father asked me to keep an eye on you, and you're getting deeper and deeper into this thing. I thought he'd better see for himself how things are. And meet Chen, of course.'

'Sure. I knew it was Chen. That's what's been bugging you.'

'Lily dear, I have nothing against Chen. He's a remarkable young man.'

'You hate his guts!' Lily spat out the words. 'Go on, why don't you admit it? And I know why you hate him.'

'Lily!'

'Remember Wu Dalang in the story? They all said stay away from Wu Dalang, because he's small and he'll resent your size, and he'll try to harm you. Well, you're another fucking Wu Dalang.'

'I'm tall enough, for Christ's sake. What're you on about?'

'You're not as tall as Chen, and that's what's bugging you. You hate him, because he can look down at you.'

'Lily! For God's sake —'

But she went on and on, her razor tongue cutting and slashing. With a final 'Don't you mess with us, you little bollix,' she stormed out and slammed the door. I could hear her snorting 'Fuckin' Wu Dalang' as she went down the corridor. Whatever about the Beijing spring, it was working no magic on our Lily. If anything the pressures were making her nastier.

I was both distressed and depressed after the confrontation. But of course Lily's genius was that when she went for you there was always the tiniest grain of truth in what she said, and she knew how to make a mountain out of it.

I tossed and turned that night wondering could she be right. I went over my dealings with Chen, and all I could think of was that I had helped every way I could. Staying discreetly in the background, of course. And Chen seemed to appreciate my help. And the help had made a difference, of that I was certain.

Did I like Chen? Well, he wasn't that easy to like. He was one of those leader types, and he knew how to get people to do things. Still, a lot of people around seemed to like him. Repeat the question: did I like Chen? Well, he seemed to like me OK. That's not the question. Well, he had an opinion of himself. And he could sometimes be patronising, like about Joyce. And he made me uncomfortable when he stood too close. A bit overpowering, then.

Ah.

Lily, you bitch. May you die roaring.

Song was bubbling with joy the next evening and quite put Lily out of my mind. The miracle had touched Song too, and she had just grown by one big increment. That afternoon, along with a couple of college teachers, Song had marched for the first time.

She was euphoric as she described the experience: 'I'll never forget it, PJ, as long as I live. We waited in that side street for our turn to join. Then we moved forward, singing the 'Internationale'.

'Well I'll never forget the feeling when we swung around the corner into Chang'an. I nearly died when I saw the crowd, and they all cheered and cheered, and they sang the 'Internationale' along with us as we marched.

'We felt so proud, I started to cry. Maybe I'm sentimental, PJ, but the others were crying too – the tears were streaming down their faces as they marched. I think, maybe, in all my life I had never done a thing so – so significant, so important. For my own people. For my country. I never had a chance like this to show how I felt about democracy. About – about liberty.

'I felt at that moment, the Chinese people are very great: they're not slaves, like the government wants them to be. And I felt that from us marching there would come, somehow, the future of China. I know that moment when we turned that corner will always be the best moment of my life.'

I had seen it of course. I had been in the crowd of bystanders as the marchers swung around into the boulevard, nine abreast. Song had been in the front row, where they carried at waist level a banner stretching the width of the march. The scene recalled Delacroix's painting, *Liberty Leading the People*, where a young woman strides across the barricades holding high the tricolour, accompanied by a boy in his teens. Those young Chinese had that same heroic manner; their faces had that nobility which a great moment can impart.

'So that's it, is it, Song?' I said. 'You're committed now. Sucked in, like all the others. Right?'

'A lot of the teachers are joining in, PJ. I can't stay back any longer.'

'But you were so afraid. After – after what happened to Lee. God knows we've both been scared.'

'I'm still afraid,' Song said. 'But it's different now – if I die, we'd all be dying together. And it would be for China. So I'm afraid, yet I'm not. You understand, PJ? You don't mind?'

'Would it make a difference if I minded?' I said. 'No, Song, I don't mind, even if I'll worry myself sick. But I'm staying out of it. You know why. I don't want them saying foreign devils are behind it.'

'I wish we could get Sven to stay out of it,' she said. 'And Lily, too. But she's impossible.'

I had been too embarrassed to detail Lily's assault on me, especially the bit about being jealous of Chen. But Song clearly knew there was no moving Lily, as long as she and Chen were an item.

'It's Sven that's causing the real trouble,' Song said. 'It's not that he's marching – Chen won't let him. But he's trying to make love to all the women. Chai Ling slapped his face – he didn't even care that she's married. He thinks that because we don't believe in the God that we'll open our legs for him, that we have no moral standards. Do you think we have no moral standards, PJ?'

'You're stricter than nuns, for God's sake. I never met the like. To tell the truth, I've never quite understood why.'

'It goes back to ancient China, where they thought sex was something bad, and people couldn't talk of it. In those times girls were taught to build high walls around their hearts. Even now, if you give a woman something, you're not really supposed to touch her hand. Remember the legend about the girl who chopped her hand off because a man had touched it?'

'But why, Song?'

'Control. We've been controlled for hundreds of years. I think it began with the Song dynasty, around the time of your Middle Ages. You couldn't say what you thought, and you couldn't do what you wanted. Especially in sex – it was just a way to have children. That's when they began binding women's feet so they couldn't wander. That too was control – the leaders all had their concubines, but women everywhere were prisoners.'

Song sighed. 'It's the same today. The government still have their concubines. But they control us. Do you know they still separate husbands and wives for years, sending one to work in Shanghai and the other to Sichuan? And they can arrest

133

you for making love if you're not married. Here it's the rule of man, not the rule of law. They can arrest you if the local leaders decide. And they do. But you and I are discreet, and nobody really knows, so they'll not bother us.'

'How about Sven?'

'Now that's a problem. He's so indiscreet, and so stupid, he has no idea of the trouble he is causing.' Song sighed. 'Do you know what they're calling him? *Da yang ju* – Big Penis. And we all laugh at him behind his back. But the trouble is, it gives the authorities the chance to say the protesters are morally lax. That they are all going to bed with foreign devils. Which they're not. Nobody wants to hurt Sven's feelings, but I think Chen will have to tell him to stay away.'

CHAPTER THIRTEEN

S VEN'S ANTICS WERE forgotten in the anxieties of the week that followed. The protest movement was quite simply running out of steam, and students were drifting back to classes, which was precisely what the authorities aimed for.

The wily old government leaders, while bickering among themselves, played a brilliant game of appearing to enter dialogue with the students in the hope of wearing them out before Gorbachev's state visit. They sent nonentities to meet the protesters; they promised answers to their demands, answers which never came. They promised a public, televised meeting with student leaders, which was to happen on Monday, May 8. Nothing happened. Then it was promised for Wednesday. Then the students were told to wait until May 13.

'It's like trying to punch a cotton pillow,' Chen said.

By Thursday all but one of the Beijing colleges had reopened. Only Beida held out. And in Room 400 of the college's Democracy Building, the *de facto* operations room for the whole protest movement, the student leaders were meeting. They were at the end of their tether.

'If we could only keep going for four more days,' Chen was saying. 'That's all we need till Gorbachev comes. Look, the streets are already full of foreign journalists for the visit. We can embarrass the government in front of the whole world, and force them to talk.' He sighed. 'If we could just keep the protest going.' He looked across at me and asked in English, 'What would western students do, PJ?'

'It's not my place to advise you, and you know that, Chen,' I said in English. 'You only asked me here to draft a press report on your decisions. Otherwise I'm not to be involved. Remember?' Song interpreted for the others.

'A few of us have been thinking of a hunger strike,' Chen said quietly.

'What?'

'*Jue shi* – hunger strike.' He turned to Lily. 'Didn't they do it in Ireland? And did it not rouse the country? We could do the same – have a hunger strike in Tiananmen Square.' He turned to the group and spoke in Chinese, presumably repeating what he had said to me.

There was absolute silence in the room. I had to say something. 'Chen, you forgot to mention what happened to the hunger strikers in Ireland. They died. And those who didn't die went blind.'

I turned to the others, Song translating: 'This is the first time death has entered your plans,' I said. 'It's not my place to speak, but this time I must. As a journalist I know what hunger strikes are like. Please, please go home and think this over. Up to now it was about marching, carrying banners. But this is about death.'

Chai Ling was on her feet. 'We have to face death for a life that's worth living,' she said. 'I am ready to go on hunger strike.' This was the first time I had heard Chai Ling speak, and I thought she had a lovely voice. More lovely even than Song's. She looked so fragile she might already have been refusing food. Immediately her husband Feng was by her side. He took her hand, but said nothing.

A bespectacled young man called Li Lu stood up. 'My grandfather died in prison. He too was looking for life, a decent life for all of us. For such a life I will brave this death, along with Chai Ling.'

Wang Dan and another man I knew only as Ma stood up together. They did not say anything – they just stood.

Wuerkaixi stood up to join them. He spoke quietly, but the orator in him was obvious. 'In the old days,' he said, 'when the emperor did a wicked thing, the scholar official remonstrated with him. When the emperor would not listen, the scholar-official took his own life as a witness to the higher good. We are the scholar-officials of today.'

Lily stood up. When I saw the look in her eye, I decided to say nothing.

And then everything just seemed to come apart for me. Song was suddenly squeezing my hand, harder than she had ever squeezed it before. Then she stood up. When I realised the import of it, I thought I might faint.

'I starved once before,' she said quietly. 'That was for myself. I can do it one more time, if it's for China.'

'That's it, then,' Chen said. 'I guess it's a hunger strike.'

Song would not be moved. I was once more astonished how such a gentle person could be so unyielding.

'But how can I *not* go on hunger strike?' she asked me, as I was filing my copy for AP. 'I can't leave my students alone to starve, once it all begins. And it will be the only chance I'll ever have to do something great for China. I'll never get the chance again.'

137

But the fear was in her. All that night I could sense it. It was almost like that first night we had spent together. We clung to one another, almost unmoving, as we had done that first fearful night.

'Will I die, PJ?' she whispered once.

'No!' I snorted. 'They'll give in. They have to, now.' But I was dying inside, for I was sure the authorities would never give in.

Images came to me of Song, hollow and cancerous looking, of her eyes opaque as she grew blind, and I shrank shivering from those images and breathed in her incomparable odour as if I would never breathe it again. Then she started to shake, and I felt her tears wetting the pillow and I was trying to dry those tears with my lips.

And then, perversely, I was wondering to myself, with astonishing selfishness, who would translate for me if Song went on hunger strike.

In the morning Song went back to her colleagues at Beida to spend the day preparing for the hunger strike. There were banners to print, blankets to collect and headbands to make for the more than forty who had by now volunteered. And a farewell meal to arrange for the next day, before the strikers set out for Tiananmen Square.

Before breakfast I stopped by the hotel's fax room and found two messages. One was from Associated Press, saying they now had two reporters in Beijing to cover the Gorbachev visit, so they would no longer need me. However, they'd accept colour stories – descriptive pieces on the atmosphere of the visit – if I wanted to do any. I didn't much mind being dropped, as I had more pressing things on my mind by then.

The other message was from Mick. The Chinese embassy in Dublin had refused him a visa until the 'turmoil' in Beijing was over. He was therefore depending on me, more than ever, to look to the safety of Lily.

'Goddammit, this is becoming intolerable,' I said to Norman at breakfast. 'To land me with this bloody gorgon, who brooks no control from anyone. He must have known that when he sent her out here. Probably wanted rid of her till she grew up and got sense. Well, she's not getting sense out here, that's for sure, and I doubt if she'll ever grow up. Hunger strike, I ask you. We need her on strike like a hole in the head.'

'What y'going to do with her?' Norman asked.

'Do with her? What can I do? I wish I could get her the hell out of Beijing, back to her Daddy in Dublin, where she belongs. But Norman, I can't even get her out of the square, never mind out of China. It's not funny any more.'

CHAPTER FOURTEEN

CHAI LING'S VOICE was echoing over the loudspeakers as I walked into the Beida campus early the next afternoon, the day the hunger strike was to begin. Song had said to stay away until after the farewell meal at midday.

The place was electric. Students clustered underneath the loudspeakers, listening with rapt attention. I marvelled once more at the tinkling beauty of Chai Ling's voice.

Inside the south gate a young woman handed me a paper that read, in English, *Chai Ling's Speech: the Hunger Strikers' Last Will and Testament*. She gestured at the loudspeaker in the tree above her, and I understood this was the speech that was being relayed. Or perhaps a recording. I sat down on the pavement and read it there and then, with the actual speech echoing above me. This is what Chai Ling was saying:

> In these glorious sunny days of May, we are on hunger strike. In this most wonderful time of our

141

youth, we have no choice but to leave behind us the best things life has to offer. How unwilling we are! How reluctant are out hearts!

Alas, our nation has come to this – uncontrolled inflation, endemic nepotism, high-handed despotism, widespread official corruption. An ever-increasing number of benevolent and principled men and women are forced to lead exiled lives overseas; daily, our society has become ever more unsafe. Countrymen, all our countrymen of good will, please listen to our entreaty. This nation is our nation, these people are our people, this government is our government. If we do not speak, who will? If we do not act, who will?

Even though our shoulders are still young and fragile, even though death, to us, is too heavy a burden to bear, we have decided to take our leave. We have no choice but to take our leave. History demands it from us.

We feel the purest patriotism, we offer the finest of our heart and soul, yet we have been described as 'rioting', with 'ulterior' motives, and 'being used by a small group of people'.

We would like to plead with every honest citizen of China, with every worker, peasant, soldier, intellectual, famous person, ordinary person, government official, policeman, and with those who say we are the guilty ones, that you put your hand on your heart, ask the goodness that is in your heart, what are we guilty of? Are we rioting? We go on a class strike, we demonstrate peacefully, we embark on a hunger strike, we are forced to hide – what are all these for? Our emotions have been manipulated time and again, we endure hunger to see truth, but

are met with police brutality. Our student repre-
sentatives went down on their knees to plead for
democracy, but the Government pretended not to
see. Our request for equal dialogue has been
delayed again and again. Our student leaders face
mortal dangers.

What are we to do?

Democracy is life's greatest safeguard for the
preservation of our well-being. Freedom is our
heaven-given right since the beginning of man. Yet
now we have to fight for them with our young lives.
Can the Chinese people be proud of this?

We have no choice but to go on hunger strike. It
is our only choice. We use courage that enables us
to face death, to fight for the life that's worth living.

But we are still children, we are still children!
China our mother, please take a good look at your
sons and daughters. Hunger is destroying their
youth, death is stalking ever closer to them. Can
you remain unmoved?

We do not want to die. We want to continue to
live, and live well. Because the best times of our
lives are yet before us, we really do not want to die.
We want to study well, since our nation is so poor.
It may seem that we have forsaken our nation to
die, but death is definitely not what we are after.
However, if one person's death, or a few people's
deaths, can enable more people to lead better lives,
and can help our nation to become more prosper-
ous, we then have not the right to continue living
stealthily.

When we are enduring hunger, fathers and moth-
ers, don't be sad. When we are saying farewell to

life, uncles and aunts, please don't break your hearts. We have only one wish, that is to allow all of us to lead better lives. We have only one request: please do not forget that what we are seeking is in no way death. For we know democracy is not the affairs of a few, and the realisation of democracy cannot be completed simply by one generation.

Death is awaiting the echo that is most universal and immemorial.

> When a man is about to die,
> His words would be kind.
> If a horse is about to expire,
> His cries would be sorrowful.

Farewell, comrades, take care! May those who die and those who live share the same loyalty. Farewell, beloved, take care! I cannot bear to take leave of you, yet there is no choice but to take leave. Farewell, our parents! Please forgive us: your children cannot manage to be loyal and filial at the same time. Farewell, our people! Please permit us to demonstrate to you our loyalty in this desperate fashion.

With our lives we have written this attestation – we must make clear the sky of our Republic.

The reasons for the hunger strike are: 1. We protest against the Government's cold and indifferent attitude towards the Beijing students' strike. 2. We protest the Government's extended delays in carrying out a dialogue with the students. 3. We protest the Government's insistence on mislabelling the students' democratic and patriotic movement as 'rioting', and all other associated misreporting.

The requests of the hunger strikers are: 1. We request the Government to begin a dialogue immediately with us in a practical, concrete and equal manner. 2. We request the Government to give this student movement the true label and fair assessment, stipulating that it is a patriotic, democratic student movement.

The time of hunger strike: May 13, 1989, at 2 o'clock in the afternoon. The place of hunger strike: Tiananmen Square.

Before I had finished reading, the echoing voice faded to silence. There was momentary silence around me, and then cheering. I thought the cheering was just for the speech until I saw the hunger strikers coming down the avenue.

They had to be the strikers because all had white cloth bands around their heads. Most also wore white tee-shirts with Chinese characters front and back. But their numbers astonished me – these weren't the forty hunger strikers I had expected: there were hundreds here. The alley news had evidently been at work.

There weren't the usual disciplined ranks, as though this was not so much a demonstration as a means of getting speedily to Tiananmen Square to begin the hunger strike. Many rode bicycles: I spotted Chai Ling herself, perched on a carrier behind the young man with glasses, Li Lu. Chen was next to them, like a great gorilla doing violence to his tiny bicycle. And there was Song, solemn-faced, balancing on the rack of Lily's bike. Song didn't see me although I waved and shouted. She was wearing her white sweater with white chinos, and of course the white headband. She looked superb all in white. Pure, that was it. She must have borrowed the chinos especially for the strike.

I felt a touch on my shoulder. It was Kui'er. 'Seeing off our warriors,' he said. 'Like we saw off Jing Ke's warriors two thousand years ago. Off to save China. Nothing changes.'

Tiananmen Square was swarming by the time Kui'er and I got there through crowded streets. Later I read the crowd numbered more than two hundred thousand. Word of the hunger strike had evidently spread like wildfire via the *xiaodao xiaoxi* – the 'alley news' – and the people had come to show their support.

I couldn't see the hunger strikers. Someone told Kui'er they were clustered at the base of the Heroes' Monument, so I followed him as he pushed and talked his way through the crowd. The new gentleness was much in evidence: people smiled and said *dui bu qi* – 'pardon me' – instead of the customary shoving and cursing.

We broke through the last of the throng and encountered a sea of white. There were at the very least a thousand youngsters lying or squatting in rows on the pavement, most wearing the white tee-shirts and headbands. White-coated medics moved among them.

'What the fuck are you doing here?' It was Lily. Her headband made her look like Pocahontas. All she needed was a feather.

'I might ask you the same thing, Lily. You've no business going on hunger strike.' My voice was slightly trembly, because this young woman unaccountably made me nervous, and I knew she knew it. 'You're not one of them,' I added.

'I am one of them, but you fucking well aren't, and that's more to the point. It's assholes like you and Sven are screwing up everything for the rest of us.'

'I've got something to tell you,' I said, to get her off the point. 'Your father's not coming. They won't give him a visa.'

'Good. Best news I've had in weeks. Now I've something to tell you. Sven was picked up by the cops last night. Caught him riding a girl in one of the college rooms.'

146

'Gawd almighty. Is that true?'

'Go ask your lover. She's over there by the steps.'

Song was sitting on the bottom step of the monument and wept a little when I came across. I sat down and put my arms around her, and sat with her in silence.

'Will I die, PJ?' Song whispered.

'I already told you, Song. They can't hold out against this.' I indicated the sea of white. 'It'll be over in no time.' I knew it wouldn't.

To change the subject, I asked her what had happened with Sven. It was worse than I'd imagined: the security police had burst into a dormitory room and found Sven naked under the mosquito net with an eighteen-year-old student. He was still trying to get his breeches on properly as they marched him off. The girl was screaming in terror when they took her away.

A cheer went up as the lights in the square came on. A cold breeze was coming up from behind the monument, and I felt Song shiver. I felt a pang of hunger, and remembered I hadn't eaten. I couldn't see Kui'er anywhere. He must have gone home.

'You should go home now,' Song said. 'You must eat, you know. You're not on hunger strike.'

'I'll stay a while longer.' I felt ashamed to walk away. And I genuinely didn't want to leave Song alone in her hunger.

The girl on the step beside Song caught my eye, smiled and give me the V-sign. 'Can I speak English with you?' she asked.

God, do they ever give up? In the middle of a bloody hunger strike, and still trying to practise their English. She looked about seventeen years old.

'Sure,' I said. 'Why don't you tell me what you're doing on hunger strike? What's your name, by the way?'

'Zijun.'

'So why are you doing this, Zijun?'

147

'To help others. To help China. Like Lei Feng did.'

'Who's he?'

'He was a good soldier who gave his life to helping others.'

'Why bother to help others? What's in it for you?'

She thought for a moment. 'When I was only six,' she said, 'my mother took me on a visit here to Beijing. I saw my first beggar, sitting on the side of the street. I didn't know what he was. Then, when we were eating in a little restaurant, someone came in from the street and asked my mother for what was left on her plate. I've never forgotten that.

'If I come out of this alive,' she said, 'I want to go to Africa and work in one of those English-speaking countries there. As a teacher for the poor.'

'Will you come out of it? Are you prepared to go to the end?'

She nodded.

'What if the authorities don't give in?'

'They will give in,' she said fiercely. 'They'll have to.'

'Aye, sure,' I said. 'They'll have to.'

CHAPTER FIFTEEN

LOUDSPEAKERS CRACKLED AND Wuerkaixi's voice echoed around us. I noticed temporary speakers attached to lamp standards, evidently a rival system to the official speakers permanently installed high above the square. He was standing not far from us, flanked by Chen and Chai Ling, on the highest step of the monument.

'They are going to take the oath,' Song whispered.

'Translate for me,' I said.

'*Wo xuan shi* —' Chen intoned. A thousand voices repeated his words.

'I take my pledge —' Song translated.

'— *wei min zhu zai wo guo* —'

'— for democracy to exist and develop in our country – for the prosperity of our Motherland. – I am determined to take part in the hunger strike. – I will abide by the discipline of the strike. – I will not stop until I achieve my goal.'

Everyone stood and sang the 'Internationale', and then it was Chen's voice over the loudspeaker. 'Let us make one more pledge,' he said. 'That in fifty years' time those of us

149

still living will meet again here in Tiananmen Square. And we will bring our grandchildren, and say to them that in this place and at this time the New China was born. Do we pledge this?'

'Wo *men xuan shi*,' cried a thousand voices, and those voices cheered and cheered again.

Chen's voice grew gentle, fraternal. 'And now, brothers and sisters, you have before you a long, night without food,' he said. 'Perhaps a few such nights before we achieve our goal. So try to rest and conserve your strength.

'There are some makeshift latrines at the back of the monument. We will do better with that tomorrow. The night is cold, and friends in the military have given us some quilts and blankets. We are going to distribute them to those who need them most.

'And please do drink the salt water that will be passed around. It is necessary if you are to endure the hunger. Try to rest, now.'

The loudspeakers crackled into silence, and there was some clapping of hands. And the youngsters settled down to their first night of hunger. Figures moved around, handing out blankets, but they were all gone before they reached us.

I shall always be glad I was there to experience the sights and sounds of that first night of the strike. I doubt if anyone slept much. A few people seemed to be trying to read under the dim lamps of the square. Some clustered in circles and talked quietly, while others clung together under quilts for warmth. Cigarette tips glowed, and the brief flare of matches seemed to leap from place to place like a will-o'-the-wisp.

For the first time I was hearing what a hunger strike sounded like. It was a great whisper coming up from the ground, broken by occasional quiet coughing, or weeping, or murmuring, or even laughter. There was the tiny tinny beat from

Walkman earphones. Sometimes a voice would gently rise in song, and it was like a lullaby.

Song and I murmured the night away.

'I'm not beautiful,' I remember her saying. 'Maybe pretty, or only a little beautiful. It is Lily who is really beautiful.'

'She has grown too hard to be really beautiful,' I said. 'Kindness and softness are a part of beauty. She has neither.'

Song snuggled closer to me. 'I will tell you the things we Chinese call beautiful. The eyes – they must be the shape of almonds. The breasts should be big, and pointed. The legs must be long, especially below the knee. The buttocks – high, not drooping. And the hair – it should cascade, like a dark waterfall. And the heart – it should be kind. Yes, you were right about that.'

Zijun coughed. I looked over and noticed she was shivering. Without a word Song pulled off her sweater and went over to her.

'But what about you?' I asked when she came back.

She giggled. 'Remember you once called me an onion? Well, I have three vests under this tee-shirt!'

We were silent for a while.

'Maybe people will start to trust again,' Song whispered. 'Maybe this will change them.'

'How do you mean?'

'We have a saying that it's your friend that will betray you – the friend you confide everything to. The friend you trust. That's since the Cultural Revolution. The people's heart is broken, because so many betrayed each other in those days. So many people are mental cripples – their souls are twisted. We're all warped right out of shape.' She looked around at the hunger strikers on the ground beside her. 'But there's trust here,' she said, 'and there's goodness. Maybe this is the beginning of untwisting China's soul.'

We were silent again, and I was pondering her words. Then

Song was humming something gently to herself. She turned to me. 'There's a song I love. Would you like I sing it for you? Quietly?'

'I'd like it very much.'

'It's about the rain that washes the chest of the earth.'

'Breast. Breast of the earth.'

'Well, breast, then. I sing it for you now.'

Without a trace of self-consciousness she sang this haunting melody. Although I had to lean close to listen, the gentle sound must have carried, for by the second verse a few of the people around us had quietly joined in. By the third verse it seemed the whole white mass of hunger strikers had joined in, but almost as if all were whispering together.

We must have dozed off after that. It was broad daylight when I awoke to find Chen squatting beside me. He had a white laboratory coat over his arm. My gut gurgled for want of food.

'The news is bad, PJ.' Chen said gently. 'It's on the radio this morning, about Sven. It's bad what they're saying about him. But it's worse than that – they're saying there's immorality down here among the hunger strikers, and that foreigners are leading it.'

Song struggled up, rubbing her eyes. 'But we haven't —'

'*Wo dong*. It's OK, Song. I know that. But he can't stay.' He turned to me. 'PJ. I hate to ask you this, but you must please stay away from now on. That's how you can help us most.' The old arrogance seemed gone. Even Chen seemed touched by the Gentle Revolution. 'PJ, will you make me a promise that you will stay away?'

What else could I do? I promised.

Chen handed me the white coat. 'If there is some most urgent reason why you must come – really it would have to be very urgent – or if we send for you to write something for the press, then put this coat on. You will then look like a foreign medic, caring for the hunger strikers, and our cordon will let you through. And if they stop you, here is a pass to show them.'

He gripped me by the arm. 'Please understand, PJ. Please? It's not easy for any of us.'

On my way home I was sick for the want of Song. I stopped by the South Cathedral, leaving my bicycle at the railings without the slightest worry it might be stolen. Inside, a solemn high mass was being celebrated at the high altar. I remembered it was Sunday.

I had often been intrigued how a Catholic church could survive, even flourish, just a block or two from the control centre of the world's biggest communist and atheist country.

Entering the church was like experiencing a time warp. There was the evocative smell of incense; the three Chinese priests facing the altar with their backs to the people chanted in Latin.

This was the Chinese Catholic Church, which had broken with the Vatican years ago, as the price of being allowed to exist in China. The Vatican Council's changes in liturgy would not have reached here. The atmosphere was the Europe of my youth, complete with stained glass, nordic madonnas and a blond, blue-eyed, colonial Christ child.

Even the customary hard men, clustered half inside the front door, kneeling on one knee, were just as I had remembered at home. *Plus ça change* . . . Except the eyes.

Other than that, only the two narrow red banners with gold characters, hanging vertically on either side of the high altar, gave any hint of China. I wondered if maybe the banners proclaimed, 'God bless the glorious Chinese Communist Revolution', and I found myself smiling a little in spite of my sadness.

I knelt and let the atmosphere engulf me.

How little I really knew about China. I remembered how my childhood image had been of little yellow people in conical coolie hats, up to their waists in paddy fields or sailing in junks or trotting along with rickshaws – the pagan Chinee for whose conversion we put pennies in the box in school. My sources would have been *The Far East*, that missionary magazine, and a film, *55 Days in Peking*, in which the actors were westerners made up with slanted eyes, and who portrayed the Chinese as peculiarly nasty.

I could still have spent the past year here without learning much more, except for a splendid Chinese woman who had let me enter into her life, into her mind and body. I was privileged beyond all westerners here. Yet while I learned more, I still did not always understand. And what puzzled me most was the sheer goodness I encountered everywhere except in high places.

'Can you be good without God?' For some reason the vexed old question started going around and around inside my mind. Surely I had seen goodness last night? Goodness without God. At least nobody there believed in a God. Yet it had to be goodness – goodness multiplied a thousand times, in a thousand hearts. Hearts without God?

No. Certainly God was in those hearts. They needn't know it. The Hidden God who is everywhere. I thought of Abu Ben Adam whose name was omitted from those who loved God, who told the angel, 'Write me as one who loves his fellow man.' And saw in a vision his name placed at the head of those who loved God.

Can you be good without God? What is goodness anyway? Getting like Pilate now – no, he'd been on about truth. Anyhow they say they're more or less the same thing. Truth and goodness. And beauty, too. But are they real, or in the mind? Is goodness just a mental construct? The authorities would call those youngsters bad – 'bad elements', threatening China's stability. Deng Xiaoping would see himself as good, working to save China. And he could point to good things achieved. So could Li Peng.

In school I had been a 'good' boy. What did that mean? It meant I had been docile, nothing more. No trouble to my teachers. Giving pennies to the missions for the pagan Chinee. But especially obeying the rules. Of course they'd have called that 'good', wouldn't they, when they really meant controllable. Down, doggie. Good doggie. Was good the same as complaisant?

Some of the school's 'bad' boys had ended up courageous editors, caring doctors, dedicated politicians. And I had ended up a 'good Catholic'. Obeying rules. Rocking no boats. Praying; paying; obeying. And navigating my marriage by some imagined fucking chart, without ever looking up from the tiller until we slammed on to the rocks.

Talking of charts, what had the Bible said? *Blessed are they who hunger and thirst after justice.* Well what are those kids doing but that? Hungering after justice, literally hungering.

It reminded me I was hungry. So I got up, made a cursory genuflection, and, grateful I was not on strike, hurried out to my bicycle to get home in time for lunch.

As I cycled north past Muxidi, I had the cycle lane almost to myself. But crowds were cycling in the opposite direction, and seemed in festive mood. They were surely going to Tiananmen Square, and it occurred to me that the hunger strikers would have a lot of support that afternoon. Then I noticed youngsters with white headbands cycling towards the square, and I knew the strikers were going to get recruits as well.

Cycling along I was bothered by that whole notion of hungering and thirsting after justice. Sure wouldn't we all hunger after justice when we've been wronged? Even children show an innate need for fairness. It had to be more than that.

155

I remembered the little one in the square who was fasting 'to help others, to help China'. The one that was concerned about beggars and wanted, maybe daftly, to work for Africa's poor. That was the key, surely. To hunger after justice *for others*.

In other words, to care. Had I ever cared, before I met Song? While busy polishing myself up for God, had I ever truly cared for anyone or anything? If caring was the key, had I been Christian at all?

And had I to come to Beijing to learn the kernel of real Christianity? To learn it from the Gentle Revolution? To learn it from young communists, from followers of Confucius, from godless youngsters?

Or to learn it from a godless old man? That struck me as I sat down to lunch with Norman.

'A stroke of genius, PJ,' he was saying. 'This hunger strike is a stroke of genius. Believe me, those protesters know what they're about. Do you realise starvation here is still part of living memory? I remember it, myself, in the so-called Great Leap Forward. And now China's children are starving once again, this time to shame their leaders. This will awaken China, as nothing else could.'

He sighed. 'What I fear is, the leaders will lose such face, in front of Gorbachev and the world, they will take a terrible revenge.'

'Something I want to ask you, Norman,' I said, in a complete *non sequitur*. 'Can you be good without God?'

I got the bleary look. '*You* probably couldn't,' Norman said.

CHAPTER SIXTEEN

FOR THOUSANDS OF years the Chinese have been in the thrall of feudal emperors who, with the most ferocious imaginable punishments of Chinese *Legalism*, controlled people's thoughts, words and deeds, dictating even the length of a man's pigtail and the size of his wife's feet. Those emperors malignly distorted Confucius' teachings on benevolence and obedience to manipulate their people and render them utterly docile.

The Chinese never fully succumbed, but, as rebellion was next to impossible, people swallowed their anger, hid their emotions even from themselves, and tried to rationalise even their worst humiliations. The cold face was their protective clothing.

The Chinese even mocked themselves in the classic story of Ah Q – the village idiot who convinces himself that his wretched humiliations are victories, so that even if he is the foremost self-belittler, at least he is foremost at something.

When communism came, there was a brief morning of hope that the miseries of serfdom were at an end, until it turned out that Mao was just another emperor, and a dangerously mad one at that. Then there was hope that Deng Xiaoping would change things, but he proved himself an emperor too. A cruel one.

That is why that week in May 1989, when the Soviet Union's leader Mikhail Gorbachev came to visit, must surely have been one of the most extraordinary in the country's four-thousand-year history. During that visit, the children of China – not the adults, not the leaders, not even the soldiers, but the babes and sucklings – took on the emperor and faced him down before the world.

Gorbachev himself was the occasion rather than the cause. It was simply that his visit to China had brought the world's media to Beijing, and the youngsters in Tiananmen Square used those media to give the world the unimaginable spectacle of an emperor losing his clothes.

In fact, few actually saw Gorbachev. On the Monday he arrived, I got a brief glimpse of a line of dark-windowed Mercedes limousines – the detested 'Benzes' – slinking into the rear of the Great Hall from the only alley which police had managed to keep clear. I was peeping through the line of police that was holding back the crowd. It was after 6pm – hours after he had been due.

All day the crowd had waited for Gorbachev, uncertain from what direction he would come. Students were perched on lamp standards and swinging off the Heroes' Monument, peering north, south, east and west to try and spot the motorcade. I had gone to the back alley because I rightly guessed the authorities would not dare take Gorbachev through Tiananmen Square.

The square would have been impassable anyhow. Although the police had ordered it vacated by 8 o'clock that morning, people had been swarming there all morning and afternoon. By the time Gorbachev was due, more than three hundred thousand had gathered, and the number of hunger strikers had risen to three thousand.

It was a day of brilliant sunshine, and the square could have been an eastern Woodstock. The crowds seemed good humoured, singing when they felt like it and marching around the square behind their banners. But beneath the good humour one could sense urgency, frustration, anger, fear. It showed particularly in the banners, a few of which were now in English, presumably for the benefit of the foreign media.

'China, will you let your children die?' one of them asked. Another proclaimed, 'We like food, but we love democracy more!' And several banners bore the words of Patrick Henry: 'Give me liberty or give me death.'

There were several outbreaks of shoving against the police on the steps of the Great Hall of the People. It could have got nasty, but the Gentle Revolution still seemed to prevail.

Ambulance sirens were beginning to be heard, as hunger strikers fainted and were taken to hospital. One could not actually see the strikers, as they had been moved to the far side of the Heroes' Monument, where they were surrounded by a protective cordon of thousands of students. The leaders had organised what they called the 'lifeline' – a cleared path out of the square for the ambulances to reach the hunger strikers. Both margins of this lifeline was protected by youngsters with arms linked.

All of this I only half observed. My mind was fixed on Song, whom I could not reach, and who was now into her third day without food. Her gut would be shrieking for sustenance. As I wandered aimlessly through the youthful throngs, I knew she was hearing the same sounds as I was. Would the singing cheer her? Would the cheering give her hope? Would the sirens bring back the fear? Was she lonely? Was she thinking of her death? Did she tremble? If I could just be there to hold her. I ached to do so. I don't think I ever loved Song as much as I did that day.

As I shambled around the square, there was no one to translate the banners for me, no one to tell me what the people were singing or what the loudspeakers were bellowing, or what rumours were sweeping across the throng.

For the first time since the protests began, I was an outsider.

From a few hundred protesters at the very beginning, the numbers had grown to several thousand, then to two hundred thousand. On Wednesday, in one of the most extraordinary moments in China's history, one million people spontaneously swarmed out of their homes and workplaces and converged on Tiananmen Square. One million. The same happened on Thursday, with perhaps a second million in the surrounding streets. And again on Friday. Karl Marx gave the name 'revolutionary praxis' to such moments as this, and pointed out that they are among the rarest phenomena in human affairs.

It was no longer just the young who were joining in. The hundreds of thousands swarming towards the square from all over the city included civil servants and Communist Party cadres behind their flags, elderly Taoist monks, Buddhists in saffron robes, workers bearing banners identifying their factories, China Airlines pilots and stewardesses, a Christian group carrying a crucifix, even a group of policemen in uniform. Sports celebrities marched, including China's complete national volleyball team. People arrived from every direction: they came down the broad sweep of Chang'an Boulevard from Haidian district; they came from the east, past where the diplomats lived; they came up through the *hutongs* and alleyways from the Temple of Heaven.

And that Wednesday afternoon I saw something I had never thought to see: marching merrily into the square behind a massive red-and-gold banner of protest, came a troop of China's soldiers. It was a sight that must have given heart to the protesters and heartache to the authorities – at least to those among the authorities who might be meditating military means.

It was no longer a protest confined to Beijing. From morning to night, trucks with numberplates of distant provinces and crammed with banner-waving people inched their way through the crowded streets towards Tiananmen Square. The railway stations erupted with campaigners from Nanjing and Tianjin and Guangdong while the radio announced that protests had spread to twenty-five other major cities.

Tiananmen Square during that extraordinary week was the colour of blood. Blood-red flags snapped in the breeze high above the square to honour Gorbachev; below them the massed crowds were an undulating ocean of crimson banners that dipped and rose and whirled and flourished. The walls dripped with blood-red posters. Red headbands crowned thousands of brows (except for the hunger strikers, who wore white); even the little ones who came during the day to visit their elder brothers and sisters had red scarves around their necks.

Yet of all red things, blood itself had not come. I prayed it might stay away.

'Exponential' – that word kept coming to mind. Every day was a new high point, with the greatest imaginable enthusiasm, the biggest conceivable masses of people. But the next day things were even greater. It made me think of Mount St Helens, that volcano in Washington State that kept on swelling and swelling until one day it blew. In Beijing, too, something must blow.

As the euphoria grew, so grew my anguish. I wandered the expanse of Tiananmen Square, thinking always and only of a white island of hunger within that sea of red. And thinking particularly of one fragile denizen of that island.

My anguish was not helped by the ambulance sirens that grew to a cacophony as the days passed. By Wednesday the BBC was saying a thousand hunger strikers a day were collapsing, or suffering diarrhoea or exhaustion, or even hallucinating, and being rushed to nearby hospitals. While in hospital they were put on saline drips, but continued to refuse food. And all of them, as soon as they could stand up, went straight back to the square to continue their hunger strike.

Eventually the dee-dah shriek of the sirens was drowning out almost any other sound. It was then I recalled the first time I had heard that hideous sound, the day I had watched a young man taken to his execution.

CHAPTER SEVENTEEN

BY THURSDAY I could hold out no longer. I had to get to Song. The sight of those hundreds of ambulances, and the BBC reports of so many hunger strikers collapsing, had been deeply shocking. I had always had a vague notion that hunger strikers could survive fifty or sixty days, as I remembered they had done in Ireland, so that the early days would hardly be dangerous.

It was old Norman who enlightened me, over a hearty breakfast. 'Those hunger strikers in Ireland would have been pretty beefy young chaps, wouldn't you agree?' He gave a wry smile. 'I mean to say, no matter how frightfully Britannia had ruled them, they'd have been well fed for most of their lives. Eh?'

'Maybe so.'

'Not the same here, y'know. These youngsters live on rice and bean curd. Born of parents that knew starvation. Nothing there to give endurance. No fat to live off – not like your lot.

163

Why d'y'think the lassies are so slender? Medical chaps here are saying most of them can't last more than a week.'

I wanted to get up and run to the square.

'There are other problems, as a matter of fact,' Norman was saying, 'which is why I think perhaps you ought to get the young lady out, if she'll come. They're saying there's going to be rain. Torrential rain. And that the rain will bring epidemics.'

Getting to Tiananmen Square that Thursday morning meant pushing my bicycle through streets almost as packed with people as the square itself. Besides the masses of people heading doggedly for the square and the trucks crammed with chanting workers, thousands lined the streets to cheer them on. There were also thousands of demonstrators simply roaming the streets in groups, not heading for the square at all, but carrying the protests all over the city.

I put on the white coat Chen had given me when I got to the bottom end of the square and began to burrow my way northwards towards the monument. When people saw the coat they stood aside, and some of them applauded. I felt ashamed of my pretense.

At the back of the monument some of the genuine medics were carrying crates of lemonade in through the picket line towards the hunger strikers. I hoisted a crate and followed along. When we came abruptly through the final line of pickets and stepped in among the hunger strikers, I stopped in shock.

At first I thought they were all dead. It was as if that murmuring pool of humanity which I remembered from a short few nights ago had frozen over and become hard and still. The white-clad bodies lay side by side, motionless, most with eyes closed. Some had a single rose at the throat. Many of the faces had grotesque red or brown blotches, and some were so swollen I could hardly see the eyes. There was a smell of piss and disinfectant. I couldn't see Song.

One of the figures near me opened its eyes, saw me, and raised two fingers in the V-sign. I put the crate down and burst into tears. I could not stop: I stood there and cried and cried.

'What the fuck are you snivelling at?' I knew that gravelly voice. 'Are y'a man, or what?'

I turned around. Lily was sitting on the ground, glaring with contempt at my tears. Now *she* looks fine, I thought. Years of meat and potatoes, and it shows. She'll last the sixty days. Regrettably.

'Aren't you supposed to stay the fuck outa here?'

'Let him be, Lily,' Chen said, standing up from beside her. He put a gentle hand on my shoulder. 'You did promise, PJ,' he said, 'but perhaps there's a reason?'

'Where the hell is Song? There's going to be an epidemic, Chen, because there's rains coming.'

'We know about the rains, PJ. We have buses arriving today, a hundred of them. We'll be fine and dry in the buses.'

'But where's Song? I came to get her out. She'll die, Chen.'

'She's gone to hospital. They took her this morning. She's at the Fuchengmen Hospital.'

'I've got to get to her.'

'If you can persuade her to quit, do. Let me show you something.'

We climbed across the prostrate bodies to a group of boys and girls wearing surgical face masks. Chen bent down and gently removed the mask from a young man. Beneath the mask the mouth was taped shut.

'These ones are refusing water now,' Chen said. 'The ones from Nankai.'

I felt the tears start again. I knelt down by the young man and shook my head. He gazed at me weakly and pointed to the characters on his tee-shirt.

'It says, "Until death",' Chen whispered.

165

We stood up. 'He means that, doesn't he?' I asked Chen.

'They all mean it. And we'll have our first deaths soon. The doctors say they're already far past their limit. They have us going around every night to turn the students over, in case they die in a coma. But the government doesn't care if we live or die. Sometimes I think they want us dead, because we made them lose face. They hate us now. Can you imagine it, PJ – old men hating their children?'

'But do you need deaths? Haven't these kids made their point long since?'

'We had a vote last night. I was for stopping, but they voted to keep going. Almost unanimously. And now Chai Ling says she'll burn herself to death if there's no signal from the government.'

He turned to me. 'I never thought it would come to this, PJ. Did we go wrong somewhere?'

The sky was greenish black and muttering with thunder as I cycled the few blocks to Fuchengmen. I entered the parking lot with drops of rain starting to fall and ambulances roaring in past me to disgorge their starving cargoes. I parked my bicycle and ran up the ramp into the turmoil of the central hall.

'Jue shi ren?' (hunger strikers?) I called to the man at the desk and he pointed to a stairway, giving me a respectful salute. Ah, of course, the white coat working its magic again. I half thought I might get me a stethoscope to go with it.

Halfway up the stairs I almost bumped into a owlish-looking man in a Mao suit. He had thick, horn-rimmed glasses, and his black hair was sleeked back. I felt sure I had met him, but where? That hair's dyed, I thought, for no particular reason. He stared coldly at me for an instant, nodded curtly and passed by. A couple of Mao-suited flunkeys and a military officer scurried after him down the stairs. I paused at the landing and looked down, to find them staring back up at me.

My heart was beginning to hammer at the thought of being with Song. There were hunger strikers lying along the corridors, still wearing their white headbands, and the wards were full of them. I thought of going back down to the desk to check the register, but then I guessed that in this chaos no one would have bothered checking them in. I thought I'd have a job finding Song, but she was in the second room I entered.

It was a narrow room. About ten hunger strikers, men and women, lay side by side on pallets on the floor, under a window against which rain lashed. The window was so dark from the storm it could have been night time, and a single naked bulb illuminated the ceiling. Cartoons played on a TV screen high on the wall. Song lay on her back under a white covering, her eyes closed, her face blotchy but unswollen. There was an upturned drip bottle hanging above her and a tube into her arm. I leaned over and whispered her name. The eyes opened and her hands reached for me. I got down to hug her: she smelled of tiredness and disinfectant. A lump came into my throat.

'It's all right, Song,' I whispered. 'It's over now.'

Tears trickled back across her temples and into her hair. Her lips moved. 'It's not over, PJ,' she whispered. 'I go back today.'

The girl on the next pallet shifted slightly, to give me space beside Song. I just sat there with my back against the wall and held her hand. I said nothing. We stayed like that a long time. The last thing I remember before both of us must have dozed off is a squall of rain lashing the window.

I awoke with Song pressing my hand. At first I didn't know where I was. She pointed to the TV. I could hardly believe my eyes: there on the screen was Chen, ensconced in a big armchair, with Wuerkaixi beside him, wearing what looked like striped pyjamas. Among the five or six others I recognised

Wang Dan. The camera panned and Gawd Almighty there was Lily, large as life. It zoomed in on her face and I could see why she had been a model. She certainly didn't look as if she was on hunger strike. And she was clearly loving every minute of this.

'What the hell is she —?'

Song gently squeezed my hand to shut me up. On the screen Wuerkaixi seemed angry: he was waving his hands about and almost shouting.

'What's he —?'

'Later,' Song whispered, and pressed my hand again.

The camera panned and zoomed, and there on the screen was the man I had bumped into on the stairs. Of course. I should have recognised him. I had indeed seen him before – on TV, but once in the flesh, at that fateful banquet. It was Li Peng, Premier of China. So the students had got their meeting at last.

Li Peng looked mad as hell. His finger stabbed the air as if it were a scorpion's tail, and he was hissing and screeching by turns. And whatever he was saying must have been grim, for even Wuerkaixi and Chen looked chastened.

Li hissed himself to a close, an announcer came on screen, and there were glimpses of Gorbachev boarding a plane. There was a murmur around the room.

'Li Peng says there's anarchy, and that we are totally responsible,' Song whispered to me. She seemed slightly stronger after her sleep. 'He says we've completely lost control, and that his government is going move against us and take control from us.'

The young woman beside us spoke in English: 'That's because Gorbachev is gone. Li feels free to attack us now. But he cannot win. That storm was a sign he has lost the Mandate of Heaven.'

'What if *we* have lost it?' Song whispered.

Before we could answer, a nurse came in and switched off the television. The young man with the glasses, Li Lu, was with her. He looked worn out with hunger, but there was an urgency in his voice as he addressed the room.

When he had finished speaking, Song started shaking her head. Even lying there she seemed to gather up some momentary energy, and she too spoke with some urgency. There was a brief altercation, then Li Lu shrugged his shoulders. He took Song's hand and pressed it respectfully, then left.

Song closed her eyes as if to get strength back. Without opening them she whispered to me, 'He wants us to start eating. He says the doctors are saying our bodies are starting to cannibalise themselves for protein, and that we'll be maimed for life with tissue damage. He says it's agreed now that strikers who collapse and go to hospital are not to return fasting to the square. They're to eat. They'll announce the end of the hunger strike after everyone has gone to hospital.' Song thought for a moment. 'I don't think this is true,' she whispered. 'Li Lu is a good person, but I don't think he really knows.'

'What did you tell him?'

'I said I can't stop my strike. Not when my students are still fasting at the square.'

Bowls of porridge were being carried in. I knew there was no point in arguing with Song.

'Will you at least stay here till tomorrow?' I asked her. 'I'll spend the night with you, even if I have to sit in the corridor.'

She nodded. Then she handed me her bowl of porridge. 'You're not on strike,' she said.

169

CHAPTER EIGHTEEN

SONG DID NOT in fact get back to Tiananmen Square the next morning. The doctors simply wouldn't let her return, and she was too weak to dispute it with them. But she would not eat.

Finally towards evening they let her go. I think they must have guessed the hunger strike was about to end. I helped Song into a returning ambulance, where she lay down on a stretcher inside. They would not let me come with her – my by-now grubby white coat must have become less convincing – so I went and got my bicycle.

The streets were still thronged, but there wasn't a policeman to be seen. At every intersection students with white armbands were directing traffic, and doing it with panache. I had to smile when I saw two of them pulling over a car to inspect the driver's licence. A company of students, arm in arm, was standing guard to protect the government compound at Zhongnanhai. It was as though the authorities had melted into thin air like evil spirits, leaving the students in charge of China.

Tiananmen Square had changed out of all recognition. There must have been more than a hundred buses lined up in rows, between the monument and Chang'an Boulevard. Laundry fluttered jauntily from clotheslines strung from bus to bus, creating a curiously mediterranean effect, like a Naples street scene. The outer buses had the air removed from their tyres.

I expected the hunger strikers to be inside the buses, but instead found them grouped in front of the monument, with buses around them like circled wild-west wagons. When I saw people eating noodles with their fingers, my heart lifted within me, for I knew the hunger strike was over.

Song was lying flat on the pavement, with a quilt over her. She was not eating.

'It's over,' she said. 'The word's gone out for food. The locals are starting to bring it. And do you know who came here last night?'

'Who?'

'Zhao Ziyang. They say he was in tears and he told them he had come too late, and he begged everyone to start eating. Do you think maybe the government is going to listen to us now?'

I didn't say what I thought, namely that Zhao was probably done for and was making one last despairing bid to end the confrontation. It would be the hard men we'd be facing from now on, and sooner rather than later.

'Where's Lily?' I asked, to change the subject.

'She went back to Beida soon as the strike was over. Said she needed a shower.'

That would be Lily, I thought. 'How did she get there?'

'She borrowed a bicycle.'

Yes indeed, that would be Lily. A week on hunger strike, and she cycles ten miles across the city. One up for Irish meat and potatoes, I'd say.

172

A couple of older women came among us, carrying between them an enormous steaming cauldron that smelled good.

'There's three thousand here,' I said to Song. 'They're going to need more than that. And we've no loaves and fishes.'

'Fishes?'

'Forget it. Take too long to explain. Has anyone got a pen?'

Song said something, and a brush and a jar of ink, probably used for writing headbands, was handed across to us. Song unrolled her headband, and tore a piece off it.

'Write just four characters,' I said: *'Strike over. Need food.'*

I kissed her and ran up to Chang'an Boulevard with my white rag to hail a taxi. I must have been mad – a taxi in that turmoil? An ancient flatbed truck inched past me through the crowd, with four men in the back, cheering and giving the victory sign. I held up my rag, and one of them reached down to haul me up.

'*You Yi Binguan,*' I said. The street lights were coming on as we rattled off through the crowd.

When we reached the Friendship Hotel the guard on the gate recognised me and waved us through, and I directed our driver straight to Number Eight Dining Room. I left them, rushed up the staircase to find all the *fu wu yuan*s clearing up after the dinner. I showed them my rag, and within no time at all what was left of that evening's dinner, plus what seemed to be all of tomorrow's breakfast and all of tomorrow's lunch and dinner, was being piled on the back of the truck. I chuckled as I imagined Norman's face tomorrow, sitting down to a lunchless lunch table. Norman liked his food.

We made one more call, to the Friendship's supermarket store. They were about to close. I threw my credit card on the counter and presented my magic rag. The woman recognised me. She read the rag, declined my credit card, barked an order, and she and her assistants proceeded to empty the contents of the store on to the flatbed of the truck.

173

David Rice

I was thinking, as we headed back, the Chinese might not know about the loaves and fishes, but they sure know about miracles.

Chai Ling and her husband Feng were having a terrible row when we got back. My first reaction was relief – at least Chai Ling had not immolated herself, but the fight shocked me as I knew them to be a deeply loving couple. They were screaming and shouting abuse, and the next thing they had come to blows. Chen and Li Lu pulled them apart, and Chai Ling sat down on the ground, crying pitiably. She grabbed a quilt and pulled it over her head, and the quilt shook with her sobbing.

Feng stood staring at her, then turned on his heel and marched off. The protective circle parted to let him pass. He paused, turned around to look at us, then collapsed on the ground. They lifted him into an ambulance.

'He's worn out from hunger,' Song said.

'What was it all about?'

'They called off the strike without consulting him, and he's furious. But no one could find him to ask him.'

It was a joy to watch the youngsters eat. They ate gingerly, as though almost frightened of the food. Medics moved among them, obviously warning them to eat little and slowly at first. Some of the youngsters were weeping, the tears falling into their bowls of rice or noodles. One young man was holding the bowl and feeding his girlfriend. Every movement of the chopsticks spoke his love.

Song was holding a bowl of noodles close to her chin, in the Chinese manner. Even now her chopsticks moved with elegance in her left hand. She hadn't touched a thing until she had made sure that her students were eating.

I felt somehow I was watching a sacrament – something almost as holy as the Last Supper. I didn't think Jesus would have minded the comparison.

174

The loudspeakers above us crackled, then bellowed into life. A high-pitched ranting voice echoed deafeningly around the square. It rose and fell, and crackled and roared, and went on and on. The supper had frozen into a tableau as the students listened. I saw chopsticks poised motionless.

A deeper voice came over the loudspeaker. Whatever it said, there was a sudden gigantic roar from the students. I saw a young man dash his bowl of noodles to the ground. One of the shards landed at my feet. There was crying, screaming, fists being shaken at the loudspeakers. Youngsters lying near me were weeping and beating their fists on the pavement.

'What *is* it?' I said to Song.

'It's Li Peng and Yang Shangkun. They've declared martial law.'

The fear was back and it was bad. I could see it in Song's face. I could feel it in the pit of my stomach and in the damp of my armpits. We sat silently hand in hand, together on the pavement, while those loudspeakers bellowed out their savage message over and over again – that martial law would be enforced from 10am tomorrow, Saturday.

Above the black silhouette of the Great Hall of the People a full moon gazed down on us through a luminous cloud. I found myself thinking the thought of Omar Khayyam: when that same moon comes around once more, will it look for us in vain?

The rumours buzzed about us like flies, and Song translated whatever ones she managed to catch. Army units are already in Beijing and are moving towards us, one rumour said. They've got tanks, said another. The tanks are being stopped by thousands of people swamping them in the streets, said a third rumour. Then the grimmest rumour of all: the tanks have got through the people and are heading our way.

Many of the young people were crying in terror of what might be coming. Some clung to each other, weeping and waiting. I was wishing I could be miles away, but I couldn't leave without losing face. I'd like to think I stayed for Song's sake too, but I'm not a brave man. Probably mixed motives, as always with me. I do know that if Song had agreed to come away, I'd have been gone like a shot.

The loudspeakers faded, their evil echo lingering. After a few minutes the student's own public address system came on. Chen's voice seemed to give new courage, and the next thing thousands of students were swarming out to the perimeter of the square. They were going to form a human shield against the tanks, Song explained.

As the night wore on, hope slunk back. 'Maybe they won't come,' Song whispered. 'Or maybe not till martial law starts tomorrow.'

All that night the students were singing the 'Internationale', and the rousing old communist songs from the revolution, and even Beethoven's 'Ode to Joy', with Chinese words. A swarm of motorcyclists roared around and around the perimeter, though what they hoped to do against tanks, I could not guess.

The tanks did not come.

But the fear remained when dawn came. If they hadn't come by night they would surely come by day, probably as soon as martial law came into force at 10 o'clock. Song looked wan and worn. Already fragile from the hunger strike, she had now had a night without sleep. I longed to get her away, but it was dawning on me that she had grown to be as much a part of Tiananmen Square as the pavement she sat on.

The student loudspeakers came on, and Chai Ling was confirming some of the night's rumours. Yes, the army had indeed stopped moving. Hundreds of trucks filled with soldiers had been forced to stop, as crowds sat on the ground in front of them. People had swarmed all over the trucks, shouting, 'The People's Liberation Army must love the people.'

Now I knew what those motorcyclists had been about. They were the eyes of Tiananmen Square, bringing the only real information we had. People had started to call them the *Fei Hu Dui* – the Flying Tiger Brigades.

The soldiers, Chai Ling said, didn't know why they were here. They had come from Zhang Jia Kou, hundreds of miles away, and had seen no television for a month. They knew nothing of the protests. They told the protesters who climbed on the trucks to talk with them that they were coming here on manoeuvres and to make a film.

Some of the soldiers had been emotional. And some had given the victory sign, when their officers weren't looking.

Chai Ling listed the places where the army was stalled. They included the main south highway, the airport road, and the Great Wall Road to the north. I thought some of the other place-names sounded ominous: Chaoyang, Jing Yuan, and the Summer Palace were well within the city.

Chai Ling's voice faded. There was near silence in the square. The hands on my watch crawled around to 10 o'clock and Martial Law. We watched the big government loud-speakers high above us. And waited.

On the dot of 10am a helicopter thudded down along the ravine of Chang'an Boulevard, well below the tops of the buildings. It banked in front of Tiananmen Gate and swung in over the square. It was one of those French-made Gazelles – I recognised its faired-in tail rotor. We shaded our eyes to watch it hover right above us.

A huge bulk appeared below the helicopter, falling directly on top of us. Song screamed and I thought I was going to die. The thing exploded and became thousands of fluttering leaflets.

They had put it in writing, the bastards, their fucking Declaration of Martial Law.

It was a fearsome document, as I discovered when Song read it to me. All demonstrations were forthwith banned. Marches, processions, gatherings of any sort were outlawed. Even the constitutional right of assembly was done away with. No one was to give interviews, speak publicly in any fashion, or hand out any kind of information leaflet.

'The security forces,' the leaflet said, 'have been authorised to use whatever force is at their disposal, to ensure the effectiveness of martial law.'

It was even illegal to draw up or present a petition.

Foreign journalists were banned from press coverage, interviewing, photographing or filming. And particularly ominous for me was a decree that forbade foreigners from involving themselves in any activities of Chinese people that might instigate propaganda.

Those accursed loudspeakers started up again, this time to warn students against talking to foreign journalists. 'There is no point in doing so, anyhow,' the loudspeakers said, 'because all satellite dishes operated by foreign television networks are at this very moment in the process of being shut down.'

We were being cut off from the world.

CHAPTER NINETEEN

I ONCE READ that soldiers and sailors, before they go into battle, become uncommonly kind to one another. Maybe it was something similar in Tiananmen Square that day of martial law, for certainly the kindness of the Gentle Revolution was back in full measure.

Other things were back too, and back with a vengeance: rumour, sentiment and a sense of doom.

There was a vogue for autographs; youngsters kept asking me to sign their headbands and tee-shirts, and were doing the same for one another. There was a frenzy of exchanging mementos: pens, ear rings, kerchiefs, caps, key rings, whatever little possessions they had. I remembered once, as a boy scout at an international jamboree, how we went through a similar frenzy of exchanging mementos. But only towards the end – because it was ending. Here, too, something was moving towards its end, and the young people sensed it.

David Rice

The rumours and the alley news grew wilder as the day wore on. A cheer rippled around the square when word spread that Deng Xiaoping had resigned. I doubted that one: Deng held no official position, so had nothing to resign from. All he had was power, and people rarely resign from that. Anyhow, fast on its heels came the rumour that Deng was still there.

Then word spread that the government had electrified the gratings over the subways, to kill students who walked across them. There was some careful stepping at the north side of the square where the gratings were.

I was thinking the government might have done better to allow real news to be broadcast, as the rumours were doing it no good at all. They certainly were doing Deng no good. One rumour had him saying it would be worth killing twenty thousand students to get twenty years of stability. Another had him stashing millions of dollars in the US, prior to immediate retirement there.

There was a rumour that President Bush had said martial law becomes null and void if not implemented within twenty-four hours. That was popular for a while, but I doubt if many really believed it. We were clutching at any straw that floated by.

One rumour got a lot of credence – that the government had brought in soldiers of the Uighur tribe, because they spoke no Chinese and so could not be won over by the protesters. A call went out for Uighur students to report to the student leaders. They were to be available to interpret, if such troops appeared on the streets.

The sense of impending doom was increased by the low-flying helicopters that circled the square interminably. Helicopters are an exceedingly rare sight in Beijing. I had never feared such machines before, but now I felt their menace and began to detest them. Word circulated that they carried heat-seeking missiles, or that they would be dropping gas on the square. Our worst fears seemed confirmed when student headquarters began distributing surgical masks and wet towels for defence against gas. Although God knows what use a surgical mask would be, I reflected.

I just wanted Song out of Tiananmen Square, and could think of nothing else, but she seemed to have grown roots. 'I'm part of it here now,' she told me. 'I cannot walk away.'

'But you could be dead before the day is over,' I said. 'We could both be dead.'

'You go, PJ. It's not your fight. I don't want you dead.'

'And I don't want you dead either, you stupid woman. Will you cop yourself on – nobody's any use dead!'

None of us were making much sense that day. Terror is not conducive to rational thought. And as the hours crawled towards twilight, the prospect of military attack grew. And its horrors grew in our imagination.

Shortly after sundown a Canadian journalist came over to talk to me, ignoring the martial law restrictions. The word was out, he said, that the military would strike just before dawn. That way they'd have darkness for moving into position and daylight in which to attack. When I heard he had a car waiting to take him back to the Shangri La Hotel, just up from the Friendship, I saw my chance.

'Listen to me, Song,' I said. 'You stink, do you know that? I don't blame you, after all we've been through.' For a moment I thought she'd hit me. 'Look, I stink too. Listen. Nothing will happen till morning – this bloke says it's from the horse's mouth. He can give us a lift to the Friendship, so we can both have a shower. How about it?'

She hesitated. 'How would we get back to the square?'

'Taxi. There's always taxis at the Friendship. Come on – let's do it. And we'll get a decent bite to eat there, too.'

I think it was the shower swung it. Song, like most Chinese, was always squeaky clean, and she must have felt miserable with the condition she was in. Anyhow she fell for it. As to coming back, I hadn't the slightest notion of it, or of letting Song back if I could help it.

Well, we'd deal with that later. There'd be no taxis at the Friendship, anyway. At least I hoped there wouldn't be.

The streets were as thronged as Tiananmen Square. We must have been crazy to think we could easily get through, and we encountered one diversion after another. There seemed to be few street lights on, and there was a frightening quietness about the crowds in those moonlit alleyways.

As the car stalled in the crowd every few minutes, faces peered in, saw the foreign devils inside, smiled nervously and gave the victory sign.

We were a street somewhere off Dianmen Avenue when the car simply stopped dead in a crowd that squeezed it from all sides. Then I realised the dark shapes rearing up behind the crowds were military trucks full of silent soldiers. Metal glinted in the moonlight.

The soldiers were still as statues. Our car could not move, nor could the crowd. It sort of pulsated, and our windows became a mass of faces, smiling anxiously in at us. I sensed that people were dangerously hyper. It was then I realised our driver was not quite sober.

A young man shouldered himself in front of our car and motioned us fiercely to reverse. Two other students pushed their way to the back of the car and miraculously opened a fearfully narrow passage. We backed and backed: from the rear seat I was shouting directions so we did not run over a body. Had we done so, those smiles might have vanished.

As our driver accelerated away, the car bumped and hurled a figure aside, but the driver refused to stop. 'They'd kill us,' he kept saying. I hoped the youngster wasn't badly hurt.

Our nerves were ragged by the time we reached the Friendship Hotel, where I was dismayed to see three taxis in the hotel park. As we went up in the lift I was muttering that I'd think twice before riding with an asshole like that again. Song said nothing. She had the cold face back on.

'You take the first shower,' I said to Song when we got to my room. 'There's some clothes of yours in the bottom drawer of the wardrobe.'

I called room service and ordered food for us both. I ordered lots, and told them to bring us double portions of everything.

'I'm going down to Norman,' I called. 'Back shortly.' Song didn't answer. I could hear the shower hissing.

Norman's lair was poisonous with smoke. He was ensconced in his recliner, pipe in hand, a glass of whiskey beside him. He pointed his pipe silently at the television. Good Lord, I had completely forgotten. The English Cup Final.

I went to the cupboard, poured myself a generous shot of Norman's customary Johnny Walker. I sat down and let the soothing tones of John Motson's commentary wash over me. I had soon lost myself in the magic of the match, with the green sward and the blue and the red jerseys, and all the old emotions. As I watched those cheering festive crowds, the grimmer crowds of Tiananmen Square seemed for a moment far away.

In the end Liverpool trounced Everton, as I had expected them to. I sat there gazing at the commentators, wishing the spell would not break: even losing could be a happy enough thing, when it's only football. You didn't die.

Norman got up, poured himself another whiskey and topped up mine. The unaccustomed whiskey on an empty stomach was making me light-headed.

The phone rang, and Norman answered. I heard him give directions on switching a call, then he handed me the phone without a word.

'You fucking gobshite! You BOLLIX!' Lily was screaming down the phone. 'Jeeesus, PJ, I'll fucking KILL you! How dare you! How fucking dare you!'

'Lily, what is it? What are you on about?'

'You know fucking well what I'm on about!'

'Lily, where are you?'

'You hoor, you know goddam well where I am. I'm in London, and you fucking well got me here!'

'Lily. Calm down. I don't know what you're talking about. How the hell could I have got you to London?'

'It's you and your fucking Brit buddy. You swung it between you. You wanted me out from the start. Jesus, PJ, I fucking hate you. I hope you die. I hope you DIE. I hope that fucking oul' Brit dies.'

Lily was now roaring crying down the phone. For a while I could get no sense out of her. Finally, between the screeching and the snuffling, I pieced together what had happened. It seemed she had headed back to college the moment the hunger strike was over. When she walked into her room at Beida, she found two police officers waiting. They already had her bags packed and her passport and a plane ticket ready. They had simply driven her to the airport and put her on an Air China plane for London.

'On my honour, Lily, I had nothing whatsoever to do with it,' I told her. 'For God's sake, how could I? And neither had Norman. I swear it, Lily. Before God I swear it. Please believe me. Listen, let me look into whatever happened. We'll have you back here in no time.'

'Fuck off to hell, PJ!' Lily said, and hung up.

I put down the phone and turned to Norman. Then I stopped. His face had that cunning look that Walt Disney's Pluto wears when he's up to no good. And he wouldn't catch my eye.

'Norman,' I said. 'Norman! Look at me!'

He looked.

'Lily's in London,' I said.

'Is she, by Jove?'

'Did you have anything to do with it?'

'You're being ridiculous, PJ.'

I knew it then. 'You interfering old bastard,' I said, and I was mad. 'How dare you? How dare you stick your nose into this? Who the bloody hell asked you to interfere?'

'You did.'

'I did nothing of the sort!'

'Y'did, y'know.'

I was standing up and pointing my finger now. 'You stop your bloody nonsense, Norman. I never asked you, and you know it.'

'Last man to say that was Henry the Second.'

'Huh?'

'Henry the Second. After they killed Beckett. He said he never asked them to kill him. Remember? But what did he say before that? – "Who will rid me of this turbulent priest?"'

I sat down, trying to get a grip on things. Norman's face was working, that's the only way I can describe it, as if he were in the grip of some great emotion. Or choking. Then I realised he was trying to hold back a fit of laughing. I started to laugh too. Then suddenly we were doubled up with the laughing. We laughed and we laughed, until my insides were hurting.

We got it under control, then Norman started off again. Then I started too. We were shaking with the laughing. That's when the knock came on the door.

'*Jin lai*,' Norman called out.

The door swung open, and there was Song. She stared at us both, as we tried to control the shakes.

'I'm going back to the square now, PJ,' she said.

'Stay here and join us,' I said stupidly. 'Don't go back to

that fucking square. You'll only get killed. I don't want to see you killed.' Maybe I wasn't drunk, but I was in that condition described in Irish courts as 'having drink taken'.

'I'm going now,' Song said.

She turned on her heel and went down the corridor, her airline bag over her shoulder. She looked gorgeous in her clean, neat jeans and denim shirt. Don't need clean clothes for getting killed in. Shocking waste. Her, not the clothes. Half of me realised I wasn't thinking too clearly.

I scrambled after her, and jumped into the back of the taxi along with her. There was silence for a long time as the driver negotiated the *hutongs* and alleyways and their near-hysterical crowds.

'You shouldn't drink like that,' Song said.

I exploded. 'Sweet Jeeeeus,' I shouted. 'Is there no fucking woman in the world that doesn't try to control a man? I come all the fucking way to China to get away from them. And they're the fucking same here. Will you get off my goddam back!'

The driver was looking around. I was afraid he might run over some of the crowd outside, so I shut up. Song was weeping silently. I went to put my arm around her, but for some reason she didn't seem to want it.

The taxi stopped, and there was the Great Hall of the People. Jesus, I had forgotten all about it. I had completely forgotten Tiananmen Square. Wasn't something supposed to be coming? Tanks, or something? I couldn't quite remember.

Song was paying off the driver. She said a couple of words, which I guessed meant 'Take him home', so I jumped out of the car and followed her through the protective cordon and up to one of the buses.

Ah yes, tanks. That's what's coming.

'Tanks'll be here before dawn,' I said. ' But don't you worry – I'll look after you.'

CHAPTER TWENTY

I AWOKE WITH a hangover, in the back of a Tiananmen Square bus. At first I didn't know where I was until I saw the Heroes' Monument outside the window.

There was a whiff of garlic. Song was sharing our untouched food from last night among the youngsters in the bus. So that's what had been in the airline bag. She looked wretchedly wan, but how else could she look after those days on hunger strike? It was astonishing that she should be on her feet at all.

She came up to me and gave me a tiny portion of pork and garlic sprouts, nestled on a paper napkin. 'Try this, PJ,' she said gently. 'It will help you.'

I nodded, accepted the napkin and started to munch. Then I suddenly jumped up. 'Jesus, the tanks,' I shouted. 'Did they come?'

Song was back like a shot. 'It's all right, PJ,' she whispered. 'The tanks never came. And no soldiers either. It's all right. You're OK. Just eat. OK?'

I felt embarrassed after my outburst. The bloody kids in the bus were all turned around gaping at me. Then I felt angry – the Chinese have this way of staring unblinkingly at you, and it would get on your nerves, especially when you're fragile. So what, I got drunk? And so what, they never get drunk? But they're certainly not perfect. There's a lot of things wrong here too. They can't even run a bloody square properly. And they think bloody marching will solve everything.

'What the hell are ye all staring at?' I shouted.

Song was in the seat beside me, and she was holding my hand.

'I'm sorry about last night,' I whispered to her.

Before she could reply, the bus door opened and Chen climbed in. Li Lu was with him. I really wished they hadn't come while I was like this. If they could have waited until I was myself – but they could hardly have known.

'We're looking for Lily,' Chen said to me. 'Have you seen her?'

'Lily's in London.'

'She's *where*?'

'London. She rang me last night to tell you.'

Chen sat slowly down on the seat across from me. Even sitting down he towered above me, but I didn't mind any more. 'Why did she leave us?' he asked, almost to himself.

'She didn't leave. She was fired out of China by the police. That's what she told me.' As I said this, I was glad Lily couldn't call him right then. I would not have liked Chen to hear Lily's gloss upon my simple statement.

Chen looked so beaten I felt sorry for him.

'Look,' I said, 'she'll be back when all this is over. You haven't lost her. And it's probably better this way – she's safer over there while the flap is on.'

'You know, I was going to ask her to get married today.'

'Good Lord. How were you going to manage that?'

188

'There's going to be a few weddings today, in front of our own little commune here in the square. In case we die tonight, we'll have declared our love. It will not be the first time – we have a tradition in China of weddings on the execution ground. But I guess that's out for me, now. The wedding, I mean. Maybe not the execution.'

Chen snapped himself together and was once more the administrator. But still courteous. 'I have a request, PJ,' he said. 'We cannot forget the help you've given us – and you will do lots more – but I'm afraid it's the same request as the last time. You – must – stay – away.'

He drew a deep breath. 'I know you are concerned for Song. Indeed, for your sake we asked her to stay away too, but she will not. She says her place is with us. We cannot refuse her.'

He lowered his voice. 'The reason you cannot be here among us is that your name has been mentioned in a security-police bulletin. Including your photograph. It says you are one of the westerners who are inciting the students to turmoil. And Li Peng referred to it in a speech yesterday, without mentioning names. It is their excuse for refusing to listen to us. There are hundreds of spies here in the square, watching and reporting everything.'

My first reaction was momentary conceit – even Li Peng had noticed me. It must have been that time at the hospital, when he was visiting the hunger strikers there. He must have asked, who's that foreign devil? I felt vaguely flattered. Then I felt scared. What do they do to people who incite students to turmoil?

'Well then,' I said facetiously, 'I don't suppose Song and I can get married in the square today.'

'It wouldn't be such a good idea, PJ,' Chen said with a smile. 'But here is a suggestion. Why don't you stay on the edge of the square, outside the cordon, where all the onlookers are? You wouldn't be among us then, but you could be nearby to help Song when the trouble comes.'

Li Lu spoke for the first time. He spoke in Chinese.

Chen interpreted. 'Li Lu is right. We thought the military would attack already. Which means they have to be coming soon. Today or tonight. We have reports that Li Peng has ordered the square cleared by one in the morning.'

So that Sunday found me once again on the outside looking in. I had begged Song to come away with me, but she simply would not. 'I belong here, PJ,' she kept saying.

However, before I left her we laid our plan of action for when the military came. She would disappear into the crowd and rendezvous with me at the left side of the Great Hall steps. Together we would run to the south of the square, behind Mao's tomb. I would have her bicycle along with mine at the nearby cycle racks, and we would cycle away.

That's how daft we were. As if the tanks would halt to allow us hand in our tickets, pay the lady, identify our bikes and lift them out of the racks. And cycle into the sunset, of course. Or maybe into the moonlight, for nobody really knew at what time the tanks would come. Anyhow who said they wouldn't enter the square from the south end, right by our bicycle rack? Or come in both ends of the square, simultaneously?

It goes to show how wrong Samuel Johnson was when he said the prospect of immediate execution concentrates the mind wonderfully. Mine was all over the place. And so was Song's mind, or she'd have come away that morning, instead of sitting like a dummy waiting for the military.

But it wasn't just Song and myself. Half a million people in the square were quite simply waiting for the soldiers to come and kill them. When a rumour swept through that the soldiers were coming out through the Forbidden City, the crowds swarmed to the top of the square to bear their breasts to the guns.

When a story spread that a trainload of soldiers had arrived at the station, just two blocks away, the crowd swarmed down there to meet them. I got more or less carried along with the throng and found myself in a narrow street with the turreted station building at the far end. I could hardly turn with the pressure of bodies around me, and I knew that when the soldiers came out they would have no need to fire. We would be crushed or trampled to death. But I didn't particularly want to do much about it. I was there, and that was that. Just part of the crowd.

That rumour had been accurate: the soldiers really were inside the station, as I learned later. It's just that they didn't come out at that point. It was to be some time before they did. And I remember, as the crowd moved back to Tiananmen Square, there was a palpable sense of disappointment, which I shared. A new chant was in vogue which seemed to make the protesters even more emotional. As we headed back I spotted Kui'er, almost beside me in the crowd. He seemed as pleased to see me as I was to see him. It was he told me that the latest chant meant, 'We came on our feet; we'll leave on our backs.'

That's how daft we were that Sunday, but I didn't realise it then. The thudding of the helicopters above us and the bellowing of the loudspeakers and the lemming-like rushes of the crowd from one side of the square to the other all began to seem normal.

'Where's Ning these days?' I asked Kui'er.

'Tried to kill herself. Husband told me she cut her wrists. She's been sent back to her old papa in the countryside. Jilin Province.'

'Where the daughter is?'

'Yes.'

'How about the boy?'

'Has to stay here in Beijing with his papa. He's registered here.'

That day we swung wildly between terror and hope. The alley news was working overtime, and I was glad to have Kui'er to translate the many rumours that were circulating. According to the alley news, orders had been issued to clear the hospitals to leave space for the casualties that would shortly be coming from Tiananmen Square. And we heard the cleaning women of Beijing has been rostered to wipe the square clean of the blood that would be soaking it.

The underground passages beneath the square were already packed with soldiers, and all they had to do was come up from the ground and take over. So said one of the rumours. There were thousands of others in plain clothes among the throngs in the square, waiting to join with them. So said another rumour. People found themselves watching carefully any young man in the square with a tight haircut, and a few close-cropped students inevitably suffered.

Then we heard that a daughter of one of the top military commanders was here among the protesters, and that her father had refused to move against them. Which was why the military were stalled. That gave us hope for about half a minute.

We heard that the student leaders were urging people to fly kites as the best way to bring down the helicopters. It would take the helluva kite to do that, I thought. And we heard they had sent out for doves, which, when released, would fly around the helicopters and interfere with their rotor blades. Which was rather rough on the doves.

My favourite rumour was that the motorcyclists were carrying their girlfriends on their pillions while roaming the city. The girls were to distract the soldiers while their men were busy slashing the tyres of the soldiers' trucks. Well, girls on bikes had certainly distracted me many a time in Beijing.

About mid-afternoon I was eating some steamed bread that a couple of youngsters offered to share with me when the 'Bridal Chorus' from *Lohengrin* blared out from the students' loudspeakers, and I knew the marriages were taking place. The crowd in the square joined in a Chinese version of 'Here Comes the Bride', which soon mutated into the 'Internationale'.

And when the five newly-wed couples, led by Li Lu and his bride Ming, did a circuit of the square, the crowd showered them with gifts. They were the usual tiny things – sweets, pens and key rings – which people with little to give gave with such love.

'Weddings on the execution ground!' people were calling out. I felt this brought a shadow on the brightness of the occasion, but it was uttered and accepted with enthusiasm.

It started me on a fantasy about being married to Song. I imagined her with me in Ireland, hiking through the yellow gorse on a mountain track above Killaloe and breathing the heady scent of the gorse. Or standing on an Atlantic cliff at Dunquin, gazing out towards the Blaskets, watching the breezes scuttling over the surface of the sunlit sea. I wanted to see those almond eyes grow wide with wonder.

I could indeed marry Song. I could bring her home, my gold-dusted bride, and find us a bungalow in some Wicklow valley like Glenmalure where I would write my books and she would never again live three to a room. And we could have little gold-dusted children with almond eyes. And hopefully not with my nose. Her father would come to us and she could care for him with that touching filial love that was so Chinese.

I found myself marvelling once again at this extraordinary human being whose hand I could hardly get to hold in this mad turmoil. There were so many layers to her. There was the defensive outer shell of the cold face that every Chinese had, and, when you got inside that, there was the gentle yielding and the softness and the caring and the giving. And the vulnerability. And that exquisite capacity for love. And, within that again, the steel that could take on a Communist Party bully-boy, endure jail without flinching, and twice – twice – contemplate death from starvation. A steel that had enabled her to hack her way back to finish her schooling and to bludgeon herself all the way through university. And finally the sheer brilliance that had caught the eye of the authorities so that they had assigned her to teach at China's premier campus. And then the caring and compassion she showed her students.

Once you have found her, I thought again, never let her go.

As the lights came up in the square at dusk, the students' public address system came on. At first I did not recognise the voice, then I realised it was Li Lu, the young man who had been with Chen on the bus and who had got married that afternoon. With Kui'er interpreting I got the gist.

'Forty years ago,' Li Lu said, 'when the People's Liberation Army entered Beijing, our parents ran into the streets to welcome it. Tonight it is coming again, and their children shall again run into the streets, but this time not to welcome it. Instead they will sit down in front of the soldiers and their tanks.

'What is the difference? This time the People's Army is not led by Mao, but sent by a coward called Li Peng, who has staged a counter revolutionary coup, to prevent freedom and democracy, and to plunge the country into a new dark age.'

Jesus, this is treason he's talking, I thought. This is a hanging matter now. But how that young man could talk.

'Li Peng has said on television that the troops must reach the square by 1am,' Li Lu went on. A moan arose from around the square. 'So we have only a few hours left. Let us prepare now. Here are our plans.

'Your leaders will go to meet the soldiers when they come, and try to talk to them and win them over to our cause. If this does not work, then we will at least negotiate to be allowed to withdraw peacefully from the square.

'Those are our duties. Here are yours. You do not swear. You do not curse. You do not fight back. You shout together, "The People's Army loves the people!"

'Those who were on hunger strike are still weak. They must go straight to the buses and remain there. We will arrange with the soldiers to get them away safely. And when the time comes and the soldiers move in among us, remember your first duty is to care for the girls, the weak and those who were on hunger strike.

'As you know, I got married today. Tonight I will not get to sleep with the girl I love. If we die tonight we will sleep together for ever. If we do not die, then some day I will bring her back here with our children, and we will show those children where their China began – the free, democratic, happy China which will be theirs by that time.'

I wondered if maybe some day Song and I would come back with our children too.

CHAPTER TWENTY-ONE

THE SOLDIERS DID not come that night. They did not come the next night. Nor the night after that. We began to wonder if they would come at all.

After some days the waiting for the soldiers developed its own routine. As happens in prolonged abnormal situations, the bizarre became routine.

The soldiers dreaded by everyone were already among us, a part of everyday life. They sat in their trucks at the sides of streets all over the city, knocking on doors for people to boil water for them, cheerfully accepting cigarettes and plates of noodles and rice from kindly neighbours, chatting with the crowds that sat on the pavements around the trucks to prevent their moving.

No one seemed to be working. Hardly a factory or office in the city was open. Instead of the rush-hour traffic, there was an even flow all day, and it was mostly to or from Tiananmen Square. At every intersection the students still directed the traffic.

There wasn't a policeman to be seen. I heard that a lot of

197

them were in civvies down at the square, having joined the protesters. Perhaps a lot of them were also in civvies down at the square spying on the protesters. We'll never know. One thing we do know is that during those days the crime rate came close to zero.

A group calling itself the Beijing Thieves' Association put up posters around the city announcing that they too were going on strike. 'In support of the protest movement,' the poster announced, 'we, the thieves of Beijing, hereby announce that we are giving up stealing for the duration of the protests.'

So the policemen weren't really needed.

Barricades were the norm in every street. Throughout the suburbs, as well as in the streets leading to the square, buses had been placed horizontally across the road and stayed like that for days. In a few streets they would be moved aside during the day but replaced at night. In some streets dumper trucks had piled heaps of rubble from building sites; in other places the barriers were as insubstantial as those ubiquitous cycle racks, just dragged across the road. Protesters manned each barricade, guiding the cars and cyclists through the narrow gaps.

Sometimes I cursed those barricades between me and my Song. For most of the long hours of every day all I had of Song was an image of her face an inch from mine, the dark eyes unblinking, and the warm womanly smell from her skin. And the gold-dusted hand with the circular whorls. That face was the last image when I fell asleep and the first when I wakened.

Tiananmen Square itself gradually acquired the attributes of a people's commune.

In *The Scarlet Letter* Nathaniel Hawthorne observed that even the most idealistic communities discover how two institutions early become necessary: the prison and the cemetery.

These days I would add a third: the administrative office, complete with application forms in triplicate, in-trays and rubber stamps. The young administrators of Tiananmen Square were not around long enough to establish the first two such institutions – there were enough prisons and cemeteries out there yawning for them anyhow – but they did brilliantly with the third.

It was only when I was on the outside looking in that I realised how splendidly organised the Tiananmen Square commune had become. There were strict boundaries around the central compound where the buses were, marked by the permanent cordon of guardian students. There was the command centre at the Monument to the People's Heroes, from which Chen and the leaders issued their decisions. Those decisions were arrived at democratically, as far as was possible in the circumstances.

Security clearances were required to pass through the various cordons, and officials in armbands enforced them. There were official passes and even rubber stamps to stamp them (except in China they're called 'chops', and are not rubber).

The commune had organised its own feeding system, garbage collection, latrine maintenance. The acquiring and distribution of food was no mean feat in a city with growing scarcities of vegetables, milk, eggs and rice, due to roadblocks and the fact that few in the city were working. Water and basins were available for washing and bathing: in the absence of showers, the youngsters reverted to the traditional Chinese use of two basins – one for amidships and the other for washing the rest of the body.

The teachers at the various universities organised their own support system for the students, collecting donations and sending basic necessities down to the square, such as loo paper, sanitary napkins, soap, shampoo, blankets and disinfectants. Song told me they could never have held out as long as they did had it not been for the back-up from the college teachers.

There was an embryonic policing system, which showed its effectiveness when three demonstrators threw some paint at the sacred portrait of Mao above Tiananmen Gate. They were promptly arrested by the students and handed over to an official police barracks up the street.

There was a fully functioning loudspeaker system, connected to the command centre, rivalling the official system set high up around the square. (It has remained a mystery to me why the protesters never got around to dismantling the official loudspeakers. They took down all the government's video cameras around the square, but the loudspeakers stayed operational to the end.)

There was immense pride among the young people in the system they created at Tiananmen Square. 'The Square is our Republic' was a boast I often heard during those days, and it was routinely uttered in the broadcasts of the student public-address system.

I developed my own micro-routine, to fit in with the macro-routine around me. When the conviction grew that the army would attack only under cover of darkness, I took to sleeping in the daytime back at the hotel and coming down to the square in the evenings to spend the night there. That way I could be there for Song if anything happened.

The south end of the Great Hall steps became my stamping ground, a place to rendezvous with Song, who often came out through the cordon to spend an hour or so with me. I would bring her food from the hotel and was glad to see her building up her strength after the hunger strike.

I would sit there on the steps, willing Song to arrive, staring at the spot where she would come through the cordon. And then I'd see her making her way towards me, slender and graceful, and I'd think again of Yeats' line: 'A young girl, and she had the walk of a queen.'

And then she would be in my arms and we no longer cared who saw us, and I would breathe in her scent and maybe weep a little without her noticing. I would open my rucksack and take out the little things she had asked for: a fresh bar of soap, maybe, or some shampoo or a packet of STs. Then I would take out the foil-wrapped carton of noodles or chow mein that the kitchen staff had made up for her and hand her the chopsticks. I'd watch the graceful movements of those chopsticks in her left hand.

Part of my daily routine, of course, was to try to persuade Song to come away with me. She routinely said no.

I took to listening regularly to the BBC World Service on my hotel radio, and it was like a hotline to a different life. The jaunty 'Lilliburlero' and the booming of Big Ben continued to have a calming effect on me, reminding me that there was a saner world out there somewhere. It also helped me get a broader picture than I could ever get at Tiananmen Square. From the BBC I learned that even though Zhao Ziyang had disappeared from sight, the struggle between his supporters and those of hardliner Li Peng was far from over.

Most heartening news of all was that the army's eighty-seven-year-old Marshall Xu had rejected 'groundless rumours' that the army would suppress the students. It was in Beijing, he had said, only to safeguard stability. And better still, a number of retired generals had asked the authorities to end martial law. 'The army must not enter Beijing,' they had said.

Of course the army was already in Beijing, as I knew only too well since I cycled past the soldiers every day. Still, it was reassuring to know there was not a monolith out there, hell-bent on destroying the protesters. The students still had friends.

I do believe it was this knowledge that kept them going, for some of the protesters had shortwave radios and would be hearing the same broadcasts as I was. I often wondered if those at the BBC World Service were aware of the profound hope they were able to engender among those thousands of young people.

Norman, over dinner (which was my breakfast), was my other source of information. His stories were more local, of course, and could be grim. It was from him I learned that Sven was in jail, and that the Norwegian consul could get nowhere with the case because of the turmoil. The girl caught with Sven had never been seen or heard of again. And Sven's unfortunate Chinese wife had had to return to her family, since the hotel bill was no longer being paid. What Norman did not say, but which I found out later, was that she had departed with 10,000 *yuan*, a parting gift from Norman. It had to be most of the old fellow's savings.

It was this news that prompted me to pay a long overdue visit to my employer at Xinhua. I had rather foolishly taken my accommodation for granted, and I did not want to find my hotel bill, too, cut off. Or my salary, which was still being paid.

Mr Xiao was courtesy itself. The turmoil would be over shortly, he assured me, and we'd all be back at our journalist training in no time at all. Just a little more patience, and all would be well.

'Oh, and by the way,' he said, just as I was leaving, 'this came to me from the security police some days ago.' He handed me a photograph of Song and myself. Song was lying on the ground with her hunger-strike headband on. I was hunkered beside her, holding her hand.

'I wouldn't worry too much about it,' Xiao said. 'We appreciate your work here. And you will soon be doing it again. But just remember, there is very little they do not know, about any of us.

'Would you like to keep the picture, by the way? You might like to have it as a memento of your stay among us.'

All things pass. Even that massive institution called the Chinese Empire had, after four thousand years, come to dissolution at the hands of Sun Yat Sen and then Mao. Likewise there must soon be an end to the fragile little community of Tiananmen Square.

In the event, it lasted just days, but that youthful commune had an intensity of living, an idealism, a beauty, and I would dare to say a level of happiness, that bore no relation to time.

The authorities knew it could not last. And so they waited, with their oriental patience. The army waited on the streets. The leaders waited inside Zhongnanhai and quietly expected the winding down of what they called the 'event' at Tiananmen Square.

That Tuesday was undoubtedly the high point, when the first illegal march under martial law took place. Once more, and for the last time, a million people turned out on the streets. And over and over during their long march to Tiananmen Square, their chant was '*Li Peng, xia tai!*' – 'Li Peng, resign!'

As if in answer the sky turned black, like the moment of the Crucifixion, and darkness came down upon Beijing. A vicious wind roared down Chang'an Boulevard, flailing the population with dust from the Gobi Desert. Then the rains came thundering down and turned the dust to mud.

'It is the sign,' people said. 'Li Peng has lost the Mandate of Heaven.'

'No,' Song said when I met her. 'Li Peng hasn't lost it. We have.'

'Well that's it, then,' I said. 'So you're not going to win? Then it's time to come away.'

'I cannot.'

'Song, you just said —'

'Listen to me, PJ. It's not about winning. It's about doing

203

something that will never be forgotten. And because it won't be forgotten, China will finally win in the end. I know now this is what I was born for.'

'Song, you could die here.'

'Yes, I could. But life's a coin you get for free. You save it; you polish it; you guard it. And then some day it's time to spend it. The thing is to spend it on something worthwhile. Like China.'

Jesus, the bleeding blood sacrifice all over again. Hadn't there been enough of that nonsense in Ireland? I hated Song in this mood, and I prayed it would pass quickly, but right now there was no moving her.

But she was right about one thing: she was right about who had lost the Mandate of Heaven, as I realised when I saw what began to happen in Tiananmen Square from about that moment. It was subtle, and it was gradual, but it became slowly clear that the movement had passed its peak.

It was a couple of days before I was sure of it. Certainly the crowds at the square seemed thinner as the week wore on. The protective cordon around the buses grew thinner too, until it was only one or two deep. After a while the difference between the occupiers of the square and the onlookers became blurred, and Song could move in and out from the core group with ease.

The students gradually relinquished their control of traffic, and policemen once more appeared on the streets.

Tiananmen Square was showing signs of wear. The banners began to droop and the flags looked limp and sad. The tents and the buses took on a bedraggled look, and garbage was piling up around the square. Plastic bags and discarded leaflets blew about the pavement, catching in railings and wrapping themselves around the flagpoles and lamp-standards.

The young people were looking as worn as the square itself. Eyes had lost their sparkle and shoulders drooped; the chanting and cheering grew less, until it was hardly heard at all; jeans and tee-shirts grew wrinkled and shabby. The railway stations filled up as thousands of protesters from the provinces headed home. A bad smell grew in the square when the latrines gradually failed to cope. By the end of the week the reek of sewage was formidable.

The student leaders strove valiantly to keep up morale, holding rallies and pledge-taking sessions and press conferences at the monument. However they had already started to disagree among themselves. It was understandable: faced with the possibility of violence at the hands of the military and conscious of their responsibility to the young people in the square who had put their fate in their hands, these leaders, as much as the youngsters themselves, were unsure of what to do next.

Song kept me up to date with the quarrels. 'There was a big fight last night,' she told me on Thursday, 'about whether to stay or leave the square. It went on all night, and we ended up voting. Only nineteen wanted to leave. So we stay.'

'How did you vote?' I asked her. I needn't have bothered, because I knew the answer. Would she ever get sense? I hoped she would. I was at the square night after night now only in the hopes of finally persuading her to come away.

On Saturday Song was telling me how a couple of would-be leaders were trying to challenge Chen. 'They said he's been stealing the money we collected and putting it in a bank account. Chen is very upset and wants to resign, but we won't let him.

'And they're fighting again about leaving the square. Wang Dan and Wuerkaixi want to finish everything with a big rally on Tuesday and then march out of the square for good. Chai Ling was for it, but suddenly changed her mind. I don't know why. Now she's saying we should all stay till the June 20 meeting of Congress.

'But the thing is, they're not listening to her. Everyone's fed up, and they're all saying they want to leave after the rally. We'll be gone by Tuesday.'

I hugged Song for her good news. Three more days of this misery – for misery it had become – and I would have her back out of the hellhole that Tiananmen Square now was. I began to think with grudging admiration of the restraint of the military, and even to admire the wisdom of Li Peng and the leaders. They had waited and waited and waited, knowing that in the end everyone would get tired and go home. They had known all along that violence would not be necessary.

'You see?' I said to Song. 'The old men *have* grown benign.'

CHAPTER TWENTY-TWO

IF IT HADN'T been for the Goddess, we'd have been home by Tuesday. The Goddess changed everything, as goddesses are wont to do.

On Monday night there was much bustle at the top end of the square, and I could hardly get through the crowds to see what was going on. Huge carved lumps of some white substance – probably plaster or fibreglass – were being carted in on flatbed trucks across to where a tower of scaffolding had been erected.

When the sun rose over Tiananmen Square on Tuesday, there stood the Goddess of Democracy, a thirty-foot, white plaster figure at the top of the square, both hands holding a flaming torch above her head and staring across at Mao's portrait.

'They've been creating her for weeks over at the Central Academy,' Song told me when she came out to have a look. 'They've built her so cleverly that once the parts are assembled no one can take her away without destroying her. That's what Yan Zhang is telling us – he's one of the sculptors.'

Everyone was calling her the Goddess of Democracy, although she looked dangerously like the Statue of Liberty, albeit with an ever-so-slight Chinese cast to the face. At least I thought there was such a cast, but Song disagreed.

'It's a western face, and that's dangerous,' she hissed when she saw it. 'It will let the government say there's American influence here.'

'They're saying it anyway,' I assured her. But the one thing we both agreed on was that the statue's sheer effrontery would have Li Peng and Deng foaming at the mouth.

'Which isn't the best thing right now,' I said, 'especially as they've been staying their hand, waiting for us to go home. Which brings me to the point – I came to take you home. You said you'd come away this morning.'

'I cannot.'

'But you said —'

'I cannot, now.'

'Song, you promised.'

'Things are different now. Look at the crowds in the square already this morning and the crowds all last night. The statue has brought the people back. It's like it was before.'

'Listen to me, Song. It isn't like it was before, and it never will be again. These people are just gawkers, just come to look because they heard about the statue. It's only a flash in the pan. The movement's over – and you should bloody well know that. Don't be a fool. Look, you said yourself the Mandate of Heaven was lost.'

'Maybe I was wrong. But that doesn't matter – my place is here. PJ, I'm going to be here till June 20, unless we can get the Congress moved forward, which we're trying to do. We had a meeting last night, and we agreed to stay. We might even stage another hunger strike.'

That did it. I lost my temper, which is unusual for me. It was just all those nights of traipsing down to the square to be near this stubborn silly bitch, who spent most of the time with her cronies anyway – I couldn't take any more of it.

Unfortunately I said all that to her, and a lot more.

'So stick with your goddam fanatics,' I told her. 'I'm sick, sore and tired of you and your po face that hasn't smiled in weeks. Christ, you're supposed to be a teacher, supposed to be a leader, and you're letting those fucking students lead you by the balls. Or, or by whatever. Tits, I suppose.

'Anyway I'm bloody-well fed up with it. I'm fed up with you and your stupid stubbornness. The ass is worn off me cycling ten miles twice a day, just to get a fucking audience with you – if I'm lucky. And I'm fed up with that. And I'm fed up bringing you food from that goddam hotel. What the fuck do you think I am anyway?'

O Jesus, was the cold face ever back. The Ice Maiden wasn't in it. 'I didn't ask you for food, PJ. You brought it because you wished. I don't want it. I never did want it. And I don't want you here – this is not your business. Just go away, will you please? And stay away.'

'Song. For Christ's sake —'

'Just don't come back. And remember, you can't do to me what you did to Lily.' She turned on her heel and went back through the cordon to her cronies. Walk of a queen, my ass. More like a goddam Reverend Mother.

I stayed away from Tiananmen Square after that. There was nothing to take me there any more, since Song had made it so clear I wasn't wanted.

Anyhow the square and all its works and pomps had become one colossal bore – and a stinking bore at that. The BBC confirmed that after the initial curiosity about the Goddess, the numbers had dwindled to a mere 5,000 hard-core protesters huddled around the monument.

They'd never last the two and a half weeks until Congress.

It would wither away as I had predicted, and sooner rather than later Song would come slinking back to Beida. And I was going to enjoy saying I told you so.

To have treated me like that. To have been as hard and cold as that, just because I lost my temper. To have told me I'd been some kind of a nuisance all the time, when I had tried so hard to help. And that I'd never been anything but an outsider. And to throw the food in my face like that. And then to throw the Lily affair at me. But that's the Chinese for you, as Norman always said, they're different from us – 'all bloody thousand million of them'.

To tell the truth, this new Song frightened me a little. The mask on the face and the scorn in the eyes came from a culture altogether alien to mine. How would it fit into Ireland? Or would she dominate me and create a mini-China there? Hold it now – she never even said she would come. In fact had I ever asked her? Was fantasy gripping me again? The times were unreal – that's how it was. None of us were ourselves, and that included Song. And then I'd think of her face an inch from mine, and I'd remember the tenderness. I'd feel good for a while. Then I'd feel angry again. The whole thing was giving me a colossal headache, circling inside my head. She was a right bitch for getting me into a state like that.

I settled into a more normal routine of sleeping nights and mooching around Beijing by day. Anywhere away from Tiananmen Square. I was starting to hate that place.

The brightest spots of the day were the meals with old Norman. It was a relief listening to him going on about what was wrong with the Chinese, and I appreciated his guesses at what was happening inside the government.

'Li Peng has won,' he told me one day. 'No doubt about that. They're saying he has that fellow Zhao under house arrest.'

Old Norman was often way ahead of the BBC. And with hindsight I can say he was usually spot on.

On the Saturday morning of that week, I decided to take a bus out to the Fragrant Hills, hoping it would get my mind off Song. There were the usual swarms of people picnicking among the trees and traipsing in and out of the Buddhist temples, so I followed a track well into the mountains.

At some point I realised I was on the same track Song and I had taken on our first trip there. Wood pigeons cooed as I walked the path beneath the trees. Once more the leaves were glowing, but this time in the fresh foliage of spring, and beams of sunlight slanted across my path. I was in a green cathedral, and slowly I began to feel at peace. I listened to the forest murmurs, and, like Siegfried, I longed for them to tell me what was to come.

At one point I met a small, striped animal in the middle of the track. It could have been a badger, although I am not sure if there are badgers in China. We both stopped and gazed at each other for a long time without moving.

Finally the little creature sniffed the air and pottered off into the undergrowth. I stood there feeling an extraordinary sense of peace, of being at one with nature, and a touch of childhood wonder.

The lines of the poem that Song had recited almost on this spot came to my mind:

> Deeper yet deeper into the mountains go;
> Drain every beauty there of hill and dale.

Just remembering the poem brought back what had happened here. I could see again the unblinking almond eyes and smell the fragrance of that face so close to mine. I didn't feel angry any longer.

As I hiked back down the track I was recalling the tender

caring Song, which was the one I had mostly encountered. And so what if she could be strong when the occasion warranted? Wasn't that to be admired? Who wants a weakling for a woman?

My step was lighter as I came out of the Fragrant Hills, and my heart was lighter as the bus took me back to Beijing. Even the line of tanks we passed in the suburbs didn't much bother me.

CHAPTER TWENTY-THREE

IT WAS PAST dinner time when I got back from the Fragrant Hills, so I ate at the Friendship's dreadful off-hours restaurant – some cold spiced beef like slivers of leather, a bowl of rice and a couple of cans of over-priced Five Star beer. Sitting in the long narrow 'Choo-Choo Bar', as we called it, with its compartments like a railway carriage, I felt tired but in a lighter mood than I had been in for days. I was now feeling more sorrow for Song than anger, sitting down in Tiananmen Square amid all that filth with a handful of her students.

The young woman who waited on me was slow, and I was snippy with her, and then ashamed of myself for it. It was about 10.40 when I got to Building Number Four and climbed the stairs to my room. All I could think of was falling flat on my bed and getting a good night's rest. On the floor inside the door was a note in Norman's flowing hand. 'Come over at once,' it said.

When I knocked, Norman opened the door immediately, practically grabbing me in. 'Is Song at the square?' he asked.

'She is.'

'Get her out.'

'She won't come.'

'*Get her out!*'

'Is there something I don't know?'

'Goddammit, did y'hear what I said? Go down to the square and get that woman out *now*!'

I ran downstairs to the hotel's taxi rank. There were no taxis. First time I had seen it empty. I ran across to the bicycle park, unlocked my bicycle, jumped on and cycled as fast as I could. There were silent crowds at every intersection. The streets were strangely dark: most of the street lamps were off.

I cycled south with a sort of numbness, legs pumping the pedals like an automaton, and there was nothing inside me except an image of Tiananmen Square and the overpowering need to get there. 'If she won't come I'll drag her,' I heard myself muttering.

I turned east near the Xiyuan Hotel, then south again on Sanlihe Lu, that long tree-lined avenue that runs past the sylvan grounds of the State Guesthouse, where the roadside is usually filled with barbers cutting hair in the open air. No barbers tonight – just pedestrians and cyclists moving southwards with silent purpose.

As I neared Muxidi the crowds got thicker, so I dumped my bike against a wall and took off on foot. The crowd was solid. Forcing my way through, I finally emerged at the Muxidi intersection. At right angles to my path was Chang'an Boulevard, that vast artery that runs east-west all the way to Tiananmen Square, several miles east of us to my left.

It could have been a film set. That part of the boulevard that passed right in front of me was empty and most of the street lights were off, making it a sinister no-man's land.

Drawn across the boulevard, where it vanished into darkness on my left, was a barricade of buses. Hundreds of people massed behind the buses, and some people were lined across in front of them.

To my right, a little way up the boulevard, the military waited. There was no moon, and I dimly discerned helmeted soldiers in the darkness. Rearing up behind them were the silhouettes of battle tanks with their cannon arced low, and open trucks crammed with helmeted men.

'But why tanks?' I muttered to no one in particular. 'Why tanks?' I felt that momentary dizziness a condemned man must feel when he gets the first glimpse of the noose.

There was a faint acrid smell in the air that made my eyes water.

I had arrived during a momentary lull in whatever had been happening. It may have been only the briefest of pauses, but it seemed as if it had been like that for an age. It was as if time had stopped. Silent. Still. It could have been some 19th-century painting entitled, *Before the Battle*.

I could think only of getting to Tiananmen Square. Sidling along the edge of no man's land towards the bus barricades, I squeezed myself between a bus and the sidewalk railings. Immediately after I passed, the bus exploded into flames. I felt the heat sear the back of my neck, and then the tableau came to life.

The first sound was the clanking moan of tanks, and I looked back to see blazing buses buckling as tank turrets with their obscene long cannon poked their way through the barriers. Helmeted men were leaping through the gaps, and there was a sound like monster firecrackers, louder even than the roar of the flames.

A girl lifted a camera and a soldier came up to her, loosing his AK-47 directly into her. It was on automatic. She was hurled backwards and her camera clattered at my feet. It was

215

one of those little plastic things with a built-in flash. The girl lay on her back near it, a wisp of smoke or steam coming from the crater that had been her breast. She had a lovely face.

'*Zhen zi dan*! *Zhen zi dan*!' people were screaming. 'Real bullets. Real bullets.'

I stood there stunned in the glare of the blazing buses, watching the soldiers go by on the double, flashes licking around the muzzles of their guns. People thudded to the pavement around me. I didn't know if they were dying, or dead, or just trying to save themselves.

I too threw myself down and watched the boots thud past and saw the tank tracks squealing within a foot of my head. A man who had thrown himself down beside me, almost on top of me, suddenly grunted and I could feel his body lurch. Then there was something oozing underneath me and I pushed him away. The small of his back felt sticky, and a lavatory smell came from him.

One of the blazing buses exploded with a woomff. I raised my head to look: the vehicles and figures were black shapes against the orange glare. Heat seared my face and eyes, and I covered them with my hands, to discover my brows and eyelashes were gone.

The tanks had passed, and now armoured vehicles and trucks piled with helmeted figures were roaring by. One of the armoured vehicles seemed to hesitate, as if unwilling to smash into the crowd. It stopped, and the other vehicles simply went around it. Suddenly it seemed as if a swarm of bees had engulfed the vehicle. But the swarm was human, and what looked like iron bars rose and fell. I saw a figure dragged out of a hatch. For an instant he was silhouetted against the flames, and I could see hands tearing at him.

A figure leaped up on the vehicle with something blazing in its hand, and everyone jumped away, and there was a roar and a cheer as the vehicle went up in flames. A flaming figure jumped from the hatch and down into the crowd on the far side, and there was another cheering roar.

The shooting seemed to have stopped, and some of the people on the ground were starting to get up. Some just lay there. I stood up. I was foul with the blood and excrement from the body beside me. I had a momentary, insane notion that I'd just go home and shower before coming back to get Song. The notion was gone as soon as I thought it. I hurried east along the boulevard towards Tiananmen, following in the wake of the soldiers and tanks.

Here and there trucks and armoured vehicles were blazing, and people were lifting bodies on to the flat carriers of tricycles. Some of the street lights were on here, and the bodies all seemed red and white, even in the glare of the flames – white shirts and blood soaking them. But they weren't pure clean colours: the bodies seemed filthy, and it was strange how shapeless they had become in death, how they seemed to lose human form.

A young man ran past me with joy on his face, pointing to blood coming from his shoulder. He was clearly proud of his wound.

My numbness was lifting, and panic was setting in about Song. I tried to run, but because of the mass of people around me and the tanks grinding along up ahead, I could only trudge forward as part of the crowd that followed in the wake of the military, like a mass of dispirited camp followers.

Ahead of us, at the Fuchengmen overpass, automatic fire was popping at what must have been another roadblock. The crowd around me halted, docilely, waiting for the army to blast its way ahead. It was as if the military were on our side and they were clearing a pathway for us. Then we started moving forward slowly, and we could hear the squeaking moan of the tanks again. I realised I was crying out Song's

217

name over and over again. I kept seeing her face in close-up, and for some reason I kept thinking of the gossamer fluff on her upper lip.

At the overpass a boy of about nine clutched with both hands the metal railings, lying face downwards. His middle was squashed flat, the imprint of a truck wheel clear across his body. It had carried his blood and shit several metres down the street. The child's bare legs, in white ankle socks and sneakers, looked neat and clean, his toes pointing slightly inwards.

People had stopped and were gazing over the rails of the overpass to the street below. I looked down and saw the body of a soldier, turning gently at the end of a rope. His helmet was still on his head.

The next hours are blurred in my mind. In a sort of stupor I followed the army on its slow roll towards Tiananmen Square, clearing a crazy way for me to get to Song. Bouts of quite daft normality punctuated my journey towards the square, as when I found myself opposite the square bulk of the Minzu Hotel, set well back from the street, and realised I needed a piss. The uniformed doorman was outside his revolving doors as though the street in front of him were not littered with dead and dying, and as though people were not scraping squashed bodies off the asphalt in front of the hotel. His eyes widened at my filthy shirt.

In the lobby a large, loud, lavender, Louisiana lady was intoning: 'What ah wanna know is, do we git to the Great Wall or naht? 'Cos if we don't git there tomorrow, Senator Stevens is gonna yell so loud, y'awl won't know what hitcha . . .'

In the men's room I realised I was routinely washing my hands even though my clothes were foul with blood and shit.

As I came out of the hotel it occurred to me I might try sneaking down through the maze of *hutongs* and alleys to the south, beyond Xidan, and perhaps circle around to the square by a southern route. But somewhere in every alleyway I met a wall of helmeted soldiers, clean and neat and seemingly free of battle. Each time they politely motioned me to turn around and go back.

Finally I found myself back on Chang'an Boulevard, shuffling wearily along between the smouldering hulks of trucks. I wondered then if Song was even alive. I was still saying her name over and over. Not loudly any more. Just whispering it to myself. And for some reason thinking of the circular whorls on her fingers, and the fluff on her upper lip.

The farther along Chang'an Boulevard, the closer to Tiananmen Square, the more fearful became the scene. The street was an inferno of blazing army trucks and commuter buses. In some places even the trees along the avenue were on fire. The crowd swirled around the blazing vehicles, pressing on in the wake of the soldiers.

Coming up to Liubukou junction a strange thing occurred: the line of tanks ahead of us halted, and the shooting stopped. The street became eerily quiet, and the pause lasted for several minutes. Then guns started cracking again, and the clanking juggernaut inched forward once more.

But it was not moving fast enough for me. I climbed across into the left-hand bicycle lane to try edging my way up along the edge of the throng. *'Dui bu qi!'* I kept repeating – 'Excuse me! Excuse me!' – and, amazingly, people gave way and let me come through. Perhaps it was the desperation in my voice.

My eyes were streaming now from the miasma of tear gas that hung in the air. All the time I could hear the military crashing and grinding its way forward – a cacophony of moaning engines, clanking, squealing tank tracks and the crackle of automatic fire.

219

The crowd in the bike lane thinned out, and I found myself running along parallel to the tanks and soldiers. The gunfire was continuous, but the soldiers seemed to be firing dead ahead. No one paid any attention to me or the few others running along beside me. Just ahead on the left were the stone lions that guarded the red-lacquered gates of Zhongnanhai. When last I had seen it, the entrance had been a mini-replica of Tiananmen Square, with students camped in tents in front of it. Now it was crammed with several lines of soldiers. They were waving their rifles and cheering as the tanks went by. They made no attempt to interfere with me as I trotted past. Perhaps they thought I was a foreign reporter and maybe felt it would be wiser to leave me alone for the moment, unless otherwise ordered.

Suddenly – it must have been about 2 or 3 in the morning – I found myself at the north-west edge of Tiananmen Square. Flames flickered eerily through the smoke that billowed along the top of the square and across Chang'an Boulevard. It swirled around the red bulk of Tiananmen, the Gate of Heavenly Peace, and its portrait of Mao, staring down through the smoke into the square. Across in the square the Goddess of Democracy gazed serenely back at Mao, her fibreglass torch raised above the smoke. Beyond the Goddess some of the student tents were on fire.

Much of the smoke came from two armoured vehicles that blazed in the boulevard, one near the top of the square and the other across the boulevard below Mao's portrait. People seemed to be running wild out there between the burning vehicles, as if sure that no more bullets could come from them. They didn't seem to realise the firing was now coming from the newly arrived troops beside me. I watched the people look around mystified, then fall down dead. Soon there were bodies dotted across the boulevard. The rest of the people just vanished, some northwards, behind the

Forbidden City, the others down into the depths of the square.

Government loudspeakers incessantly repeated some harsh, metallic message that echoed all over the square. The booming of the loudspeakers and the billows of smoke and the flickering flames was like Valhalla in flames.

CHAPTER TWENTY-FOUR

THE COLUMN OF tanks had halted beside me at the entrance to the square. From where I stood I could see the windows of the Great Hall of the People. Its lights burned serenely, and I could imagine some mad-hatter banquet going on in there while Beijing burned outside.

Soldiers were gathering up the bodies in the boulevard and flinging them into the back of two open trucks. They all had that rubbery springiness peculiar to cadavers. A soldier motioned with his gun for me to move back. I moved back a few yards to the edge of the boulevard, underneath Tiananmen Gate. When he left me alone, I stayed there.

The tanks and tracked vehicles suddenly began rolling again, lurching forward along the top of the square. From the opposite side I could see other tanks approaching. One by one they stopped, swivelled at right angles on their tracks, so that in line abreast along the top they now faced into the square. One by one their long, cruel cannon arced downwards.

I peered down into the square but could see little beyond the white foreground figure of the Goddess. Although some street lights were on here, the smoke obscured everything. The Monument to the People's Heroes was dimly discernible, rising out of the smoke.

Song was down in there somewhere, and there was no way that I could reach her. Fire lay between us. I thought of the young people clinging to each other at the foot of the obelisk as they saw those tank cannon arcing downwards.

The loudspeakers faltered for a moment, and the faint strains of the 'Internationale' wafted from deep in the square. The loudspeakers came back on again, incessantly repeating some hypnotic message.

The tanks started forward, cannon silent, their machine guns firing down into the square. Oh sweet Jesus they're going after Song. I foolishly started to run across the boulevard, but the same soldier grabbed me and hurled me stumbling backwards. As I picked myself up from the ground he pointed his gun at me in warning.

A bus roared out of the smoke towards the tanks, like that insanely gallant Polish cavalry that had once charged Hitler's panzers. The bus's windscreen disintegrated, as it careened sideways to crash against a bollard. The tanks stopped, still in line abreast, but now they were inside the square, just short of the Goddess of Democracy. Their machine guns arced upwards: they seemed to be aiming at the rival loudspeakers which the students had hung from the lamp standards.

The official loudspeakers continued their hypnotic harangue. Then they too stopped with a final crackle. At that point the few remaining street lights went out. A strange hush descended on the square.

There arose a strange howling from the soldiers around the tanks. Like wolves. I thought of Song there in the darkness, listening to the howling. Waiting. Alone in her terror. Would those almond eyes be closed? Would there be sweat on her upper lip? Would her hands be shaking?

Above the square the sky was lightening. The faintest streak appeared behind the History Museum on the far side of the square, and for a moment it seemed a promise of hope.

The official loudspeakers started up again, and I heard a cheer. In English I asked a man near me what had been said.

'Students may leave,' he told me. 'She – they – must go out from the far end of Square. This is official.'

The lights came on again, although by now dawn was creeping into the sky. I could see that the top end of the square was now filled with soldiers. From the far end of the square a faint singing came out of the pall of smoke. As I watched, the soldiers moved forward into the square, and the rattle of automatic fire began again. However, the men seemed to be again pointing their guns upwards, whether at loudspeakers or lights was unclear.

The soldiers passed the Goddess, picking their way through the wilderness of tents at the rear of the statue. Behind them the tanks began to roll. They moved in unison, like one roaring clanking mechanical reaper stretching across the square, cutting down everything in its path. Moments before they reached the Goddess, the first rays of the sun broke through to touch her raised torch. For an instant it looked as if the torch were alight.

The Goddess shuddered. There was a tank nuzzling at her base. She wavered, crumpled, and collapsed.

The reaping machine clattered on down the square. A bus was hit and knocked sideways. It went on fire. I saw the tanks reach the tents, which folded silently beneath their tracks. I thought I heard screams. The tanks rolled on.

It was morning now. I could only hope Song was no longer in the square.

I don't know how long I stayed gazing into the square until a violent shove brought me back to reality. A soldier, holding his rifle in both hands like a stave, was pushing me to move away. Other soldiers were moving forward in a line, and it was clear they wanted us to go back along Chang'an Boulevard, the way we had come.

Once I started back, I walked quickly. I had to get to Beida as fast as possible. Perhaps Song would be back there by now. I might catch up with her if she had got out from the bottom of the square and had looped back to Chang'an.

As I trudged westward along Chang'an, three tanks came behind me from the direction of the square I had just left. They were going at an incredible speed for tracked vehicles, and I felt the wind of their passing. With tracks screeching like dying animals, they disappeared into the smoke ahead. It was evident the drivers had learnt what could happen to a vehicle that slowed down or hesitated: these tanks were clearly not going to stop for anything.

What that could mean I realised when I reached the Liubukou intersection, a mile further west. I heard the screaming before I got through the smoke and tear gas.

In the very middle of the intersection was a pink spaghetti-like heap of squashed human entrails, with black bits of crushed bicycle frames tossed among them like seasoning. The marks of tank tracks were a straight, hard line through the ooze.

An animal howling mingled with coughing from the smoke and gas that still hung in the air. My own eyes were streaming again. A girl in pigtails was kneeling and beating her fists on the roadway: beside her, students were trying to tie a tourniquet on the thigh of another girl. Both her legs were gone, bones squashed flat by the tank tracks, and the stumps ended in a horror of red sausages and blue jelly and jagged bone-ends. Blood was pulsing from each stump in rhythmic gouts.

I pulled off my shirt, tore off one of the sleeves and used it as a tourniquet on the other thigh, garrotting it tight with a bit of bicycle-frame from near by. We lifted her on to the flat wooden bed of a goods tricycle. She died as we did so, head lolling back, mouth gaping, eyes staring.

'What happened here?' I asked the student who had tied the tourniquet. With gestures and halting English he told me how the students had left Tiananmen Square by the south end, as ordered by the military, had looped around Qianmen and were heading northward towards the university district. Their path took them at right angles across Chang'an Boulevard. A crowd of students had been straggling across the boulevard when the tanks came out of the smoke and just kept on going. There was no way they could have stopped anyway, going at that speed, he said.

There was no more I could do. I checked for Song among the squashed bodies, but could not see her. I put my torn shirt back on, left and coughed my way along Chang'an. As I passed the Minzu Hotel the doorman was still standing there. I thought of that Roman sentry found standing to attention in Pompeii, who had remained at his post as the Vesuvian ash engulfed him.

At Fuchengmen and most of the other intersections the smouldering skeletons of buses slanted across the boulevard where they had been hurled aside by the tanks. Smoke and the remains of tear gas were a miasma over the street.

I intended to turn right at the Muxidi crossing and head northwards to get my bicycle. How I could have thought of anything as mundane as a bicycle, I do not know. But I did. Muxidi was where it all had begun the previous night, and it looked now as if the populace was having its revenge. A line of closed armoured vehicles was stalled at the intersection, and some were on fire. Soldiers were jumping from them with their hands in the air, people grabbing them by the arms and dragging or marching them down towards the canal bank. The soldiers were young and frightened. Some were bleeding.

Some were crying – whether from fright or tear gas I could not be sure.

A man came up to one of the soldiers that was being led away and brought a lump of concrete down on his head. The soldier went down.

I turned away and headed northwards, parallel to the canal. And there was my bicycle, safe and sound, among a hundred others. I had not even thought to lock it. Probably if I were to go back after World War III my bicycle would still be there, melted down perhaps, but certainly not stolen.

I cycled back to the university district at Haidian. The little knots of students I passed on my way home had the expression of refugees in war documentaries – a blankness, all feeling driven out by horror. They trudged rather than walked. There were still some bedraggled banners, and one white banner had bloodstains on it. A few youngsters gave me the victory sign, almost shyly. I scrutinised every group as I passed, but I did not see Song.

I passed through the university district, where silent crowds were on every corner, just standing and staring. A truck smouldered outside the entrance to People's University, and the pungent smell assailed my nostrils.

As I rounded the street corner to the Beida campus' south gate, I could hear gunfire and screaming. A crowd massed around the gate, spilling across the street, but it did not look like a battle scene. It took me a moment to realise that the sounds came from loudspeakers up on the gateway: the students must have been playing sound recordings of what had happened at Tiananmen Square or Muxidi. The crowd stood silently, faces expressionless, listening as if in church. The cold face was back.

I pushed my way through the crowd and wheeled my bicycle through the gate. There was no sign of the usual guards. I mounted and cycled up the avenue past the new library building, gleaming white among the brown crumbling dormitories.

Clutches of students stood where pathways intersected, and they gazed at me unseeing. At Song's dormitory I threw the bicycle down and ran up the four flights of concrete stairs between the junk and the cardboard boxes and the bicycles.

The V-sign was still on Song's door, but nobody answered my knock. I knocked again, louder. A woman came out from the room opposite, wiping her hands on a cloth. She shook her head: '*Mei you*,' she said.

'Did you see her at all?' I asked. 'Any sign of her around here last night?'

'*Bu dong*.' She shrugged uncomprehendingly. '*Mei you*.'

As shock and numbness wore off, panic took hold. I seemed to have had no feelings for the past twelve hours, but suddenly fear for Song became a ferocious tightening of the chest and an urgent thumping somewhere deep down in the gut.

I ran down the stairs and pedalled back out past the crowd at the gate and down the street to the Friendship. She could be waiting there for me, in the lobby of Number Four, where she so often waited before. As I came through the glass doors of Number Four, the stares of the doorman made me aware of how I looked, with my filthy, sleeveless shirt and blood all over me.

Song was not in the lobby. The sofa where she had so often waited for me was empty. It was where we had first met, when we sat to arrange the Chinese classes. I ran past the elevator and up the stairs to my room. Perhaps she was inside – if she had brought her key. She wasn't.

I threw myself on the bed and curled myself around my throbbing gut, trying to force myself to think clearly. She could still be on her way home. Either that – I looked at my watch and it was nearly 11am, so that was unlikely – or else she was in some hospital.

Or else she was dead.

I had to go searching again. I got up from the bed, walked slowly downstairs to my bicycle and cycled bone-weary along the street back to Beida. It was only then I realised I had not even thought of showering or changing my filthy clothes. I just carried on, turned in the gate and sought out Song's room again. Still no answer. I put my shoulder to the flimsy door and pushed it in. There was no one. It looked as if her room-mates were gone away. On the bottom bunk bed were Song's blue jeans, neatly folded, and her maroon pullover. I lifted the pullover and after all these weeks her scent still clung to it. I buried my face in the wool, breathing in the faint fragrance of Song, and started to cry.

Before I left I tapped on the door across the corridor, indicating with signs that Song's lock needed repairing.

I headed south towards downtown Beijing, following the route Song would surely follow on her way home. There was a hush in the streets: the knots of people at street corners were completely silent. Everywhere were the overturned, burnt-out trucks, all with the strange acrid smell.

Sometimes a truckload of soldiers would roar down the street, and in the distance there was the occasional crackle of gunfire. There were no more students heading home. At Muxidi a bulldozer was nuzzling the burnt-out buses aside; bits of crumpled railings lay all over the street between there and the Fuchengmen overpass. The overpass was lined with helmeted troops, and the ugly bulk of tanks rose behind them.

There was no way forward: a policeman directed cyclists down the slope to the right. That would bring me to Qianmen Street and eventually to the southern end of Tiananmen Square. I obeyed wearily, but at the South Cathedral I again found my way barred by troops and was forced right again. No one was getting near the square. I found myself wandering aimlessly in the streets to the south of the square, as dazed and as hopeless as anyone else. Finally I sat down on a stone step outside a door and put my head in my hands.

God's curse upon you, Li Peng. God's curse upon you, for silencing my Song.

God's curse upon you, you child molester, who molested them with lead and left them dead. God's curse upon you, you cannibal, you Chronos devouring your own children. God's curse upon you, you Herod who slaughtered the innocents to keep your crown. God's curse upon you, you coward, that betrayed the little ones entrusted to you by China, for fear that a dwarf called Deng Xiaoping might take away your golden handshake.

You, who met mercy as a parentless child, when Zhou Enlai fostered you and made you his son, could show no mercy to China's children.

God curse your owlish face that insults the wisdom of that bird, and curse your false black hair that truly reflects your falseness. The curse of God on you, Li Peng, you malign bastard masquerading as a government minister. His curse upon you and your geriatric cronies who think they possess China. Like the gods of Valhalla, your twilight is upon you. The humans have come.

I hope you die, but not soon. God grant you live long enough to know in full measure the contempt in which you are held by the children you did not get to kill. And in your long, last agony, may you see the face of that child cut in half at Muxidi, and may you see his belly squashed flat so that yours might stay full, and may you see the cleanness of his socks and shoes that never waded through blood as yours have done.

May the words of Mao Zedong be true of you: 'He who injures the students will come to no good end.' And may the roars of your dying be heard by those children of China whom you did not manage to massacre, now grown and taking over a China you thought was yours and building it into a land you could never have dreamt of.

God damn you, Li Peng. May the God you don't believe in damn you to the hell you thought was not there. And Deng Xiaoping with you. I hope there's a hell. And if there is, may you both go to that special place that Dante reserved for cannibals that eat their children.

I got up and shambled down the street in quest of Song.

I was passing a mass of scaffolding on South Dong Dan Street when I realised the scaffolding was around a hospital. I could just about understand the characters for *Tong Ren* – the Everybody Equal Hospital. As good a place as any to continue my search for Song: in the wards and in the morgues.

CHAPTER TWENTY-FIVE

THE BODIES AND the blood were everywhere. It was certainly the Everybody Equal Hospital. The bodies lay in rows in the foyer, packed like large sardines. Some were alive; some were dying; and some were clearly dead. The sweetish smell of a butcher's shop hung in the air.

A few figures in white coats moved around, adjusting drips, wheeling stretchers, moving slowly as if in a trance. People wandering among the prostrate figures, maybe seeking relatives, too seemed in a trance. As I was. I stepped mechanically from one body to another, peering into each face to see if it was Song.

When they were wheeling one of the corpses away, I called 'Hold it!' and they stopped until I pulled back the cover and looked at the mangled face. I had said it in English, but it didn't seem to matter. Perhaps the tone was enough.

'Go on,' I said. 'It's not who I'm looking for.'

Similar scenes met me in every corridor: bodies along each wall, dead, dying or bleeding, with a narrow walkway up the centre between the outstretched feet. Occasionally someone

233

moaned from pain, but what I remember was mostly the silence, and the smell.

In several of the corridors I had to step over pools of blood that were seeping from the bodies and spreading across the floor. There were marks where people had already slipped: blood is very slippery. Even in the wards where there were regular patients in the beds, bodies were around them on the floor.

I peered into every face in that hospital, the quick and the dead: those with eyes closed, and those with wide open eyes that returned my gaze; those with jaws shot away; those with shattered cheekbones; dead faces with holes through eyeballs or temples; live faces unmarked but twisted with pain. None belonged to Song. I peered and peered until all those faces merged into one and became for me forever the Face of Tiananmen Square.

I went systematically from the top corridor to the basement, and no one bothered to stop me. People wandered the corridors on the same errand as myself, stooping and peering as I was doing. They all had the same blank faces. Not cold faces now. Blank faces. I had one too.

I even wandered through an operating theatre and no one bothered me. I looked at the face on the table, trying to identify Song behind the mask that covered the nose. It wasn't she.

When I got to the basement I found I was alone. I wandered through a storage room following the sweet smell until it led me to a cold-room that was evidently serving as a morgue. The smell of excrement began to predominate over the butcher-shop smell. The bodies were spilling out through the open door. They were mostly naked here and lying belly upwards, male and female indiscriminately, sometimes legs apart and showing the genitals. It was when the rat came out from underneath that I started vomiting, and I threw up over a male cadaver just inside the door. There was no space between the bodies to vomit into.

When I had finished vomiting I started climbing over the bodies, trying to step on the limbs rather than the torsos, searching always for that one face. A few heads had plastic bags over them. I picked only the ones that had female torsos, and when I pulled each bag off I found that the face inside had been more or less shot away, by a dum-dum bullet, I guessed. Without a face to go by, I looked at the torso more carefully to see if it could belong to Song. But a dead body hangs together so differently from a living one that it took me a long time to be sure none was she.

I came up from the basement and wandered back through the lobby towards the door.

I went across the street to the little park and sat on a bench. There was a scent of newly mown grass. A few small children were playing on the swings and on the seesaw. Their laughter reached me.

A soldier was on guard at the nearby Xiehe Hospital, where I went next. He held his AK-47 rifle horizontally in both hands, to bar my way. I just nodded and went off down the street, circled the block, and found a back entrance through some kitchens.

I methodically did the rounds in that huge hospital, just as I had done at the Tong Ren. It could have been the same place – the same shell-shocked faces, the bodies lying in rows, the butcher smell. But no Song.

At the next three hospitals after that I used a rear entrance, as there always seemed to be a soldier or several soldiers at the front entrance. At the Fuchengmen Hospital the back entrance led me into a courtyard, where I saw two men lift a body off a trolley and toss it into the back of a tarpaulin-covered truck. I went across to look in and saw that the truck was packed with dead bodies. I wanted to climb in to look at them, but when I went over, one of the men motioned me away.

A crazy sort of panic set in, that if I didn't hurry, Song would be carted off in one of these lorry loads. So I started almost running through the corridors of Fuchengmen, glancing as quickly as possible at all the faces on the ground. Soon I was hardly taking anything in, and I might well have passed Song by without noticing.

After that I raced to the Railway Hospital, and started the same mad gallop through the corridors. That's where I collapsed.

When I came to I was lying among the bodies in the foyer, and a young man in a white coat was holding my head and giving me a sip of water.

'*Hui qu ba*,' he said gently. 'You go home,' he added, when he saw my incomprehension. His hands-wide gesture at the crowded foyer clearly said, there's nothing you can do here. I tried to stand up and my feet nearly gave way. My whole body was shaking. I steadied myself and went out past the soldier at the door.

A taxi was just disgorging two Mao-suited cadres, and I went down the steps to it and simply climbed in. '*You Yi*,' I said to the driver.

I guess I got to the Friendship and found my way to my room. I may even have had a shower and possibly got something to eat. The thing is, I can't remember any of it.

The first thing I do remember is two people being in the room with me. I wasn't sure how much time had passed, but later understood it was Wednesday. I must have slept and slept. One of the people was Norman and the other was Fintan Clark, a young man from the Irish Embassy whom I knew.

'. . . The embassies think it could be civil war,' Fintan was saying. 'The 38th army taking on the 27th that did the killings. That's why we're getting you out.'

'Out where?'

'Home. I already told you.'

'I'm not going anywhere,' I said. 'There's someone I have to find.'

Norman spoke. 'PJ, people are saying, if someone hasn't made contact by now, then the person won't be doing so. He – she – will be dead. Or fled.'

The words were like lead. I said nothing for a long time. I found them hard to take in. Then I started to think. 'She'll not have escaped anywhere,' I said. 'She had nowhere to go. She never made plans for getting away.'

'A lot of the leaders have gone into hiding,' Fintan said. 'And they're saying there's an escape route being set up to get them out of the country.'

'She wasn't a leader, Fintan. No. She's still here. Maybe dead, maybe alive. I've got to stay and find out.'

CHAPTER TWENTY-SIX

THAT VERY DAY I started my hospital crawl again. Norman provided me with a list of all the hospitals in Beijing, and I went methodically from one to the other. On his advice I used taxis and returned in the evenings for food and rest.

'Can't have y'going to pieces, like last time,' was Norman's comment. 'Weren't much use to the young lady in that state, were y'now?'

Things had changed a lot in a couple of days. The foyers were cleared, and, although the corridors still had wounded lying along them, there were no dead bodies to be seen.

Not that they weren't there, as I found when I was in the Ji Shui Tan Hospital. Once more I discovered the morgue, or some sort of spill-over place for extra bodies. It was across a yard at the back of the hospital. It was the stench that led me to it, the noisome odour of rotting human beings that brings the gorge lurching up into the throat and, once smelt, can never be forgotten. It's a stench that makes you want to be a thousand miles away, where things still live. The authentic stench of Li Peng, lord of this death.

I pulled open the wooden door, and in the dim light per-ceived five or six bodies lying across the floor. They looked totally different from any I had seen before: they were grey-green and monstrously swollen, like shiny slugs. One poor wretch still had jeans on, and the thighs and buttocks had swollen inside the jeans so that they must shortly burst. If Song was in there, I did not want to find her.

I lurched back from that doorway with a hand over my mouth and fingers tight against my nostrils.

That last morgue brought home to me, as nothing else could, the likelihood that Song was dead. Yet I couldn't imag-ine that face in death. All I felt was a determination to see every living face in every hospital in Beijing.

I searched up and down and back again for days. I covered every square foot of hospital floor in Beijing. When the police turned me away, as regularly happened, I found a way around them. I laundered the white coat and started wearing it again, and it got me through many a door.

With hindsight I realise that at this time I was blotting out the immensity of the tragedy that had taken place around me. I was refusing to think of the thousands of young people dead and burnt or buried, and of so many Chinese families bereft. Of China's hopes dashed once again, and of the Dark Ages now back for another generation. I think perhaps it was the only way my mind could cope with it – to narrow the focus down to the one person significant to me.

I took to carrying the security-police photo of Song which my boss had given me and showing it to staff in the hope that they might remember having seen her. I took the photo back to the Tong Ren and the hospitals I had first visited, in the same hope.

If people had even said they had seen her body, I might have found some peace. But wherever I went, people took the photo, looked at it and handed it back with a shake of the head.

A lot changed around me during those days, but I was hardly aware of it. The threat of civil war receded, the tanks finally clanked out of Beijing, and, apart from an armed and helmeted soldier at every street corner, the city began to function again.

The cyclists looked neither to right nor left as they rode across the tank-track marks that still disfigured Chang'an Boulevard. Tiananmen Square stayed closed, and people scurried past as if it were haunted.

Arrests began, and people started to disappear.

A 'wanted' list, complete with photographs, was published. It appeared in all the newspapers and was run again and again on television. Chen, Chai Ling and her husband Feng were right at the top, along with Wuerkaixi, Li Lu and Wang Dan. Song was not on it, but I had not expected her to be.

The wanted list was actually good news. It indicated that the leaders had not been caught, and I could hope they were being handed from one safe place to another until they got out of the country. Maybe Lily would be reunited with her Chen sooner than she had ever dreamt. Not, I supposed, that it would improve her temperament.

The executions started on June 17. Television showed death sentences being handed down by judges in military uniform and the condemned being led away by soldiers complete with helmet and cold face.

The posters with the red slashes began going up on the walls of Beijing.

When someone goes missing, believed dead, we need to find the body. I had reached that stage about Song: if I could have seen her body in the hospital, accepted her wounds and her death, I might have begun to get on with life.

But that is not how it was. I didn't know if she had been machine-gunned to pieces, if she had bled to death or been clubbed to death, or had her face blasted away by one of those dum-dum bullets, or if she was languishing in some obscure ward or in some prison cell. I tried to envision what might have happened, but I could only see that close-up face, the live almond eyes gazing into mine.

Beijing became for me a chasm into which I stared. And all I got back from the chasm were the echoes of my efforts. I kept doing the rounds of the hospitals, until the harried staff knew me and my picture of Song by heart and must have been sick of us both. There was nothing new there.

That picture became my most cherished possession. I would gaze at it and remember Song as she began her hunger strike, and I would remember the song she sang then, and I would weep. I wept easily those days.

And then I would sometimes think of the happy times and the joy of seeing the cold face slowly but surely melt and give way to the smiles and the laughter. I remembered the time early on I had told her that Irish people all had webbed feet, evolved from centuries of rainy climate. Poor thing, in those days she still believed my lies, and naturally wanted to see my feet.

'Ah well, that's another thing about the Irish,' I had said. 'Our religion doesn't allow us to expose our feet to anyone.'

I had forgotten all about it when one day, shortly afterwards, I invited her to swim at the hotel pool. After our swim we were resting on the edge of the pool, our feet dangling down. She leaned down and had a good look at my feet. Then she came up and gave me one of her withering looks. 'Hinh!' Later we laughed many times about my webbed feet.

The end came one day when I was going into the Railway Hospital. A young man in pyjamas was being dragged down the steps by two helmeted soldiers. He was doubled up and shrieking in agony. Behind him came two more soldiers with a figure on a stretcher.

The soldiers pushed the screaming man into the back of a

covered lorry. The man on the stretcher was loaded in beside him. I could see other half-clothed figures in the lorry.

Norman had the answer, over dinner. 'They're going around the hospitals, pulling out the wounded and taking them away,' he told me. 'However they claim they're trying to make a distinction between the accidentally wounded and those involved in the turmoil. Well, good luck to them. Or good luck to the wounded chaps, anyway.'

He took a sip of his beer and looked at me. The upper lip didn't seem that stiff right then. 'She's gone, PJ. You must know that by now.'

I just nodded.

Norman sighed. 'Maybe it's just as well,' he said. 'You wouldn't want her dragged off like that, would you? Screaming in pain, and all that? And ending up in a slave camp in Xinjiang, perhaps maimed, for the rest of her life. If indeed they'd have let her live.'

I was certain he was right, but I needed to close those eyes that for ever gazed into mine, and that would take time. Even while I accepted the end of Song, I kept clinging to an irrational hope, as people hope that the drowned one somehow has managed to swim to safety against all odds and will somehow, sometime, somewhere reappear.

Life goes on and Xinhua was wanting me back. The very next morning I got a letter from Mr Xiao asking if I could resume the journalism training on Monday. I would be happy to hear, he added, that none of our trainees had gone missing in the recent turmoil. I was indeed happy to hear that, but how could I possibly give my mind to training journalists when I could not for even a moment get it off Song? If I could no longer function in the job I came to do, then I should return to Ireland. But if there was the slenderest chance that Song still existed, or even if I thought there might be such a mad chance, how could I think of leaving?

That was my thinking as I stood reading Mr Xiao's letter at my hotel mailbox early that morning. A thin sliver of rice paper fluttered to the ground, having obviously been caught among the couple of letters in the box. I reached down and picked it up: it had five or six Chinese characters on it, written in ballpoint. It could have been stuck in the mailbox for ages. I shoved it in my back pocket.

'Can you read that?' I said to Norman, over breakfast.

He took the scrap of paper, took off his glasses and scrutinised it. 'First two characters are *ai* and *zheng*. I'd recognise them, because I had to face them some years ago. Together they mean "cancer".'

He tossed the scrap of paper on the table. 'I can't manage all these damn characters. Far too many, anyway. Don't know why the Chinese bother with them. Y'know, they have to know about twenty thousand? Bloody ridiculous, when there's twenty-six letters in an ordinary decent alphabet.' He put his glasses back on.

'*Tong Ren*,' I said. 'I've seen those two characters. Isn't that the hospital – the Everybody Equal hospital?'

'Y'could be right.'

'So all we need are the middle two characters.' I caught the *fu wu yuan*'s eye, and he came over. He was the unfriendly one with glasses.

'Excuse me,' I said. 'Could you tell me what those mean?'

'Ward. Ward, for sick persons. Like in hospital.'

'Cancer ward,' I said slowly. 'Cancer ward, Tong Ren Hospital. Norman, *this was in my mailbox*.'

Norman stared. 'D'y'think —?'

But I didn't wait to think.

CHAPTER TWENTY-SEVEN

THE CANCER WARD at Tong Ren was in an annex. It had a separate entrance from the main hospital, in a side street, which I had not even noticed in my several visits. I only found it by producing my sliver of rice paper with the characters on it. The woman at the desk looked at it and sent someone to take me around to the small annex door. The door opened on to a stairwell that led to several wards, one above the other, the existence of which I had been unaware. It was almost a separate hospital.

Song was in the top ward, at the very end on the right.

It was a repeat of the last time I had seen her in hospital, when she had been on hunger strike. She was lying back with her eyes closed, so I sat down on the edge of the flimsy bed. She opened her eyes. 'PJ,' she whispered. And the hands reached up to me.

Once I smelled her I started to weep. I had planned not to, so I closed my eyes, but the tears forced themselves through. I just held her hands until it was done. She was weeping too.

At length she tried to struggle to a sitting position, but grimaced and grabbed her chest in pain. 'No, I'm OK,' she said, when I held her, and at length she was sitting up. 'It's just – that's where the bullet went in.'

'Should you be sitting up?' I asked.

'They want me to, for a while every day.'

'But why a cancer ward? You said it was a bullet.'

'They're passing me off as a breast-cancer patient, so the soldiers don't take me away.'

'So why didn't you contact me?' I asked. 'I've been turning Beijing upside-down for weeks.'

'I got a nurse to write you a note a week ago. Before that I was in and out of consciousness. The note had to be smuggled out because they don't want anyone to know I'm here. When I heard nothing I thought you'd gone back to Ireland. Wait, first I have to know, are my students safe? The three at the square?'

'I honestly don't know. And there's no way to find out. Everyone's gone to relatives in the provinces, to avoid being arrested.'

The tears came again.

I gazed at her as she sat there. I had never seen her so frail, even at the height of the hunger strike. Her face gave a hint of where the lines would be when she grew old. I turned around and sat in close to her, so I could put my arm around her shoulders. She smelled tired and slightly sourish, but it was her smell.

'You said a bullet. Tell me.'

'Beside this breast.' She pointed. 'It missed my heart by two centimetres, the doctor says. Came out my back.'

'Then it wasn't one of those dum-dums. That would have taken your heart with it.'

'It came from a tank, I think. Or from a soldier behind the tank – nobody's sure.'

'So what happened exactly?'

'Well, when we heard the army was coming we ran up Chang'an and met the tanks at the Liubukou junction. We linked arms across the road in front of the first tank, and it stopped and the others stopped behind it. We must have faced them for about two minutes. Then the front tank started moving again, and Chen said break now and run for it. That's what happened, except I found myself standing alone in the street in front of the tank. I don't know why I hadn't run. I was sort of paralysed and angry at the same time.

'It came right up to me and stopped again, and I could see the eyes of the driver looking at me through the slit. I just stood there, and everything went quiet. I heard afterwards we stayed like that for about three minutes. Then I felt a thump like a fist hitting my chest and I turned around to run. But I found my chest was all warm and wet and sticky, and I couldn't breathe. The ground started coming up at me.

'That's all I remember. They told me afterwards that Chen and the students ran back and dragged me from nearly under the tank tracks, and the tank stopped to let them do it. And they raced me to the hospital on one of those trike platforms. They thought I'd die before we got there.'

'But you didn't.'

'The hospital operated immediately, when they heard about me and the tank. Put me ahead of hundreds of wounded. Which wasn't fair, but it saved my life. I only heard afterwards, because I was unconscious. I nearly died anyway. The doctor said I should have – he never heard of anybody surviving a bullet where that one went.

'They say I was in and out of consciousness for days, even after they moved me in here to hide me. I'll recover now, but there'll always be a big hollow in my chest and in my back. It's very ugly. Will you mind?'

I just hugged her and we both wept some more. 'I was behind the tanks when they stopped,' I whispered, 'but I never knew it was you stopped them. I'm so proud of you. Wait till your dad hears it.'

'He's dead.' She whispered it, while we were still embracing.

I pulled away and looked at her. 'You never told me. When was it?'

'I heard it the day after you went away from the square. A student came down from Beida with the message. He died in Harbin. Heart.'

I hugged her tight. I felt grief for her loss, but deep down I was feeling a tiny selfish sense of relief. Now maybe Song might leave China with me.

Song was getting tired. I got her to lie back and I just sat there holding her hand.

A big woman in a white coat came up along the ward to Song's bed and spoke sharply to her. Song said something in reply. The woman turned to me. 'You have no right to be here,' she said in English. 'Please go away, and do not come back.'

'Song,' I said, 'tell her who I am. Tell her I'm next of kin now. For all practical purposes.'

Song told her in Chinese, and the woman turned to me again. 'Professor,' she said, 'I don't care who you are. Or what you are. You are endangering my patient. Do you realise what would happen if you had been followed? How do you know you have not been followed?'

I didn't know what to say, so I said nothing. The woman's manner softened.

'Professor, I have no wish to keep you apart, but you must wait until all of this is over. It could be a long time. The alternative could be her death. Or her life, as a slave in Xinjiang. The Prison Province. Do you understand what I am talking about?'

Song said something in Chinese, and the woman listened. She turned to me again: 'Song Lan asks if you would get some of her clothes from Beida. I will permit that, because she has been needing clothes. She will tell you what she wants. You will wrap them up in a bundle, put her name on them in Chinese. Can you write her name?'

I nodded.

'When you bring her things,' the woman said, 'you leave them at the porter's desk. You will not come up here.' She put a gentle hand on Song's shoulder, nodded to me and went off down the ward.

I dug in my pocket and found my ballpoint and an old paper napkin from the Friendship. I wrote down the things she wanted. We hugged for a bit, as it was hard to part after having just found each other. Then we realised how very, very hard indeed it was, and we hugged harder and cried some more.

But in the end I had to go.

I took a taxi to Beida. I was using taxis all the time now, as I had no idea where my bicycle was. I had left it somewhere during that crazy search for Song and could never recollect where. Anyway I hadn't the energy any more for those long rides around Beijing.

The victory sign was gone from Song's door and the lock had been fixed. There was no answer to my knock, and I was relieved to find the key still worked. The room smelled damp and deserted, so Song's roommates must have gone off to the provinces. Song's maroon sweater and jeans were still lying on the bottom bunk. Some of her other things were in her pathetic cardboard suitcase under the bunk, while the rest were in the hammock hung close to the ceiling. I put everything that was needed into the cardboard suitcase. As I lifted the maroon sweater I buried my face in it for a moment.

God knows Song didn't have many possessions, and the case was quickly filled and light to carry. My watch told me it was after midday, so I walked the short distance to the Friendship Hotel and joined old Norman for lunch. I wanted to share my joy.

When I told him I had found Song he took my hand in both of his. I was afraid he might weep – that stiff upper lip was getting more wobbly by the day. Mercifully he didn't: we'd have both been frightfully embarrassed afterwards.

'But do stay away,' he advised. 'Do what the woman said. She knows what she's talking about.'

The chat was good that lunchtime, or maybe I enjoyed it more because of the euphoria I was feeling. Not that the things Norman told me were grounds for euphoria. There had been two reasons for the massacre, he told me, and neither reason was a need to end the turmoil.

'It was ended by then, anyway,' he said. 'There were only a handful of youngsters left in the square – a few thousand at the most. And the authorities knew it was over. So why did they go in and kill them?

'Main reason was to create a climate of terror, so that what had happened would never happen again. A massive dose of terror would guarantee twenty years of stability. But of course terror is only achieved through death. Through a lot of deaths. That was their thinking. There's no other explanation for what they did.'

'You mean,' I said, 'Li Peng meant it: that it was worth killing twenty thousand for twenty years of stability?'

'I think it was Deng said that. And the word was 'get rid of' – *gan diao* – not 'kill'. But if Li Peng didn't say it, he acted on it. And look around you. He's got his stability.

'By the way, it's not twenty thousand. The embassies are

saying between five and seven thousand deaths. God knows how many wounded. Poor devils.'

'You said there were two reasons. What's the second?'

'Envy. Envy of the young.' He thought for a moment. 'It's a private theory of mine, PJ. I'm coming more around to it as I grow old myself. The old hate the young. Not all the old, but the old who have power. They hate the young for the things their own power cannot give them, like youth and beauty and health. And sex, of course. You're in a bath-chair, and y'see beautiful young people who don't need bath-chairs, and they have everything you haven't. And are arrogant, to boot.

'You cannot have what they have, *but you can take it away from them*. If y'have power, and have sufficient excuse, y'can destroy them.'

'I don't believe they'd ever do that.'

'Wouldn't they, indeed? You wouldn't, perhaps. But don't forget that power corrupts.'

He reached for his pipe and began to fill it. 'Look at the Great War. It's my belief those generals did the same thing, not saying, of course, that the generals were conscious of it. Fellows like Haig and Lord French. Remember what people called them? "The Ferocious Old Gentlemen." They were all quite elderly, but they nonchalantly sent hundred of thousands of the most beautiful of England's youth over the tops of the trenches into quite meaningless slaughter. And kept sending them, month after month, year after year, until the flower of England was gone. There's no explanation for why they kept doing it, except envy of the young. The Huns and the French did the same, of course.

'The old envy the young more than the young realise. I should know, at my age.

'Now what do we have here, except another bunch of Ferocious Old Gentlemen? They're all as ancient as the

251

Ancient Mariner. Half of them are in bath-chairs. And those youngsters did make them lose face frightfully. Remember "Little Bottle"? That's the most unforgivable of all. So it could be revenge, on top of the envy.'

He took a puff of the pipe. 'Don't quote me, by the way. As you journalists are wont to say, I'm off record. Besides, I'd like to continue my lifestyle here, as a Ferocious Old Gentleman myself!'

When I got to the hospital I did something I ought not to have done. It would be some time before I would see Song again. I wanted a last glimpse of her. Just to see that face, and remind myself that she was really alive, after those weeks trying to face the near certainty that she wasn't. I hesitated for quite a while, moving from the front desk, where I was to leave Song's suitcase, to the back door leading to the cancer wards. And back again.

Then I decided. There was really very little risk. I opened the door and ran up the three flights of stairs. As I got to the ward I was thinking, why didn't I bring flowers?

I went up along the ward, and there was a different woman in Song's bed.

I turned around to look for her, and right behind me, coming up along between the beds, was the woman in white. She stopped and held out her hands in a gesture of hopelessness. I went up to her and gripped her shoulders.

'They came just after you left,' she said. 'They must have been following you.'

CHAPTER TWENTY-EIGHT

ESPAIR AND GUILT are as near to death as living can get. I had experienced both, but never like this. I had had hope up to then. Even in my most crazy searchings around the Beijing hospitals, there had always been the slender possibility, at least in my own mind, that I would somehow find Song. Or, at worst, discover her body and know that at least she was at peace. But now there was no hope at all.

Even Norman could offer me none. 'Apart from Wu, I haven't that much influence any more,' he told me. 'And Wu has to watch his back. My few contacts were mostly Zhao's people. Zhao's finished now. Indeed, they could come for me, as they did in the Cultural Revolution. Though I doubt they would. I'm not important any more.'

The people at the Irish Embassy couldn't do a thing. How could they? Their only link with Song was that a grossly irresponsible Irishman had got himself involved with her and had brought her to ruin.

Sometimes I found myself wishing Song had died. The images of Xinjiang mesmerised me: that vast slave province in remote western China, from which few come back, the province where slave camps take the place of towns; where China banishes its dissidents and its victims into an oblivion worse than Hitler's *Nacht und Nebel*. Xinjiang – even the name sounds like the clash of funeral cymbals.

I could see Song growing gaunt and grey in Xinjiang, bearing her brutal burdens along with the pain of her shattered chest because of my stupidity.

What had I ever done in China but fuck up everyone, wrecking Lily's chance of love, compromising the protesters by my unwanted presence at Tiananmen Square and hunting Song down so irresponsibly that I had betrayed her hiding place and brought about her ruin? But sure hadn't I fucked up my marriage before that, so that my wife ended impaled on a steering wheel the very night she walked out? I was not just a loser: I was a destroyer.

Even now I was letting down my trainees at Xinhua. I couldn't bear to go near them, and, after one call from Mr Xiao, Xinhua left me alone. I think maybe they guessed at my anguish – perhaps Norman had told them – but I have no doubt it was just one more example of the sensitivity and consideration of the ordinary Chinese.

For days I wandered Beijing, going to the old haunts. I was cycling again, this time on Norman's ancient bike that had gathered dust for years in the hotel cycle-rack. A couple of tyres and brake blocks were all it had needed.

In the avenues of Beida I twice thought it was Song cycling ahead of me, and I would hurry to catch up. But the face would be another's. Those avenues were alien now, and cold-faced students shrank from contact with the foreign devil. That's how it was in terrified, post-massacre Beijing.

In Yuan Ming Yuan Park I sat on the seat where I had once held Song's hand. But I saw no sparkles on the water now, and the gold-dusted hand with the circular whorls was not there to hold. O Christ Jesus, where was it now?

Even my own Friendship Hotel was an echoing empty place, devoid of most of its denizens since the embassies had pulled out their nationals after the massacre. I sometimes thought of the words of Tom Moore:

> I feel like one
> Who treads alone
> Some banquet hall deserted,
> Whose lights are fled
> Whose garlands dead,
> And all but he departed.

It never entered my mind that the police would come for me as well, but, when they did, it was at first almost a relief.

They were waiting in my room one evening when I returned from cycling. I opened the door to find an impeccably dressed officer, slim and cold faced, standing there. Brown leather gloves were pinned under his left shoulderboard. On each side stood a policeman, one with an AK-47. The other had some kind of electric cattle-prod. The officer silently signalled for me to turn around: my arms were pulled back and I felt the cuffs go on. No one said anything.

I was marched to the lift, taken out to a car with dark windows and taken off to God knows where. But I hardly cared at that point. I was numb rather than terrified. The terror came later.

I ended up in a courtyard with rows of wooden cages along one side. They seemed to be wooden frames, with heavy-duty wire netting, almost like fencing, strung across them and serving as bars. The whole thing looked like a battery farm for outsize chickens. I was led to one of the cages, my cuffs were removed, and I had to bend to get through the hinged flap. It was then locked with a padlock.

When I tried to stand, my neck and shoulders bumped the wire roof. I sat down and discovered I could not stretch out: the square cement floor was only two-thirds the length of my body. I was neither able to stand nor lie down.

Halogen lights turned that night into dazzling day. I tried unsuccessfully to sleep crouched with my knees pulled up. I tried to call up Song's face and to imagine her fragrance. I couldn't.

In the morning a bowl of rice was pushed through a small opening in the wire.

The cement floor sloped gently towards the back of the cage. I pissed into the lower end. For shitting I had to pull down my pants and manoevre my ass above the lower end of the slope. In lieu of loo paper there were my fingers. Hygiene was effected by a man with a powerful hose, who hosed down my cage each morning. The water and turds were carried through a space at the bottom of the netting.

There were people in some of the other cages, but their wire and my wire created a moiré pattern that made it hard for me to see them clearly. No one seemed to cry out, or even whimper. Occasionally they would come for one of the occupants and take him away. There were screams then.

I was probably there for about three days, although I will never know for sure how long it was.

I screamed when they finally came for me and dragged me out. As I straightened my back after crouching for so long, the pain was excruciating.

With a helmeted guard on either side, I was marched into a building, along several corridors, up some stairs, along another corridor, and into a largish green room with a raised platform at one end. On the platform, behind a desk that ran its length, sat three men in olive-green uniforms with red and gold shoulder boards. They had officers' peaked caps, on which red and gold badges glinted. All looked in their thirties or forties, and all wore the cold face. Each had a glass jar of tea beside him. The room stank of carbolic soap.

On the floor, at a small desk to the right of the platform, sat a young woman, also in uniform and with her cap on. She was pretty in a mousy sort of way. She too had a jar of tea.

There was a chair in the middle of the room. I was placed standing in front of it, facing the officers, with my helmeted guards on either side.

The po-faced man in the middle shuffled some papers and began to read in a shrill, barking voice. He seemed to go on for ages. Finally he stopped and nodded to the young woman.

Her voice had that sing-song cadence. 'You are charged with having carnal intercourse with a female Chinese person,' she said. And blushed slightly. 'Furthermore you are charged with exposing yourself indecently in public at Purple Bamboo Park. This tribunal is to hear the evidence.'

I couldn't believe my ears. So this is what I had been in a cage for. And this was what poor old Sven had gone through. But I stood there and said nothing. My first feeling was a flooding of relief that I wasn't in for high treason or for inciting rebellion, or whatever they were arresting everyone else for. Just for screwing and for unzipping in public.

But as the court droned on, fear crawled into my belly and sank its claws in my gut. This wasn't about screwing – I knew damn well it wasn't. It didn't matter a damn what they charged me with. This was about Tiananmen Square. It was revenge on foreigners for being involved there. And since it was Rule of Man, not Rule of Law, they could invent any charge they thought fit. They were going to do with me whatever they wanted, and there was no one to stop them.

Po-face in the middle was shuffling some more papers and reading from time to time in a monotone. It went on and on. There was a pause. In a louder voice he barked out an order.

257

The door behind me opened, and someone entered, walking up to the dais. Jesus, it was the unfriendly *fu wu yuan* from the hotel. The tall one with the glasses.

Po-face barked again, and the *fu* spoke at some length, pointing at me. The woman summarised: '*Tongzhi* Wang Jin says he entered your room at the Friendship Hotel on the morning of October 2 of last year, to perform his cleaning duties, and found you together in bed with *Tongzhi* Song Lan, spinster, employee of University of Beijing.'

I could have wrung that fucking *fu*'s neck. I bet he was the security police plant in the hotel, and there was probably nothing any of us got up to that he hadn't reported. Come to think of it, he'd be the one that fingered Song, after translating 'cancer ward' for me.

The *fu* went on and on, and I guess other evidence of my unspeakable crime was piling up. But no further translation was proffered. He was dismissed. Then, one after the other, two young people were brought in. One was unknown to me, but I recognised the other.

It was Kui'er, and he was in police uniform.

To this day I don't know what he said. He was pointing at me and snarling things in Chinese. That face that could grin so cheerfully was now ugly with hate. I think it was at that point my world caved in. It was then it came home to me that in this looking-glass world nothing was as it seemed. I was in darkness and there were neither footholds nor handholds to cling to. I felt so bone weary I could have died.

The pain in my back was excruciating. I was just grateful they were not making me say anything or asking me to admit my guilt.

My gratitude was premature.

Po-face stood up, and I had the impression proceedings were coming to an end. He barked something, and the woman interpreted.

'These proceedings are hereby interrupted, to allow the accused to write out his confession. He will have it ready by 10am tomorrow, Friday.'

Po-face gathered up his papers and spoke again. The woman translated in her sing-song voice.

'The accused is hereby informed that prisoner Song Lan has already confessed and has accepted the penalty arrived at by the court. She has also denounced the accused as being equally guilty with herself and has demanded, in the interests of justice, that the accused receive an equal punishment to that which she is receiving.'

O sweet Jesus, not Song too. That's it. No, please don't let it be Song. It couldn't be Song. Song wouldn't.

Song would. And did.

Through my tears I saw Po-face ram his papers into a smart leather briefcase and march out, followed by his minions. The girl gave me a frightened little nod as she passed.

I had been longing for the court to be over. However, once it was, my overwhelming feeling was horror at the prospect of returning to my cage. O God, anything but that. I'll do anything not to. Still weeping and now in terror, I shambled once more down those corridors and stairs. I doubt if I had much dignity.

I nearly cried out for relief when we took another set of steps down to what must have been a basement. Then I thought, O my God, basement means dungeons. Maybe torture chambers. But I hardly cared at that point. Anything would have been better than the cage.

Mercifully they put me into an ordinary cell, like one you would see in a film: a stone room with a barred window high up, a chair and a table, a pallet on the floor and a bucket in the corner. Even Chinese characters scratched on the walls. Torn-up newspaper beside the bucket. A bare bulb hanging from the ceiling. And that carbolic aroma in the air, with a faint hint of shit.

An orderly came in and left something on the table. The door clanged shut and I was left to make my confession.

For the first while I remember crouching in a corner. Then I pulled myself together and crept over to lie down on the pallet. I pulled my knees up into my chest as I lay there. If the fear would stop gnawing at my gut. I wept again. The light was fading beyond the little barred window. I closed my eyes and wept behind the eyelids.

Slowly my mind came around to Song's denunciation of me. The fear had kept the thought at bay for a while, but now it forced itself on me. I felt devastated that she could do this to me, but almost immediately it struck me that they were probably lying about it anyway. They would say that sort of thing, wouldn't they, just to drive a wedge between us and get us to destroy each other?

But at least Song's alive. Relief flooded in again. And ebbed again, just as fast, when I thought of the Xinjiang slave camps. Song was probably there by now, starting the first hours of her decades of slavery. Then more horror: Christ, I'll be going there too. Aren't they talking about equal sentences?

It took me a while to calm down. Yes, it was almost certainly a lie that Song had denounced me. Of course they'd say that. What better way to get me to denounce her, or at least admit my guilt? And since I would never see her, I would never know.

Or maybe Song had just admitted screwing when confronted with the evidence, and they had added their own bit about denouncing me and demanding equal punishment. I couldn't really see her doing that off her own bat.

Then maybe I could. Maybe she did denounce me. Maybe after days in cages like that, or days and days of interrogation, or perhaps even days of torture, she'd denounce anything. I know *I* would. I'd probably already have sold Song to get out of those cages if they had given me half a chance.

Or maybe Song had simply thought out the best possible scenario. If she's condemned to Xinjiang, it's hardly just for screwing me. It's for Tiananmen Square and the hunger strike and humiliating Li Peng. Maybe Song reasoned that I wouldn't get the slave camp for just fucking. So pin it on me and get a few desperately needed brownie points.

But she's wrong there. These bastards know my involvement at the square, and the screwing is only an excuse to do me in.

So what was I to do now with my confession? I knew well it was back to those cages with me if I didn't write one. And life in the cages until I did.

I curled up and buried my head in my hands.

CHAPTER TWENTY-NINE

WHEN I AWOKE I didn't know where I was. I had been dreaming of Song, and she was in prison clothes with her back to me, and every time I approached her she'd rattle her chains and walk away down a long corridor. I would shamble after her but could never get any closer. Then she turned and her face had been shot away. I woke sweating and gagging. I tried to stretch, and there was a sense of space, so I wasn't in the cage. I could hear clanging and tramping.

When sunlight slanted through the little window, putting a square of light on the opposite wall, I remembered where I was. A flap opened in the bottom of the door and a bowl of rice was pushed in. I got up and went over to get it: it was still painful for me to move.

I sat down at the table, and saw the sheets of paper. Christ, the confession. O sweet Jesus, I haven't written a thing. My heart started to thump. What if it's nearly 10 o'clock and they come for me? They'll put me back in the cage. O God, no, not in the cage. Please. I wanted to vomit.

I pushed the rice aside and grabbed the sheets of paper. They were ruled in rows of light blue squares, to accommodate Chinese characters. Each sheet had a red star at the top. There was a cheap ballpoint pen with them. My hands had started to shake and I could hardly hold the pen. What will I write? 'I confess' – no, 'I, PJ O'Connor, do hereby confess —' To what? O my God, what do I say? What do I confess to? 'To being in bed with —' Gotta put her name down, or they'll throw it back at me. Tell my hand to stop shaking. 'To being in bed with – with Comrade Song Lan.'

I sat looking at it, and couldn't think of anything else to say. I was still looking at it and trying to keep my hands from shaking when they came for me.

It was the same tribunal; same Po-face; same girl. I stood facing the desk, almost like in primary school, facing the teacher's desk with my homework not done. But a teacher out of a nightmare with powers and punishments I could hardly begin to imagine.

Po-face shuffled papers for a while, then snapped his fingers and my confession was handed up by one of the guards. He looked at it for ages, then summoned the girl with a downward flick of his hand. She went up to him and there was muttering and whispering.

I was wanting to go to the lavatory and began to regret I hadn't used that bucket earlier. I had been in such a frenzy trying to write my confession. Po-face barked at me.

'The comrade judge asks are you trying to be funny?' the girl translated.

'No. I – I wasn't –'

Po-face exploded in a harangue of high-pitched barking that reminded me of Li Peng on television. Perhaps he was modelling himself on the same Li. It went on and on, and I hung my head. Like the schoolboy with the bad homework.

The harangue stopped, and fingers were snapped at the

girl. She could hardly have remembered it all, so I presumably got a precis.

'The comrade judge says you are insulting him and the court. You are making fun of this tribunal, and you will regret it deeply. How dare you, he says, tell the court only that you were in bed? What did you do within the bed, is what the court requires you to confess.

'And the comrade judge says how dare you write just three lines. That is also an insult to the court. You were given several pages. A proper confession must be long and detailed.

'You will go back and write your confession for 10 o'clock tomorrow. It will be a good confession. Otherwise you will be punished severely.'

Po-face stood up, barked and exited with his troop, boots clicking on the concrete. The girl gave me another mousy nod as she passed. I was marched back to my cell. I had the feeling I had narrowly missed going to the cages.

I used the bucket ate my rice, and took up my pen, in that order. My hands were still shaking. I sat looking at the sheets of paper, wondering what they could possibly want that would fill several pages. A good confession, that's what they wanted. God, I hadn't heard that since I was a kid at Catholic school. Make a good confession.

So I tried again, and I wrote what I had done 'within the bed'. Making love was what I had done, and that's what I wrote. A proper confession has to be long and detailed, that's what they had said. Still, I presumed they didn't want details of, well, who was on top, or what we actually did before we actually . . . I tried to imagine Po-face's face if that sort of thing was read out to the court. And the poor girl blushing. No, details must mean, what were the circumstances leading up to it. But I could hardly write about the drug thing that happened that night.

Finally I managed two whole pages, about how Song and I had got to know each other, and how Song has stayed over for convenience, and how we just couldn't help making love. That sort of thing.

The court wouldn't wear any of it. The next morning Po-face harangued me again. 'How dare you use the words *making love*! There is no love in that. The Chinese people do not regard such behaviour as having anything to do with love. It is an insult to the word love.' He'd have made a great Redemptorist preacher from the old days, would Po-face. He even had the face for it.

'You did not make love,' Po-face barked. He was requiring the girl to translate every sentence now. 'You committed sexual intercourse, outside of wedlock and outside of China's laws.' The poor girl blushed dreadfully at the word intercourse. I thought I detected Po-face moistening his lips with his tongue. I suppose it might have been funny had it not been for the fear.

Anyhow I was sent back to rewrite my confession for the following day. 'Outside of China's laws', my eye. I knew damn well there were no such laws. As Norman had always said, they make up the rules as they go along. But it's their rules, and I had better go along with them.

I only realised afterwards that I had long passed the point of whether or not I'd consent to write a confession. All my concerns were to get it right and get it over with. I was co-operating with these bastards, co-operating with all the energy that fear can conjure.

In the end I wrote and rewrote my confession nine times. The final one ran to eleven pages. It included pages of self-criticism and admissions of degradation, acknowledgements of the decadence of my western morals, shame for my unspeakable wickedness, and *a firm resolution never to sin again*. (It was I who thought of those final words, which I remembered from my Penny Catechism. They seemed to make a good impression on Po-face.)

The only thing I didn't do was denounce Song or put the blame on her. They didn't ask me to do so, for which I was grateful. I'm not sure what might have happened had they asked me. In the event I managed to suggest that it was I who had led her astray in her innocence, and Po-face seemed pleased at this further admission of western perfidy.

Nine rewrites, one per day, took nine days. It took a lot of Chinese man-hours to run that court just for me, but I suppose it gave employment. What would Po-face have done without the likes of me to provide work for him, I wondered.

On the final day, after my confession had been formally accepted, the court adjourned so that it could be translated into Chinese. We then all reassembled, and my confession was stamped with several chops, and copies presented to me in both Chinese and English. I never found out what I was supposed to do with them. Maybe they were keepsakes.

Po-face then stood up and barked. The young woman translated: 'The sentence will be carried out at midday tomorrow.'

That was when fear became terror.

All that night I lay curled in the foetal position. The sentence would be *carried out*, the girl has said. She hadn't said it would *commence* – which is what you'd say if it was a prison sentence.

It couldn't be. Jesus, they're not going to do me in. Come on – they're mad, but not that mad. No, they wouldn't do that. Not to me. Not for just fucking. Or even for what happened at the square. But look at what they already did in the square. No way. No. I'm a westerner. I'm an Irish citizen – as if they'd even have heard of Ireland. But no. No way they'd do anything like that.

Terror can't be described, only experienced. Like looking through an airplane window and seeing an engine in flames. Or crouching in a front-line trench and hearing the shells zeroing in. Or the moment before your car hits the truck head on. Terror means gazing into the iris of death.

I even tried to pray.

When morning came I got no rice. When the boots thudded in the corridor I thought I was going to faint. The door clanged open, I was turned around and handcuffed, and marched along the corridor and up the stone stairs.

I was momentarily dazzled when I came through the door into the courtyard. When I saw what awaited me my knees actually did give way, and I had to be held up by my two guards. I discovered later I had wet my pants.

What awaited me was one of those tumbrels – an open truck with waist-high sides – and a helmeted policeman with a large white placard, which he proceeded to hang around my neck. There were red characters on the placard.

One of the truck sides was lowered. I was so paralysed with terror that I was unable to climb in, so I was hoisted in, one guard pulling my arms and another pushing from below. They put me leaning against the truck side, a guard on either side holding me, as I could hardly stand.

The dee-dah sirens began, lights started flashing on two police cars which drove out through a gateway ahead of us, and then we were in the street. People glanced curiously up at us, then looked again when they saw it was a foreign devil in the tumbrel. I saw one little boy excitedly pulling at his mother's arm and pointing at me.

A curious thing happened. The terror turned into numbness, and I felt I was watching myself from a distance. We moved slowly through the streets. I was taking in everything. I noticed the white tower of Bei Hai Park passing us by on the left. Its curious shape had always reminded me of the white king in a chess game, and I was sorry I had never got around to climbing up to it. The sun felt warm on my head.

At some point I realised we were going north towards Haidian, and Purple Bamboo Park moved slowly by. That was where English Corner was. I remembered the little one who had wanted to speak English with us, who had asked if I had children. I had said none that I knew of. Where was she now, I wondered? Perhaps she had died in Tiananmen Square.

I also remembered Kui'er.

At the top of the street the motorcade did a U-turn and came slowly back down towards the park entrance. The street widens there, and the vehicles pulled into the parking area. There were stalls selling things outside the park gates.

Police whistles blew, and I saw people dismounting from their bikes and gathering around. Soon a crowd had gathered. The sides of my truck were let down, so that I was standing on a kind of flat scaffold.

My handcuffs were taken off, I was turned around to face the crowd. A sheaf of paper was put into my hand. My hands weren't trembling any more.

'Read each sentence, then wait,' a man said in English. I looked at the paper, and realised it was the typescript of my confession.

A police whistle blew again, someone shouted something, and they were all looking at me. I got a shove in the back, probably from a rifle butt.

I started to read. I was surprised at how strong my voice was. 'I, Peter Joseph O'Connor, of the city of Dublin in the Republic of Ireland, now resident in the People's Republic of China, and an employee of the Chinese government, do hereby confess that I have unlawfully committed sexual intercourse with an unmarried Chinese female person who was a virgin.'

I stopped and waited. A young woman's voice rang out, just behind me and to my right. I knew those sing-song cadences from my days in court. I only hoped the poor girl wasn't blushing too much at what she was having to translate.

The voice paused, and I got another shove in the back. I began again. 'On the night of October 1 of last year . . . '

The whole confession must have taken much more than an hour, with pauses for the interpreter after each sentence. The crowd leaned on their bicycles and just stared up without expression. They hardly blinked. I don't know if they were disgusted or bored.

When the last words had been uttered, whistles blew again. There were shouts and I saw policemen urging the crowd to move along. I was pushed to the edge of the platform and a policeman below signalled for me to get down. I was moving almost like an automaton, but I turned around to look at the girl, and she give me the frightened nod. Then broke into a shy smile, for the briefest instant. That was when I was sure I was not going to die.

I got down and was marched to one of the police cars. Po-face was sitting in the back, and I was put in between him and another man who climbed in after me. Po-face's nose wrinkled: I suppose I didn't smell too good.

Po-face barked, and the other man translated. 'You are to be expelled from China. You have one hour at your hotel to get the things ready. The police will come at 3 o'clock to take you to the airport. They will have your passport. The ticket is paid for by Xinhua, to be taken from your salary.'

The other car started and moved out into the street. Our car was right behind it. There were no sirens this time. The Friendship Hotel is only a block or two away, and we were quickly outside Building Number Four.

A helmeted policeman – or soldier, I can never tell them apart – marched me to the lift and accompanied me to my room. He signalled for me to go in, and the door stayed open. He stationed himself just outside, holding his AK-47 horizontally.

I sat down on the sofa and started to weep convulsively. I wept because I wasn't dead. And because Song wasn't dead.

And then because she was worse than dead, in slavery. And because I must leave China and never hear of her again. I wept till my lungs gasped for breath and I couldn't weep any more.

Then I saw the telephone and lifted it. There was a yell from the soldier, so I put it down again.

The little clock on the table said 2.25. The soldier came into the room and pushed me towards the bathroom with the butt of his gun. He pointed to the shower. I took off my clothes and went through the motions like a zombie.

By ten minutes to three I was sitting on the edge of the sofa, just waiting for the crash of the lift gates and the thump of boots along the corridor.

The crash of the lift came a minute or two before three. I waited. There was no thump of boots, but quiet footfalls along the corridor. The footfalls stopped outside my door.

It was Norman, with Song leaning on his arm.

Norman spoke. 'You've got five minutes with her, PJ. Police are downstairs – I've asked them to wait. Then y'have to go. Colonel Wu's gone out on a limb for this young lady. And so, by the way, have I. And if an exit permit's humanly possible, he'll get her one.

'Oh, and by the way, it seems they knew y'both carried drugs for Madame Lukas. It was Wu convinced them y'never knew it yourselves.'